"Ta-daa! Our best little wabbit… Is this the bunny girl you asked for?"

Former member of Item
Saiai Kinuhata

"It's okay. Hamazura, this is a hospital. It's okay if you get a nosebleed."

Former member of Item
Rikou Takitsubo

CW00417502

"…What an eyesore…
Always better to get the
bullshit out of the way
quickly."

Member of Group
Accelerator

"Oh, just resolving an incident, same as always."

Member of Group
Motoharu Tsuchimikado

"Who needs to be knocked out this time?"

Member of Group
Awaki Musujime

"N-no!! It doesn't make any sense to get a nosebleed right now!! Not like bunny girls are that.."

Former underling member of Item **Shiage Hamazura**

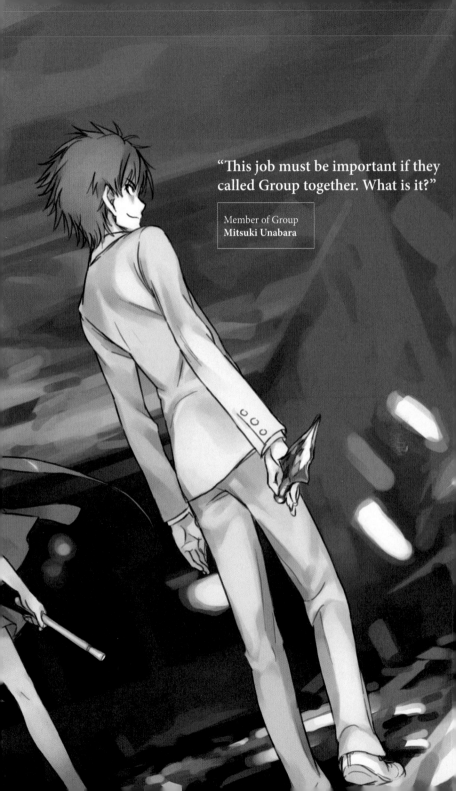

"This job must be important if they called Group together. What is it?"

Member of Group
Mitsuki Unabara

A Certain Magical Index

19

KAZUMA KAMACHI

ILLUSTRATION BY
KIYOTAKA HAIMURA

"Isn't it just plain easier to walk
up to the enemy and fire away?"

Mercenary sniper who hails
from outside Academy City
Stephanie Gorgeouspalace

"I request a match."

General Board member in
Shiokishi's service **Sugitani**

contents

VOLUME 19

KAZUMA KAMACHI
ILLUSTRATION BY: KIYOTAKA HAIMURA

NEW YORK

A CERTAIN MAGICAL INDEX, Volume 19
KAZUMA KAMACHI

Translation by Andrew Prowse
Cover art by Kiyotaka Haimura

TOARU MAJYUTSU NO INDEX Vol.19
©KAZUMA KAMACHI 2009
First published in Japan in 2009 by KADOKAWA CORPORATION, Tokyo.
English translation rights arranged with KADOKAWA CORPORATION, Tokyo,
through Tuttle-Mori Agency, Inc., Tokyo.

English translation © 2019 by Yen Press, LLC

Yen On
1290 Avenue of the Americas
New York, NY 10104

Visit us at yenpress.com
facebook.com/yenpress
twitter.com/yenpress
yenpress.tumblr.com
instagram.com/yenpress

First Yen On Edition: June 2019

Yen On is an imprint of Yen Press, LLC.
The Yen On name and logo are trademarks of Yen Press, LLC.

The publisher is not responsible for websites (or their content) that are not owned by the publisher.

Library of Congress Cataloging-in-Publication Data

Names: Kamachi, Kazuma, author. | Haimura, Kiyotaka, 1973– illustrator. | Prowse, Andrew (Andrew R.), translator. | Hinton, Yoshito, translator.
Title: A certain magical index / Kazuma Kamachi ; illustration by Kiyotaka Haimura.
Other titles: To aru majyutsu no index. (Light novel). English
Description: First Yen On edition. | New York : Yen On, 2014–
Identifiers: LCCN 2014031047 (print) | ISBN 9780316339124 (v. 1 : pbk.) |
ISBN 9780316259422 (v. 2 : pbk.) | ISBN 9780316340540 (v. 3 : pbk.) |
ISBN 9780316340564 (v. 4 : pbk.) | ISBN 9780316340595 (v. 5 : pbk.) |
ISBN 9780316340601 (v. 6 : pbk.) | ISBN 9780316272230 (v. 7 : pbk.) |
ISBN 9780316359924 (v. 8 : pbk.) | ISBN 9780316359962 (v. 9 : pbk.) |
ISBN 9780316359986 (v. 10 : pbk.) | ISBN 9780316360005 (v. 11 : pbk.) |
ISBN 9780316360029 (v. 12 : pbk.) | ISBN 9780316442671 (v. 13 : pbk.) |
ISBN 9780316442701 (v. 14 : pbk.) | ISBN 9780316442725 (v. 15 : pbk.) |
ISBN 9780316442749 (v. 16 : pbk.) | ISBN 9780316474542 (v. 17 : pbk.) |
ISBN 9780316474566 (v. 18 : pbk.) | ISBN 9781975357566 (v. 19 : pbk.)
Subjects: CYAC: Magic—Fiction. | Ability—Fiction. | Nuns—Fiction. | Japan—Fiction. | Science fiction. | BISAC: FICTION / Fantasy / General. | FICTION / Science Fiction / Adventure.
Classification: LCC PZ7.1.K215 Ce 2014 | DDC [Fic]—dc23
LC record available at https://lccn.loc.gov/2014031047

ISBNs: 978-1-9753-5756-6 (paperback)
978-1-9753-5757-3 (ebook)

1 3 5 7 9 10 8 6 4 2

LSC-C

Printed in the United States of America

PROLOGUE

A Boring Exchange Between Villains

Key_Shop.

Academy City's District 15 was its largest shopping district but also its main broadcasting base. Many a television station and media-related facility lined the streets here, altogether giving it the highest property values in the city.

There was a giant mixed-use building among them, like any apartment complex combined with corporate office space. But this one was so lavish you could probably buy an entire detached house for less than it would cost to rent a room in it.

It was the home of a man called Department Store, and it was also his place of business. The evening landscape seen out the window along one wall was jaw-dropping—if this had been a restaurant, it could have expected quite a few patrons just for the view, regardless of whether the food was good or not.

"Don't get too jealous," the room owner, a man who looked college-aged, said with a shrug from his chair.

"It's not like this place is comfortable; it's just another hideout. I'd have to abandon it if it got raided. Can't really relax here."

He had no sense of caution toward Accelerator.

Red eyes, white hair. He had a crutch in one hand, but he didn't come off as weakened by that in the slightest, since the aura he emitted implied he'd rip your body apart if you offended him. This was a

Level Five esper—and still, the room's owner looked at him without caution.

The young man was probably used to it. After all, considering the products Department Store dealt in, no decent person would ever try to do business with him.

"Well, I won't ask what happened. Just pretend I'm a cute waitress come to take your order. No need to hold back," DS went on, not appearing particularly irritated at how Accelerator maintained his silence. "What might you be after? A getaway car? Keys to a hideout? Or a money exchange, maybe? If you want to launder some stolen cash, today's rate is 0.8. It was 0.75 before, so it's a good deal, eh? And since you're the type who stands out in crowds, I could show you some disguises or introduce you to a cosmetic surgeon."

He listed these off the same way a server might explain the recommended dishes of the day. Academy City was surrounded by high walls, so it wasn't possible to flee from inspecting eyes by simply running. It was more important to prepare a safe hideout—or look for a way to sneak onto a freight train in disguise to get outside city limits. (Of course, even with tricks like that, success rates were low.)

After hearing this, Accelerator was silent for a few moments.

Eventually, he gave a slow look around the large room. "A hideout, eh? If this is one of your hideouts, then does that make this a model room?"

"Well, it *is* my main product. Hideouts are what I built my business on. I'm confident in what I deal in, and I'm very particular about them. I've got 'keys' for everything from high-class apartments in prime real estate to campers parked in District 21's hills. Want to see the catalog?"

But Accelerator didn't bite. His eyes were fixed on something to the side. A blind spot, hidden in a corner of the room by the vast landscape out the window, protected behind furniture—and something hung there like a sandbag.

"*That* one of your products, too?"

"Hmm? *Is that what you're interested in?*" DS glanced that way as well, seeing what was hanging in chains, his face turning slightly bitter. It was the look someone might give off when a friend discovered their private interests. "Unfortunately, I'm not offering that as an option right now. It's more like a hobby of mine."

It was a girl, about fifteen years old.

Nothing but white skin and underwear, her hands locked up, hanging there unmoving.

The girl was black-and-blue in some spots, but she just swayed there slowly, her strength expended, without a shred of embarrassment. Accelerator heard breathing, so she was still alive, but there was no light in her eyes.

Still looking at her, Accelerator stated, "That's an awful hobby. Doesn't that get expensive?"

"Somewhat, yes. Hey, seriously, don't break it. This might be a disposable hideout, but I hate having to deal with corpses. And even without the liability, it was crazy expensive. You kill her and you're paying seven hundred thousand, at least."

"Looks pretty beat-up for that price. Doesn't look like you whored her out, though."

"I said it was a hobby, all right? That one's for punching. She isn't good enough for regular fucking. Or are you into the flat-chested ones? You don't look it."

Then, with the hand opposite the one holding the crutch, Accelerator grabbed an envelope from his bag and tossed it onto Department Store's desk. Ten hundred-thousand-yen bills slipped out from the opening.

When he saw it, the young man's lips twisted into a pained grin. "Hey, now."

"Prepayment. I've got my own shitty jobs to do. I'm on edge. Can't guarantee I won't accidentally commit murder."

Department Store clicked his tongue. "Just so you know, it's seven hundred thousand just for killing her. Dealing with the body is separate."

His tone was slightly disappointed. She was a hobby item, but he didn't seem attached enough to her to be stubborn. He probably figured he could buy a new one anyway.

"What's so interesting about that brat anyway? You the type who can't get it up unless another man's messed up the girl first?"

"Oh, I get it. Looks like you misunderstood me," denied Accelerator casually. "I didn't buy the woman hanging over there."

"?"

"*I bought you.*"

Department Store didn't immediately understand what Accelerator meant.

Gurrrch.

Not until he heard the wet sound of his own nose breaking anyway.

"Gh, gah, *ahhhhhhhhhhhhhhhhhhhhhhhhhhhhhhh*?!"

Department Store screamed in pain, rolling out of his chair. There was a small bag on the floor near him. He realized that was what Accelerator had thrown at his face, but it didn't make any sense. Accelerator had a crutch in one hand. The throw couldn't have been that strong. But the pain was intense, like he'd taken a pitching-machine baseball to the face.

Holding his broken nose as blood spurted out of it, Department Store managed to get off the floor.

"Y…you bast…*Fghh*…What…? What the hell are you doing?!"

Department Store opened the expensive-looking desk's drawer and pulled out a gun. But even when he pointed it at Accelerator, the esper didn't react. In fact, he only grinned; the hand that had thrown the bag now at the choker on his neck.

As he smiled, he said, "By your standards…one human is worth seven hundred thousand, right?"

"…!!"

Department Store gaped as realization dawned on him.

Accelerator continued, though, as if to confirm that this was indeed the worst thing he could think of. "Bastard on the phone. Making me do all the stupid shit. I paid you the money, and I'm a little pissed off right now— *You don't mind if I kill you, right?*"

Department Store, apparently overwhelmed with terror, pulled the trigger with his trembling finger. But Accelerator licked his lips and charged at him.

There was the sound of flesh tearing and bones breaking. Then something more than a simple scream—something more like a howl.

Five minutes later.

Poking the bloody ball of flesh with his toe, Accelerator exasperatedly switched off his choker. He didn't have a scratch on him. As long as his ability was free, he could reflect every attack under the sun.

Still on his crutch, he used his other hand to take out his cell phone. After dialing, he put it to his ear.

"I'm done, I guess. These shitty jobs are all so boring. Eh? What do I need? Let's see. A recovery team to pick up a chunk of flesh that gives off a smell which will make you vomit with even the slightest whiff, and…"

Accelerator paused for just a moment.

He looked over at the hanging girl and turned his choker on again.

With just the flick of a finger, the distant chains binding the girl snapped.

"…and a set of women's clothing. Size? I don't know. Just bring some 'one size fits all' crap. You assholes have no sense, so it wouldn't matter even if I gave you a more detailed description. And put women in the recovery team. I see one man with them, and I'm kicking his balls off."

After saying what he needed to, Accelerator ended the call. He grabbed a few random bills from the desk, then crudely threw them at the girl, who was now collapsed on the floor with the chains cut.

Without looking in her direction, he switched off his choker, shifted his weight onto his crutch, then called out in an impassive voice as he headed for the exit, "Live how you want now. Whether the rest of your life succeeds or fails is up to you."

"…"

The girl in the underwear, who hadn't shown much reaction until now, finally rolled her head to look at Accelerator's back. Moving her red, cut-up lips, she asked quietly and suddenly, "Who are you…?"

"A villain," he answered in a singsong tone as he went through the front door. "A villainous piece of shit."

That was his daily life—their daily lives.

Accelerator, Motoharu Tsuchimikado, Mitsuki Unabara, and Awaki Musujime.

The four were called Group, and on this day, Group would once again root out the darkness in this city.

CHAPTER 1

I Believe in Your Kindness, at Least

Dark_Hero.

1

October 17, 6 PM.

Accelerator was by a window, sitting on the floor of the hotel room he was using as a hideout. His reason for sitting against the wall was simple—the devices he'd constructed and arranged on a spread-out newspaper. He couldn't do this sort of work on the bed.

As he continued his task, he kept his cell phone nestled between his neck and shoulder. A small girl's voice came through it. *"Anyway, I think we're having meat stew tonight, says Misaka says Misaka, reporting the results of her reconnaissance and stuff."*

"You don't say. When did Yomikawa get good enough with rice cookers to pull off a crazy stunt like that?"

The device on the newspaper was a crutch.

It resembled a tonfa, but with a modern design, which he equipped by fitting it around his right forearm. He called it "a device" because it now featured several new improvements, such as a few small motors and a weight sensor.

At the moment, the crutch was standing up on four legs like a microphone stand. Accelerator poked at it.

...I think I've managed to put it back together now, but I wonder

if the weight sensor can handle detecting my center of mass by itself. Maybe I should've jammed in an angle-adjusting gyro or something.

This precise analysis continued in his mind as he responded on his cell phone. The person on the other end was Last Order, a girl who appeared to be around ten.

"If you want, I can try negotiating to have her make some for you, too, says Misaka says Misaka, glancing toward the kitchen."

"Yeah, sure. As long as it tastes just as good after freezing it, packing it, and shipping it through the mail."

When he put his right arm through the crutch and grasped the handle, the four stands flitted like insect legs. Still sitting, he jabbed the crutch into the floor. Despite being nearly parallel to the ground, the mechanical legs began to accurately grab hold of the surface and support him.

Just barely scrapes by with a passing grade.

"You said you could come visit this weekend, says Misaka says Misaka, making sure."

"...As long as my plans don't change."

When he manipulated the grip again, there was a clatter as the crutch suddenly retracted. It was made like an extendable police baton.

Wearing giant bracelet-like pieces that wrapped around his arm from the elbow down, Accelerator moved his right wrist to see how the setup moved as a whole.

Guess that passes, too. Can't walk without a crutch, but it gets in the way when I'm using my ability.

As he muttered his impressions of the device, Accelerator moved the grip again to extend the crutch.

Jshhh!! The four-legged pole extended energetically, sending several tools that he'd left on the newspaper flying.

...Could maybe use it as a weapon if I amped up the power...No point, though. Don't need any when I'm using my ability, and if I had to lift the crutch in an emergency, I'd fall over.

"Misaka is so excited for Saturday that she can't wait— Ohh!! Yomikawa brought in the meat stew!! says Misaka says Misaka, making a report of the highest priority!!"

"Yeah? Your life is just full of detours, isn't it?"

And then it happened.

The telephone rang—not his cell, but the one installed on the hotel bedside table. Accelerator looked over to it. Before he could pick up the receiver, the ringing stopped. It had rung exactly three times, as though it was preplanned.

That was the signal.

An RV or some other similar vehicle had probably pulled up onto the shoulder near the hotel.

"*What's wrong?! asks Misaka asks Misaka, bending her head at the telephone sound.*"

"…It's nothing. Just room service," he lied, placing his weight onto his homemade crutch and slowly standing up. He became conscious of the sensation of a small handgun tucked into his pants on the back of his waist again.

Then, from the other end of the call, Last Order abruptly said, "*Are you okay?*"

She didn't know about Accelerator's job. And she didn't need to know the details to worry about him.

"*Don't do anything dangerous, asks Misaka asks Misaka.*"

"Do you even know who you're whispering to?" he replied to the voice on the cell phone, as though thrusting it away. "No need for consideration like that when you're talking with a guy who wouldn't die even if a nuke hit him."

Accelerator hung up, then stowed his cell phone in his pants pocket.

Without turning around, he headed for the guest room's exit.

Newspapers and tools were strewn about the room, but minions from some organization or another would surely be along to tidy up anyway.

Motoharu Tsuchimikado was walking through the District 7 shopping arcade, a large avenue along the way from his school to his dorm. Tsuchimikado had blond hair, sunglasses, and a Hawaiian shirt over his school uniform, making him a fairly conspicuous person—but at the moment, there were some people present with even more visual impact than him.

Specifically, part-time maids, handing out fliers for restaurants.

As he walked through the shopping district, he watched the working girls, and his eyes relaxed slightly behind his sunglasses.

"…The times really have taken a turn for the better, nya…"

Not a moment after he'd muttered it, a powerful straight punch pushed into Tsuchimikado's tall back. His little sister, Maika Tsuchimikado, was responsible. After eliciting a violent *wha-bam!!* noise you wouldn't expect from her delicate little fist, she was currently, for some reason, sitting politely with her legs folded underneath her atop an oil drum–shaped cleaning robot.

The girl, however, hadn't physically contorted her stepbrother's spine out of jealousy.

"…You can't call those professional maids. How dare they mix up maids, waitresses, and hostesses. How is this for the better, eh? That one even has Gothic fashion mixed in somehow. Do you think kneesocks make everything okay?"

Maika growled her questions, blue veins popping on her exposed forehead, since her bob's bangs were combed back. Her own clothing consisted of a long-skirted maid uniform, mainly in dark blue. Unlike the ladies handing out fliers, it had a plain but highly practical design.

"M-Maika? That jagged black aura around you is making me feel like there's a boulder in the pit of my stomach…"

"What I mean is: It's all well and good the term *maid* has spread throughout the world, but it's a problem if it spreads in the wrong way. Now people look at us lewdly just for wearing these clothes."

"L-lewdly?!"

His stepsister's remark got a huge reaction out of him.

This reaction was not, however, because he couldn't forgive the unspecified large number of bastards who would apparently look at his little sister so rudely.

"But…But is that so wrong…? Maids are healthy in the first place, aren't they? Unerotic maids—what reason could they possibly have for existing?!"

"...It looks like I'll need to show my shitty brother what professional maids are made of."

"No, stop, *gwoohhh*; my stepsister is using her body to show off pro-maid techniques to me?!" called Tsuchimikado, his words a string of lewdness, as a tiny fist beat him to a pulp.

Just then, a camper passing right by him gave a short honk of its horn. It looked like it had been trying to hurry a passenger car taking its time in front of it, but that wasn't it.

It was the signal.

The camper had probably put on its blinker and gone down a side road—and it would park there for a time to wait for Tsuchimikado.

Without waiting to see where it went, he immediately started walking toward the nearby convenience store.

"Nya. I gotta go grab some refills for my mechanical pencils."

"Hmm? I'll come, too."

"Wait, you're gonna help me?! I actually have a ton of homework today, nya. I'm not even sure both of us together could finish it, but you're really smart, so you could probably do the work of one and a half people. A brother-sister team-up operation should manage to finish by tomorrow morning."

"...I don't think I'm going to your room tonight...You're already up a creek without a paddle if you're asking your middle school sister for help on high school homework. But at least there's still leftovers. You shouldn't die of starvation. And with that, adieu!"

Still sitting politely atop the cleaning robot, Maika banged on its side with her small palm. Its sensors seemed to pick up from the gesture, since the robot swerved in the other direction, as though being controlled by a steering wheel.

"Heartless brute!!" shouted Tsuchimikado in front of the convenience store, his spirit shattered. After hanging his head, he went into the store, properly bought what he said he would, and then went down a side road away from the shopping district.

He opened the door of the camper that he found parked there.

Inside was an earlier visitor, a white-haired Level Five, lying on a simple bed as though sulking.

Looking at that Level Five, Tsuchimikado said:

"...So what's today's homework?"

Awaki Musujime was in District 10. The place had a host of research facilities related to nuclear power and microbiology, as well as an incineration plant for laboratory animals, but even within this district stood a particularly infamous building.

The juvenile reformatory.

It wasn't the sort of place a girl wearing the uniform of Kirigaoka Girls' Academy, an elite Ability Development school, would normally be seen, but she couldn't be picky—her comrades were interned there.

They were *comrades* in the sense that they had tried to complete a grand project together.

One that some might call a criminal act.

Thanks to a Level Four–Level Five duo from a school for young ladies as influential as Kirigaoka—no, possibly even more so—they'd already aborted the project itself.

Many of her comrades had been defeated through overwhelming power, then confined within this juvenile reformatory. And Musujime alone was free—only she, the project's mastermind, the one who should have been the first to be caged.

An implicit rule had been handed down to her.

She would use her incredible ability, Move Point, to fight against even deeper darkness in Academy City. If she acquiesced, they would both physically and socially guarantee her comrades' safety—and if she didn't, that guarantee went away.

One day, she'd outwit this city.

She'd win this game that was supposed to be perfectly unbeatable so she could grant her comrades freedom once again.

That alone was Awaki Musujime's goal—and there was nothing else to it. Rather, there was nothing left. Even her attachment to their rogue-like "grand project" had already vanished. There was no longer a proactive reason that kept her moving anymore. Right now, it was the endless negativity and the crushing circumstances that forced Musujime ever forward.

It doesn't matter to me, she thought. *I'll do whatever this city wants, to a point.*

But she would no longer stop, even if the result waiting for them was the utter collapse of Academy City's leadership. If that came to pass, they could blame themselves for pushing her that far.

Musujime walked down the street, lost in thought in the dim moments just before sundown.

And then it happened.

Her cell phone ringtone went off in her skirt pocket. It was a different chime from a few days ago—she didn't care about this sort of thing, so when her roommate had recommended this ringtone and then changed it for her, Musujime left it as it was, making it her default ringtone.

She gave a soft sigh, then took her cell phone out of her pocket.

After pressing the Accept button and placing it next to her ear, words from her roommate, which she'd grown accustomed to hearing, flew at her.

"Musuuu!! Where are you wandering around?!"

The voice was sugary sweet, like it belonged to a girl who hadn't reached puberty yet.

Her roommate's name was Komoe Tsukuyomi.

And in spite of her voice, surprisingly enough, she was a high school teacher.

"Today is the day that you'll try your very best until you can make vegetable stir-fry, so Teacher has been waiting with an empty stomach juuust for you. Please come back right now and take ooon the challenge. You have to acquire at least one specialty at sooome point, Musu."

At first, it might have seemed like her roommate was just trying to hand off the housework, but Musujime had been made aware in a short time that this sugar-voiced teacher had no such goals.

It was clear when the teacher continued:

"It isn't like girls need to do housework or anything, but life is long, so it's worth learning new skills to broaden your horizons. It's not only cooking. Your teacher never heard what sort of life you want in the future, but it's best to experience all kinds of things so you'll be ready when you finally do decide what path you want to take. But you should only seek out experiences on the absolute condition that you don't waste your own time or hinder the path you really want to take."

Musujime suddenly stopped walking. Here in the twilight of District 10, she realized that, at some point, the dark pressure weighing gently down on the pit of her stomach had gone away.

Something in her was surprised—not on the surface, but something deeper inside.

Surprised that there was still someone who would speak to her like this.

"..."

Musujime wondered how to answer the teacher's repeated "vegetable stir-fry, vegetable stir-fry," but then a camper drove by right near her. The vehicle stopped next to a juice vending machine, and a man got out of the driver's seat, heading to it.

Their eyes never met even once, but she knew the intent.

It was the signal to start work.

She'll be mad at me—no, mad for me, she thought, before speaking again into her cell phone.

"...This is going to sound blunt, but something suddenly came up, so it doesn't look like I'll be making any vegetable stir-fry."

"What?! Again?! Then what now? Your teacher was waiting for that stir-fry! To be honest, I figured you'd mess up a lot, so I bought so many vegetables that the refrigerator is insanely packed!"

"That's good, isn't it? Vegetarians live longer, you know," said Musujime offhandedly and then hung up.

After looking at her phone for a few moments, she put it back in her skirt pocket and started toward the camper. When she opened the door, there was a white-haired Level Five napping on a plain bed and a blond man in sunglasses sitting at the table playing a portable game where miniskirted maids equipped with gigantic laser cannons went on rampages.

Giving the passengers a nasty look, Musujime spoke.

"…Since this is a camper, there must be a kitchen, right?"

Mitsuki Unabara was in a District 7 hospital. It was past six PM, but visiting hours seemed to run relatively late, perhaps part of the hospital's policy. At the moment, it was right before closing.

The hospital room he was in was an individual one, but he wasn't the patient. He'd come to visit a girl who had been hospitalized here.

"…You still seem to like that *face*, Etzali."

The brown-skinned girl, sitting up in bed, spoke to him with a voice that sounded deliberately low. Her wavy, shoulder-length hair was black, but somehow it seemed different compared to the hair Japanese people had. The girl—Xóchitl—hailed from Central America.

"And you still seem like you're in a bad mood. Do your synthetic-fiber pajamas not suit your skin?"

As Unabara spoke, he placed a large wrapped object he'd brought with him on the side table.

"This is Aztecan native clothing. I struggled to procure it…But, well, you'd probably stand out if you wandered through the hospital in this. You can secretly change after lights-out and sleep in them."

"Are you looking for gratitude?"

"What in the world has been getting on your nerves?"

"I guess you won't understand unless I spell it out for you." Xóchitl's head swiveled, and she glared into Unabara's eyes again. "What's been getting on my nerves? You grinning like nothing even happened."

"?"

"The original copy…You picked it up, didn't you?"

Xóchitl's gaze lowered to stare at her hands.

Slowly opening and closing her five fingers, she said, "Originally, my body—save for one-third of it—was supposed to be a complete dummy…And what happened? You tore every bit of it off before I even realized it. I'm still coming to grips with the difference in our skill and capacities as sorcerers."

Before, a certain sorcerer's society had ground away two-thirds of her physical body and made it into raw materials in order to weaponize and wield a powerful original grimoire. And Unabara was the one who had privately saved her.

Xóchitl moved her gaze from her palms to Unabara.

"…You're holding on to the original copy, aren't you?"

"It's here."

Unabara used a hand to open the collar of the suit he was wearing.

There was something like a holster there, like for holding a gun, but a rolled-up book written on animal skin was stuck inside. Before Xóchitl could examine it more closely, Unabara returned his suit to normal.

"Even after turning my flesh to dust, I couldn't control it—and you can command it without doing anything?"

"Well, no…Frankly speaking, it feels like it's taking everything just to keep it suppressed."

Unabara's voice was relaxed, but he understood a fraction, at least, of exactly how fearsome this original copy was.

And of how irregular Xóchitl's situation had been—she'd been made into a mere specimen in order to use something like this as a piece on a game board.

"What happened?" asked Unabara.

It was the question he'd held onto ever since they'd reunited. He'd spoken it now because he decided Xóchitl's body and mind had stabilized enough to do so.

Xóchitl fell silent for a moment, turning her face away from Unabara. With her brown-skinned cheek facing him, she muttered:

"You know of our fight against the American research institution, right? Against Scholarship City."

"Yeah, and the particulars, too. I heard an official announcement say it had been destroyed by terrorists who had purchased an older, low-cost fighter jet."

"The truth, of course, was that we launched a magical attack on it." That was all she said before going quiet again, but just for a few moments.

An open, straightforward battle between Central America's largest sorcerer's society and a nation that was, on the surface, the global police force. She would have contributed to that war from the back lines.

"I screwed up," she said, as though delivering a boring report. "At the last possible moment right at the end, I violated orders a tiny bit. The price I paid was letting them mess with my body quite a bit. Considering our society's codes, they were in the right."

That couldn't be true. Unabara had been a part of that society for a long time, but he'd never heard of any instances where they'd crush someone's body to fuse it with an original grimoire, no matter how grave their crimes.

"There was nobody to stop them? Tochtli? She was your war buddy, right?"

Unabara knew it was over and done, but he couldn't help saying the name of another girl—Xóchitl's colleague.

But Xóchitl shook her head.

"I haven't seen her since before they carried out my sentence. I was just a weapon until you extracted the grimoire. Maybe Tecpatl would know—he was in command of the operation—but I haven't seen that creep since then, either."

Xóchitl leveled her gaze again at Unabara's suit...where the original copy was stored away.

"In the end, it wasn't a matter of the magician's natural gifts. It seems like the idea of trying to use a grimoire's original as a convenient tool was too much to ask, given the limits of the human body. Even after all that, I was at the mercy of the grimoire's every whim."

"...I think I agree with you on that. Original grimoires aren't something you can simply use as a trump card. Even if you use teamwork to bring out a power you don't understand, it would still only invite destruction…Actually, with Group and me…Joking aside, if I caused them any trouble, they'd probably put me through the ringer."

For some reason, Xóchitl was quiet for a moment.

"…Teamwork, huh?"

"?"

"Never mind. When you talk about your friends now, I'm sure the first people you think of are people I don't know."

"Xóchitl—"

"Don't try to tell me I'm wrong."

The brown-skinned girl blocked Unabara from speaking, as though creating a thick wall between them.

"Whatever your reasons were, the fact is that you defected to Academy City, and now you're doing secret work as one of their pawns. You knew that would constitute a betrayal of the ones you once called friends. I mean, look at me— You took me down. That was some great teamwork, eh?"

Xóchitl spoke quietly, admitting that she'd lost while rubbing salt in the wound anyway. When she saw Unabara's expression tighten slightly, she finally made a satisfied—but slightly gloomy—face.

"Isn't that right?"

After saying that, Xóchitl averted her face slightly from Unabara.

She pursed her small lips, and in a voice low enough that she didn't know whether he could hear her, said:

"…Etzali, my brother."

For an instant, time stopped.

And before Mitsuki Unabara could make any reaction, the hospital room door flew open with a *bang!!*

A blond young man with sunglasses, Motoharu Tsuchimikado, burst into the room.

"Unabara, you bastard!! How the hell are you gonna explain what she just said, nya?!"

"Etzali, stand back!! They must be new hunters from the

organization!! Damn, did they decide they needed to get rid of me along with you?!"

Before Unabara could advise her that, no, this visitor was a complete weirdo but not an enemy, Tsuchimikado stomped closer to him, veins popping out of his temples.

"Unabara...!! Does this mean that you had a little sister back in your homeland all along? Then what are you doing falling head over heels for a middle school girl in Academy City attending Tokiwadai?!"

"Wait, I...What are you talking about?!" Unabara's shoulders gave a major jolt.

Xóchitl, who had previously been cautious of Tsuchimikado, stopped moving immediately after hearing him talk, then turned to stare at Mitsuki Unabara again.

"...A middle school girl? You don't mean you betrayed the organization for a reason like that, do you?"

Unable to deny this, Unabara started sweating bullets. He avoided looking her in the eye. After all, it wasn't as though he was infatuated with that girl just because she was in middle school. It wouldn't have made a difference if she'd been in high school or college instead—he wasn't some huge lolicon who had risked his life because of his inclinations.

"Wait, she called me her brother just now, but our relationship in the magic society was more like teacher and student—that's all!!"

"In other words, a stepsister!! That's actually even better, nya!!"

Amid Unabara's and Tsuchimikado's cries, Awaki Musujime peered into the room from outside.

We came here to gather everyone together for a job, but if it was going to be like this, wouldn't solving this on my own have been a better idea?! she considered, relatively seriously.

She spoke to Accelerator, who was leaning on the wall nearby, without looking at him.

"Brother, sister—what are they even talking about? I swear, we're about to head for a battlefield with bullets flying everywhere, so I wish they'd act a little more appropriately."

But there was no reaction from Accelerator.

Dubiously, she looked over to him and realized his lips were moving slightly.

She focused on listening to his whispers.

"(...It's every person's fate to be pushed around by a younger brat at some point.

It looks like things in there are getting ridiculous, but I don't have the right to get in their way like an idiot.)"

"Oh, how awful. Am I the only non-lolicon in Group?"

Then, Accelerator, Motoharu Tsuchimikado, and Mitsuki Unabara all turned around and focused on the one who'd made the remark, Awaki Musujime.

In their natural voices, without any particular prior planning, they said:

"Great, the girl who is obviously a shotacon is calling *us* perverts."

"Yeah, nya." "Indeed."

"Pfft?! *Cough-cough!!* Wh-wh-wh-wh-wh-wh-wh-what grounds do you have to prove that I'm a shota—*mfgh*—shotacon...?!"

The upperclassman-type, huge-chested high school girl Awaki Musujime began to panic, but the other three, perhaps too tired to explain everything to her, merely shook their heads. The meaning was loud and clear: *Did she really think she'd been successfully hiding it this whole time?*

...Xóchitl didn't appreciate how their reactions had all been in unison, but Unabara didn't notice that subtlety. After saying good-bye to the copper-skinned girl, he left the hospital room.

As they walked down the hallway, he asked:

"This job must be important if they called Group together. What is it?"

"Oh, just resolving an incident, same as always," answered Tsuchimikado, so casually that it seemed he might break out into a whistle at any moment.

"Some terrorists have holed up with some hostages—and we've been ordered to kill them all."

2

Meanwhile, two people, a boy and a girl, arrived at the store in the same hospital building. Basically, it was a shop mainly offering light snacks such as juice and sugary treats, but it also featured a lineup of novels for passing the time as well as water guns, though where someone would use one of those in the hospital was unclear.

The girl's head moved quickly, checking all the products, while the boy watched her idly from behind.

The boy's name was Shiage Hamazura. He had brown hair, and his outfit consisted of a beat-up tracksuit and jeans. He had the features of a dumb street thug, but that's exactly what he was, so he couldn't help it. A street thug who had taken out Academy City's fourth-ranked Level Five, Shizuri Mugino.

The girl's name was Saiai Kinuhata.

She was about twelve years old, also brunette, though her hair was far less frizzled and dry. She wore it in a bob cut that just barely reached her shoulders. Her outfit was a short wool dress that looked like a sweater, which exposed a dangerous amount of her white-skinned thighs. The sort of girl you'd feel constantly uncomfortable sitting across from during a train ride.

As Kinuhata looked at the several kinds of flowers placed directly on the store's floor, she said, "We came all this way to visit her, so, like, how could you forget flowers, Hamazura? Do you actually enjoy us always thinking you're a total Hamazura, Hamazura?"

"Hey, stop bending over to look at them. Your ass is basically putting on one hell of a show back here, you know."

"But you can't quite see them clearly in this pose— Totally amazing, right? It's a completely different league compared to your run-of-the-mill sluts."

Damn, cursed Hamazura to himself. *It was planned all along!!*

After thinking hard for a few moments, Kinuhata picked out flowers he couldn't name and called the store clerk over. Once she got them all bundled into a bouquet, it fell, of course, to Hamazura to carry them.

As they walked to the elevator leading to the general hospital building, Kinuhata said, "All right, that does it for the flowers. Did you, like, remember to bring any other gifts for the visit?"

"A couple. But Takitsubo's getting discharged soon, so it's not like I went all out trying to get my hands on crazy time-killing toys."

"I would super-appreciate it if you'd stop with the bunny suits."

"What kind of person do you think I am anyway?"

"An absolute pervert who's totally into bunny girls."

As they squabbled, Hamazura and Kinuhata got into the elevator and took it to their destination floor. After walking down the hallway and knocking on the door, a familiar voice came back at them.

When they opened the door, they saw their friend, a comrade who had survived a fierce battle alongside them in the past.

Rikou Takitsubo.

Hamazura remembered her as a girl who always seemed sleepy. Her black hair was cut evenly at her shoulders. Normally, she wore a pink-colored tracksuit, which could apparently serve as hangout clothes as well as pajamas. Sitting up in bed, she was, again, in her usual tracksuit.

"Hey, girl, how you feeling?!" asked Kinuhata with ease, already knowing things were getting better for her, as she swiftly dismantled the bouquet and put the flowers in a vase.

In fact, Takitsubo herself didn't think deeply on it, either, saying, "They say that I should be fine now. They're already trying to make sure I can leave tonight."

"Uh—hey!! Why didn't you tell us that earlier?!"

"We bought you presents, too. I guess we shouldn't have bothered, huh?"

Kinuhata's unnecessary remark forced Takitsubo to reply with "I'm sorry—I'll still bring them home with me" and bow in apology. Hamazura pressed down on the crown of Kinuhata's head like a contestant in one of those trivia game shows where you press the button as fast as you can.

"No, that's not it. I just meant now we won't have time to set up a welcome-home party."

"…Hamazura, that aside, you're, like, def getting punched for this later."

And so, my position stays exactly the same!! Hamazura screamed to himself.

Kinuhata, who of course didn't notice this, said, "They were talking about how you used the Crystals too much and just totally collapsed, so I was pretty worried. I mean, if it were some regular old-cold, then at least I would know what to expect. But with a condition like this, even if someone explains it, I still couldn't even imagine what had happened. Anyway, I'm super-glad you can go home now."

Hamazura agreed. "Yeah. I know you can't ever use your ability again, since it needs Crystals, but I'm relieved nothing else bad came out of this…Oh, right. You might not need this since you're getting discharged, but a little something to pass the time. A jigsaw puzzle."

"It totally wasn't a bunny suit, then…"

"I seriously want to make you cry for acting so surprised, are you okay with that, I'll assume you are!"

"With your weak technique, you'd need more than a lifetime to do that. Oh, right. I, like, got you this thing. Ta-daa!" Kinuhata beamed as she took something out of her package (that she was making Hamazura carry). "It's, like, a stuffed rabbit!!"

It was indeed a stuffed animal about fifty centimeters in length. On the whole, it was fluffy and fanciful, but for some reason, there was something that resembled human hair sticking out from its mouth, which really made one think *Did…it just eat something?*

People didn't choose surreal mascots—surreal mascots chose them. Hamazura was worried, but then Takitsubo said, "It's cute."

"Whaaat?! I thought for sure you'd make a comment about it being impractical!! Is this the result of the former Item members having such a tight bond despite their personalities always clashing?!"

"I want to make you cry like always for acting so surprised and totally trembling like that, are you okay with that, I assume you are, well here come the tears."

"He-he-he, with your frail body it would take more than a lifetime—*dghaghaghaghaghaghagha*?! Stop, you idiot, quit doing acupressure with my foot—*gwahhh* it hurts I'm gonna die okay okay I'm crying I'm really crying!!"

Hamazura slapped the floor like a pro wrestler giving up to a strange technique, pinned as he was.

Finished with her assault for now, Kinuhata wiped the sweat from her brow and said, "Actually, the real crime is how the totally perverted bunny girl maniac Hamazura apparently managed to forget even for a moment the respect and fear he should be showing us. So, like, do you get it now?"

"...If you were a sheltered, arrogant rich girl, that might have made me squirm a bit, but it's no joke coming from someone who's maxed out her physical attack power while working her shady job. Besides, it's not like bunny girls are the *only* thing I'm into."

"Really, now?" asked Kinuhata, grabbing the stuffed rabbit Takitsubo had been holding. Then she went around behind the other girl and positioned the stuffed rabbit so that her head eclipsed it.

When she did, the stuffed animal's ears alone looked like they were jutting out from the impassive patient's head...And then Kinuhata, who had created the situation, delivered her finishing lines:

"Ta-daa! Our best little wabbit. Li'l Rikou is the type who will die of loneliness. Is this the bunny girl you asked for?"

A moment later.

Something inadvertently dripped out of Shiage Hamazura's nose.

He swiped a hand up to his face unconsciously and was shocked to find that it wasn't snot. But now wasn't the time for that. When he looked, he saw Saiai Kinuhata, the one he was pretty sure had planned this all along, and Rikou Takitsubo, the one who'd been forcibly involved in the scheme, both drawing away.

"...Hamazura...You...You, for real, like bunnies that much...?"

"N-no!! It doesn't make any sense for me to get a nosebleed right now!! This is something else, something... It must be because your damn foot massage went terribly wrong!! It has to be!! Bunnies, I don't, not like...!!"

As Hamazura desperately denied it, the impassive comforting presence, Rikou Takitsubo, softly put a hand on his shoulder.

"It's okay. Hamazura, this is a hospital. It's fine if you get a nosebleed. A doctor will make you better right away."

"Oh, ohhh…!! You're the only one who would worry about me at a time like this!!"

Hamazura was about ready to collapse from this small act of kindness.

"It's okay, Hamazura," she continued. "I'm pretty sure this hospital cares for mental sicknesses, too. Even if you get a nosebleed from a bunny, there's nothing at all to worry about."

And now he was about to collapse for a different reason.

3

Four people were in the camper: Accelerator, Motoharu Tsuchimikado, Awaki Musujime, and Mitsuki Unabara.

"The terrorists causing the incident are apparently a group called Spark Signal. It looks like one of the organizations operating behind the scenes in Academy City like we do has gone out of control," said Tsuchimikado, as if it was all worthless to him.

Unabara frowned. "What's *Spark Signal* supposed to mean?"

"The walls surrounding Academy City constantly emit highly directional electromagnetic interference at an extreme upward angle to prevent information from being sent and received through EM waves," he explained. "Cell phones work all right even a meter away from the wall, but it basically cuts off all communications that would normally go past it. Our radars and stuff are based outside the wall, and normal communications have to be routed through the external connection terminals. There are security robots patrolling the top of the wall, though, and apparently they communicate with them via data cables that hang off them and connect with floor rails.

"But there are exceptions. The higher-ups seem to have a secret way of sending messages. Plenty of people do all kinds of things to try to leak Academy City intel to the outside world, after all. Our terrorists are evidently experts at stopping that."

Musujime's expression showed slight displeasure. She'd made contact with someone on the outside during the incident surrounding the holdout. Maybe she'd fought against Spark Signal in the past.

"Apparently, they're on the same level of secrecy as Hound Dog," continued Tsuchimikado, causing Accelerator's eyebrow to twitch. Tsuchimikado ignored him and continued. "And now the team formerly known as Spark Signal has created a hostage crisis. They're holed up in the largest particle accelerator in the world, here in Academy City. It's nicknamed the Hula Hoop."

As Tsuchimikado went on, he pressed a button on a device that seemed to be a TV remote.

A map of Academy City came up on the large screen inside the vehicle. There was one section that had a different color. But it wasn't one of the school districts. It was the ringed wall wrapped around Academy City's border.

"The city built a giant circular accelerator two hundred meters underground that goes along the outside wall. The former Spark Signal terrorists hijacked the control facility, also underground, removed the accelerator's limiters, then booted it up. I hear they're accelerating protons at thirty percent the speed of light right now... Naturally, if something happens that they're not okay with, they'll kick the output up past critical levels. That will apparently cause the circular accelerator tunnel to rupture, then blast the rest of it, plus one-third of Academy City, with radiation."

"Though exactly where around the ring it'll explode would be up to fate," he added.

In summary, everyone except for those in the most central areas of Academy City was in serious danger.

While he listened, Unabara tilted his head. "The particle accelerator must use a lot of electricity, right? Couldn't they just cut it off from the power plant?"

"It takes a considerable amount of power to bring it to an emergency stop," answered Tsuchimikado. "Because of that, the facility is equipped with an independent power plant. The former members of Spark Signal are, naturally, using it to keep the accelerator up and running."

"...So even though they have control of the building, they haven't made it go haywire immediately," Musujime murmured. "Which means they must have demands, right?"

Tsuchimikado shook his head. "I'm sure the leaders in the Academy City General Board know what they are, but they didn't let us in on that much intel. They'd probably tell us not to think about anything above our paygrade and that we should simply slaughter everyone opposing them."

"If there's no time limit for resolving this," Accelerator cut in, "the situation must not be that urgent."

As Tsuchimikado listened, he pressed another button on the remote. Separate from the large circle running around the outside of Academy City, two more rings appeared, each of them smaller. They were concentric rings, but tilted, so that they all met at one point on the perimeter.

"Can't say that for sure. The Hula Hoop accelerates particles through the first, second, and third rings, depending on what phase it's in. It goes from smallest to largest. As far as we can confirm, the terrorists have already moved to the biggest one, the third circle—the accelerator running around the city's edge."

"What does that mean?" Unabara demanded.

Tsuchimikado grinned. "Judging by the facility's specs, the third circle doesn't get used for low speeds like thirty percent the speed of light. It's used for experiments that need at least seventy percent... It seems like we're not being given all the information here. They could just be showing off, or it could be to hide information to keep a seriously crazy panic from breaking out."

"Meaning the situation might be even worse, but they didn't bother to inform us," spat Accelerator, sounding fed up indeed. "This ain't doin' it for me. Maybe it is serious, but it's not like they came crying and begging without caring what it looked like. Just leave 'em alone. Until the leaders actually do that, we can just sit back and relax."

"There is one piece of intel that will convince you."

Tsuchimikado pressed a button on the remote, causing a new window to appear on the screen. It showed a school bus. One of its front tires had gone flat, and the door had been destroyed by something.

"Before those former Spark Signal asses attacked the Hula Hoop, they captured about thirty elementary school kids who were going to go stargazing as an extracurricular activity, plus their teacher and the bus driver, taking them all hostage. Very convenient negotiation tool for them. The kind they can kill one by one as time passes and their demands continue to be refused."

"..."

"They could have used the Hula Hoop employees as hostages, too, but they need them—they have to force them to actually use the accelerator. If they spent those resources as time went on, they wouldn't be able to drag out this standoff. Instead, to avoid that, they increased their supply of hostages by searching elsewhere. The leaders probably have their collective panties in a bunch over the Hula Hoop facility's time limit, but I wonder how they feel about this other limit...Do you think they care much about the lives of children?"

"Bullshit," interrupted Accelerator. "I don't see why I have to go along with this."

There wasn't a trace of sympathy in his voice.

He was, after all, a villain. The strongest Level Five, whose heart was fundamentally black as tar.

"...What an eyesore," he grumbled in a tone that suggested other people, and life itself, meant nothing to him. "Always better to get the bullshit out of the way quickly."

4

Shiage Hamazura and Saiai Kinuhata were in the nighttime shopping district.

...Not that there were any particularly amorous developments waiting for them—it was simply to prepare for Rikou Takitsubo's welcome-home party. Still, it had been an incredibly sudden thing.

"Wait, a welcome-home party? What exactly are we going to do?"

"I reserved a private salon in District 3, so we're going to, like, get a whole bunch of party goods together, then go back to the hospital and totally grab Takitsubo. After that, we'll head straight there."

"A private salon, huh…," muttered Hamazura offhandedly.

The service Kinuhata had booked was basically like renting a glorified high-end karaoke booth. Since it meant anyone could easily buy a secret hideout this way, private salons were particularly popular with upper-class children…Some might wonder what value a service like this had, but with the majority of student residences being confined to dormitories in Academy City, places completely shielded from surveillance were prized.

However, a single misstep brought the danger of these sorts of facilities turning into a hotbed for sex crimes, so its existence wasn't purely a good thing, giving teachers and guardians more than enough reason to be pretty tense…

As he was contemplating this, Kinuhata, walking next to him, volunteered, "Hamazura, what are you gonna do after this?"

"Eh? Well, I think we can order good food and stuff on the private room's intercom, and maybe we could check out some silly party favors that lots of people can—"

"Not that," Kinuhata interrupted. "Item, the organization we belonged to, is basically done for. Which means you totally don't have to work for us anymore. That's why I'm asking…Like, what are you going to do after this?"

"Sorry for answering your question with one, but what about you?"

"Well, I'll probably keep trucking along as usual. Item's, like, super-gone now, but when we were active, they pushed a lot of Stargate-related assassinations on us. We're actually trying to put a new team together…If the higher-ups—the phone people—have anything to say about it, we're probably in for more super-bloody jobs. But there's totally zero merit to bringing Takitsubo in again, now that she's out of commission, so you don't need to worry about that."

Kinuhata's answer came smoothly. She didn't seem to have many objections to her situation.

"…Huh."

"So, Hamazura, what are you going to do?"

He glanced up into the air. He could see numerous stars in the night sky, even in the city, now that the sun had fully gone below the horizon.

"I feel bad for Hanzou, but I don't feel like going back to Skill-Out at the moment. I don't know what I can do right now, but I have to do something to put Takitsubo back in the normal world. She can't use the Crystals anymore, and I kind of get the feeling *our* world isn't going to let her hold out in that state forever. Which means I've gotta think of what to do next."

It wasn't a very sensible answer—it was exactly the kind some stupid thug would give. But in this case, it was clear his thoughts weren't just something he was carelessly making up.

Shiage Hamazura had once defeated a woman who was a Level Five esper.

But the battle had been far from simple. Driven to the brink of death, forced to the very, very end of his rope, he'd willed himself to move his trembling legs and stand up to her. And *this* was what had kept him going. There was no reason his answer didn't carry any weight.

He may have been a dumb street thug in every other sense of the word, but in this aspect alone, he was different…

For a few moments, Kinuhata watched Hamazura as he gazed up at the night sky.

"…In other words, you're going to pour all your passion into forcing your hobbies onto Takitsubo, ripping off that overly practical tracksuit of hers, and making her wear a bunny suit."

"Hey, is that the character I am now? Set in stone? Since we have the chance, let me clear the air. I admit I like bunny girls, but you've got the wrong idea. The most important thing—like with swimsuits, it's the beauty of unbalance, of being seen in a place you shouldn't be wearing a swimsuit, so if it was some kind of motor show companion, I would be totally fine with—"

"Ugh, would you please, like, stop it, Hamazura? I totally get it. You want the world to form a pact that will force every girl on earth to wear a bunny suit. I wish you'd just, like, stop looking at me like some kind of pervert when you think stuff like that."

"Come on," said Hamazura, shaking his head. "I've got good eyes for this stuff, so let me be totally honest with you. A bunny suit would never work on you."

"...Well let *me* be totally honest with you, too. Takitsubo may be in high school, but I, a middle schooler, am totally sexier than her."

"No, you're dead wrong!! You just can't tell it because she always wears that tracksuit—but I know if she takes it off, it would be incredible!! And I know that if you stripped, we wouldn't discover anything that's the least bit surprising!!"

"I totally want to murder you right now; I assume you're okay with that. It's okay, right? All right, time for murder."

Roar!! Something like wind began to gather in Kinuhata's hands.

Her ability was Nitrogen Armor. She was a Level Four who could freely control the nitrogen in the air. Its effective area was extremely narrow and, at most, could reach out a few centimeters from her palms...But its power was immense. She could block sniper rifle bullets barehanded or flip ten-pound tables with a single hand.

Hamazura wanted nothing more than to avoid letting her use something so terrifying to hit him, but...

"Hrm?!"

...before he could take any sort of action, Kinuhata was herself surprised. The moment she'd gathered enough nitrogen in her palms, the pseudo-winds flipped her dress skirt all the way up.

An instant before he could see what was underneath—in other words, her panties—Kinuhata slammed one hand down on her skirt front.

"That was a super-close one...Almost gave Hamazura something to fap to tonight."

"...You just said one of the top-five worst things I've ever heard anyone say in my life. Anyway, to be honest, I've got no interest in a little brat's tasteless underwear, so don't worry. When I imagine sexy, I think older ladies—you know, the type who would look good in bunny suits, and..."

"..."

Then, Saiai Kinuhata, a girl who hated to lose at anything, grabbed the front of her miniskirt with both hands and, without any warning, motioned them upward.

"Hamazura, Hamazura. Look, watch, totally flashing ya!"

"*Uwooohhhhhhhaaaaaa?!* I can...I...I can, can...I can't see anything!! What was that, a feint? You let go of your skirt an instant too early, and your arms were the only thing that lifted up; don't scare me like that—"

After making such a straightforward reaction, he noticed Kinuhata was smirking at him.

"Oh, really? Still wanna say you've got no interest...hmm?"

"You tested me...!! But that reaction was merely shock from the surprise attack; I w-wasn't hoping for anything weird—"

"Flashing ya again!"

"*Fnnghhhhhhhhh!!* D-damn! I know it's just a spiteful fake-out, but damn it!! Why the hell am I—?"

"What's this? I've got you in the palm of my hand. Once a Hamazura, always a Hamazura. Get it? It's ten thousand years too soon for some less-than-primitive sex-obsessed animal to debate whether the great Kinuhata is sexy or not, for real. To be honest with you, you're way full of yourself. Try evolving into a regular animal first."

"...No."

Hamazura, beaten and sinking into the darkness, then lifted his face up once again.

In his eyes was the intent to fight.

"I've changed!! I'm no longer an ordinary man fated to die in despair!! I will rise again!! Come at me, Kinuhata! This time, this time for sure I'll overcome the temptation of your thighs!!"

"Hee-hee. You've, like, never had any role to play other than Generic Villager A. And you think you can stand up to me? You say

some super-funny things, Hamazura. It's time for you to, like, suffer for your sexual instincts!!"

Here we go, flashy, flashy!! came the evil demon lord Kinuhata's ultimate attack.

With a shout of "Ohhh, Takitsubo! Give me strength!!" the hero Hamazura awaited the support of the brave heart that lay deep within him.

But then Kinuhata's little finger must have caught on her miniskirt.

Because on the third try, this time, her dress skirt actually did shoot upward.

Her woolen, sweater-like skirt flapped up, revealing the small white cloth inside that should have been tightly guarded. Her way of standing, with her two thighs pressed together, was surprisingly girlish, and her underwear, which rested on the top of her thighs, squeezed slightly inward. And he could see it all perfectly.

And thus, the hero Hamazura was defeated.

As red liquid spouted from his nose for the second time that day, the hero uttered his final words.

"Cowaaaaaaaaaard!! What was that supposed to be? Duck, duck, goose?! A triple play?! I was fully ready for an attack from the front, but you brought me down from a different angle. Your strategy's like the elaborate twist of a genius short story or the textbook on how to design a haunted house!!"

Of course, this wasn't actually a strategy. It had been a complete and total accident. Kinuhata, whose arms were high in the air even after gravity returned her skirt to normal, trembled for a moment in silence.

"Hamazura, you're totally dead!!"

"You've broken my spirit, and now you've come to finish off the flesh?! Can the demon lord have no mercy?!"

Hamazura ran, and Kinuhata chased.

Soon after, the delightful sounds of destruction rang out through Academy City's shopping district.

5

The camper that Accelerator, Motoharu Tsuchimikado, Awaki Musujime, and Mitsuki Unabara were riding was headed for District 23.

The world's largest particle accelerator, the Hula Hoop, was constructed over two hundred meters underground, forming a ring along the outer wall surrounding Academy City's border. Similarly, its control center was in one of the school districts bordering the wall—at the farthest end of District 23. It was, of course, more than two hundred meters belowground as well. The terrorists had captured the facility, and now they were using human shields while making their demands through the internet.

"Come to think of it, what happened to that voice on the phone that always calls?" noted Accelerator. "Don't they always drop everything to ring us up whenever shit like this happens?"

"Hell if I know," said Tsuchimikado. "If they don't want to make contact, there's nothing we can do to raise them. They're probably on another job—or vacation."

"Aw," piped in Musujime. "Does it worry you that we can't contact them?"

"I will smash your teeth, jaw, and tongue in."

Accelerator and Awaki Musujime glared at each other, but Group wasn't the type of unit that cared.

As Unabara sharpened his obsidian knife to a sharp edge, he asked Tsuchimikado, "What is Anti-Skill doing?"

"They were planning to insert a counterterror team, but it looks like they've been forbidden from actually mobilizing," answered Tsuchimikado, who was disassembling the bigger parts of his gun and doing a simple operation check. "To be fair, though, normal Anti-Skill officers acting in this situation could very likely just make things worse. The Hula Hoop is over two hundred meters underground, and it's got defenses like a nuclear attack shelter so that the gamma rays don't flood out if a rupture occurs. The walls go without saying, but you can't even punch through the doors with regular cutters or explosives."

"Could we not just use an elevator shaft or something of the sort?" asked Unabara.

"There's a ton of partitioning walls for them, too. They're like automatic doors—they have little cutout pieces, so they can precisely close up while avoiding the elevator wires. The ducts are basically the same."

"If we dawdle, it'll clue them in," thought Musujime aloud, efficiently positioning the corkscrews that she used as weapons in her pockets. "Try to damage the doors or walls without thinking, and the former Spark Signal terrorists are liable to react by blowing a hostage's head off."

Unabara wiped off the dirt stuck to his knife's blade, asking, "What's it like on the inside?"

"Didn't you hear me? The walls are thick enough to stop gamma radiation. Regular EM waves won't get through, either. We also can't drill a hole to slide in a snake camera. We've got the layout of the building, but we don't know how many people are positioned where."

"…What about those nanodevices?" asked Musujime.

An unpleasant air settled over the camper.

Nanodevices called the Underline were scattered throughout the whole city, keeping a ceaselessly watchful eye on everything. Naturally, the Hula Hoop should have been under surveillance as well, but…

"We should assume that when the emergency doors are completely shut, they block the electron beams used in the network system… Not that I'd be surprised if there was an even more secret trick they're using to get around this issue."

After finishing that line of thought, Tsuchimikado paused, then continued. "Also, we don't *officially* know about those nanodevices existing. Even if the higher-ups had information, it wouldn't make it around to us."

"…It's difficult not knowing how many we need to kill to make this operation a success. We very well may be shot in the back after thinking we're in the clear."

"Then we should have someone who doesn't mind getting shot

make the assault." Tsuchimikado waved his handgun, dismantled and now put back together, gesturing toward the simple bed.

Accelerator was sitting on it. He could reflect any and all attacks.

"I'm not about to let this beach-bro jagoff order me around, but doing this alone might be easier than letting you people watch my back," noted Accelerator, eyeballs flitting around to return the glare. "But how do I get in there? You want me to bust through two hundred meters of bedrock *and* those defensive walls?"

...When he put it that way, it really made the proposal seem impossible, but of all the people who could potentially make it happen, Accelerator was candidate number one.

However, Tsuchimikado shook his head. "Better not. Spark Signal is one thing, but it'll be a pain if you mess up and harm the hostages or the operating accelerator. Let's play it by the book. We'll have Musujime use her power to ignore three-dimensional limitations."

Musujime's Move Point ability was classified as a relative of teleportation. It could bring a target object or person to a location of the user's choosing, while ignoring obstacles such as walls and ceilings.

But then Musujime frowned. "You want me to accurately warp something as heavy as a person to a spot I can't see, in a building I've only ever seen a rough layout of, over two hundred meters underground? I think the chances of him ending up buried in a wall or the ground are about fifty percent. But if you're still game, I won't stop you."

"I'm not asking you to do something as difficult as that." Tsuchimikado grinned. "District 23 is chock-full of aviation and space-related facilities, so most of the ground is covered by flat runways. But that would be a waste of real estate. They wouldn't have any space to set up the actual airplane development facilities and whatnot."

"What are you getting at?" asked Musujime.

"...What I mean is: Basements and underground facilities run pretty deep here. Nothing's directly linked to the Hula Hoop, but we can close the distance between us and the other side of those walls and the dirt in the ground. You use your Move Point from that location and launch our strategic weapon right into their midst."

The camper had entered District 23 while they were discussing this.

Normally, entry of civilian vehicles was prohibited without a specific pass or belonging to certain businesses, but their RV rolled on through like it was natural.

District 23, with its many scattered runways, had comparatively few tall buildings. The camper stopped next to a building that was only as tall as a school gymnasium, but its sides stretched out quite a bit.

The four got out.

When Accelerator placed his crutch's four leg pieces onto the ground, Musujime's eyes widened in surprise.

"Did you build a brand-new crutch? What a good worker ant."

"Shut up and get walking," he grumbled half-heartedly. "What are you, some annoying hag who assumes people are having an affair just because they changed clothes?"

Accelerator entered the low building. It was a proving ground for air force–related weapons, but naturally, the four had come here for what lay underground.

Using a pass that he had gotten from who knows where, Tsuchimikado disengaged the lock on the employee elevator. The lift carried them straight down about 150 meters.

It was there that Accelerator felt a tingling sensation around his temples.

…Am I getting a bad signal now because we went so far underground…?

Unconsciously, he put a hand to his choker, but there was nothing he could do about it.

Outside the reopened elevator doors was a large floor shined to a sparkle, like a department store or office building. There were no windows, but there was so much illumination it felt like it was possible to forget this was underground. Quite a few people would believe it if someone had told him this was the twelfth floor of a famous department store.

Accelerator and the others weren't headed for any specific room, but for the wall at the opposite end of the floor.

After checking the map displayed on his cell phone screen, Tsuchi-mikado rapped on the wall with the back of his hand as though knocking on the door to the president's room.

"Here we are. Diagonally down, at thirty degrees eastward and about eighty meters away, there should be a Hula Hoop control facility hallway. It doesn't look like there's any closer place than this. It should be a wide-open space down there, too."

"Eight meters…," repeated Musujime.

"On paper, it seems like even a certain middle school student in Judgment could manage this."

"…Don't even go there. I just need to do it, right?" Musujime glared at Tsuchimikado, who had purposely made her recall a cer-tain twin-tailed teleport esper. She headed for the wall then turned back to Accelerator and said, "Going in right away, then?"

"Hold up," said not Accelerator but Tsuchimikado. He slid a fin-ger across his own neck. "Something's going on with your electrode choker, right?"

"…"

"Wait fifteen minutes. I'll try using the vertically hanging wires in the elevator shaft as a makeshift antenna so that EM waves will reach into the facility."

"I can help you with that," said Unabara, adding that he didn't have anything else to do anyway.

Tsuchimikado shook his head. "You're standing in for our man on the phone. If you make an emergency call, it should temporarily con-nect you with the General Board. Get in touch with them, and just to be safe, warn them not to send in agents from any other units. I don't want a separate crew to start doing things without us realizing and winding up caught in the aftermath when they get themselves killed."

"Why me?" asked Unabara, confused.

Tsuchimikado grinned. "Because your face will probably be most popular with the old guys."

"Need I remind you it's only a rental."

The boy, not originally even an Asian much less a Japanese person, used an index finger to scratch the cheek on his gentle face that Japanese people would probably find appealing.

Tsuchimikado turned around, back to Accelerator.

"Listen up—the operation starts in fifteen minutes. I think you'll be fine, but just to be sure, check on your electrode choker again and make sure there's no other malfunctions that could potentially happen. We can deal with you dying, but not if it means those hostage kids get killed."

6

The Hula Hoop: the world's largest particle accelerator.

Constructed two hundred meters underground, the facility could accelerate photons to a maximum of 99.22 percent the speed of light and maintain that state for three hundred seconds.

Still, even this large-scale facility had its limits.

Forcing it to operate at speeds or times higher than it was designed for meant the Hula Hoop would eventually collapse, exposing one-third of Academy City to massive gamma radiation emissions.

The boy hadn't known that until this very moment.

Well. He'd also never had a masked man hold a gun to his head, nor had his hands ever been tied behind his back. From the same school bus were almost thirty of his classmates, their chaperone teacher, and the bus driver, all trembling together. This very span of time itself was one big clump of reality he'd never experienced before.

"Hold it at fifty percent light speed. The Hula Hoop is a distraction. They won't negotiate if we use it. That's why we kidnapped these kids."

"But if we go too far, won't city leadership try to bomb us along with the entire underground facility? There aren't any civilian buildings directly above us, just runways. If they wanted to, they could blow us to hell."

"That's what the Hula Hoop is for. If we show them we could

potentially cause it to explode at any moment, it'll prevent the General Board from doing anything drastic."

"I'll check the escape routes. Once negotiations are complete, with the accelerator running at about seventy percent, we'll cause an explosion in its wall, intentionally hitting the control facility with a small-scale blast. Then we'll go to Special Evacuation Area B and put on the heavy anti-radiation-powered suits to endure the emissions, and while they're fussing over setting up radiation countermeasures, we'll cross the wreckage and escape outside."

Only sinister, eerie words flew back and forth over the boy's head.

He couldn't imagine a situation where he would be released safely.

Whether this took a turn for the better or for the worse, none would be saved.

That was all he could could think about.

"Looks like it's time."

Ignoring the boy's terrible quaking, a man who acted like their leader, also in a mask, glanced at his wristwatch.

"Well, I didn't think the leadership would react without us using anyone…Is the camera ready? The real negotiations start now. Prepare yourselves."

His words were rife with euphemisms, but the masked people around him, who seemed to be subordinates, responded swiftly. The camera itself wasn't anything special; they were apparently going to use one built into a cell phone. But it was attached to a weird machine via a cable, maybe so nobody could trace the transmission.

"Video and sound are both ready to go."

"Hotline to the General Board secured. We're patching through an Anti-Skill office. We can go live on your signal."

"Great. Let's get started."

Before he even finished speaking, the leader grabbed the boy's hair in one hand. The boy screamed, more out of surprise than from pain, but the man didn't care. He dragged the boy away, then tossed him in front of the lens.

The boy wanted to object, but his words caught in his throat before he could.

That was because the leader was ready with a gun that anyone could tell was real.

"One last act of mercy. Blindfold him."

The young child struggled, but it was no use. His hands were tied behind his back, and even if they hadn't been, one little kid couldn't have put up any meaningful resistance. Before he knew it, a piece of cloth was wrapped around his head, covering his eyes.

"Get him on his knees. Start the broadcast."

In the darkness, someone grabbed his arm and forced him up. And then someone walked up to stand behind him. A cold, hard sensation pressed up against the back of his head.

He heard a small, motor-like noise as the high-efficiency cell phone camera's autofocus kicked in.

The man standing right behind him began to speak, as though reading from a speech.

"We hoped for a peaceful resolution. Again and again, we offered solutions that would cause the least amount of bloodshed. But it seems our efforts have worked against us. We seem to have given you the impression that we don't have the nerve to take real action. If that is the case, then allow me to apologize."

A chill.

The boy could feel the soft hair on his back stand up.

"In order to instill within you the ability to make sane decisions, we'd like to show you how serious we are. However, know that this was never a choice that needed to be made—and this was never blood that had to be spilled. I hope this stings your conscience and makes you regret your foolish judgment."

The boy heard a click from the gun pressed to the back of his head.

He wasn't old enough to know that it was the sound of a thumb cocking the hammer, but he understood that it was a definitive cue.

"If you do not reach a swift decision, we promise that even more innocent blood will be spilled. We won't hold back. We believe we've assembled everything necessary to change your minds. Therefore, we are considering using them all if need be. Still, we hope it won't come to that."

He wanted to run away.

He wanted to scream something.

But he knew if he did that, things would immediately take a turn for the worse.

"Now, we'll make use of the first."

And if he stayed quiet, he'd just be killed.

He knew that, but if he resisted, he'd only be killed even sooner.

He couldn't make a move.

He knew that if he didn't move, he'd be killed—but he couldn't even lift a single finger of the hands tied behind his back.

"The negotiations start now."

He was frustrated.

Realizing this emotion, which lay deeper down than his fear, the boy finally opened his trembling mouth.

"…This…"

It wasn't to plead for his life.

"…This plan will never work…"

It was the opposite.

"It doesn't matter how fancy your tricks are. It doesn't matter how scary your weapons are. Your evil deeds will never be allowed to happen."

A counterattack, at the end of the line—he wanted to do at least this much.

"I have faith. The world is a lot kinder than villains like you think it is!! You might have used a crazy plan to cover it up, but I know that a hero will catch you!! And save everyone. Someone out there, in this big world, who will save us!!"

"I see."

The leader, standing behind the boy, addressed him for the first time.

What he said was quite simple.

"Even if there was, it looks like they weren't in time for you."

The child heard a soft grinding noise.

The sound came from inside the gun, resounding directly in his skull from the muzzle pressed to his head. Because the man slowly pulled back on the trigger, a small spring was contracting.

The blindfolded boy shut his eyes anyway.

Nevertheless, until the end, he whispered to himself.

("...I believe.")

Da-bamm!! came the sound of a gunshot.

It rattled the boy's skull, scattering the scent of iron into the area.

At that very moment—

A gunshot, no more and no less, had rang out in the control facility of the Hula Hoop, the world's largest particle accelerator. Dark-red liquid splattered on the floor, and a metallic smell filled the air, mixing with a faint, drifting stench particular to lit gunpowder. An empty bullet casing fell to the ground, and a shrill clang followed.

A gun had definitely gone off.

A bullet had been fired—no ifs, ands, or buts—mercilessly, piercing flesh and bone.

Thump came a dull noise. It was the sound of the boy's small body falling to the hard floor. His children's brand clothing was awfully stained in red now. It was fresh blood and nothing else.

However.

That blood didn't belong to the boy.

It was flowing from the leader's arm, which had been holding the gun up behind him.

A third party had shot the masked man from a blind spot to the side.

"Wha...?"

For a few moments, the leader, dazed, looked at his arm—the gun blown out of his hand, and his arm bent at an unnatural forty-five-degree angle. The pain seemed to hit him shortly after.

But he never screamed.

*   *   *

As soon as the man's gaze shifted somewhere outside the cell phone camera's range, more gunshots followed. *Ga-bam-bam-bam!!* Bullets penetrated the man's entire body, sending him careening to the side.

Several panicked voices from the other masked people overlapped.

But then someone outside the video frame fired off even more bullets. The man filming with the cell phone was shot, and he fell to the floor along with the phone he'd been holding. From the Academy City leaders' points of view, who were probably watching through that camera, only the ceiling would be visible now, and then just gray noise. The lens had cracked.

Now with no video, the blindfolded boy's words came through alone, in a quiet, quavering tone:

"A he...hero...?"

"A villain."

And then, on the heels of this:

A reply came, sinister, as if to blacken out the place.

"A villainous piece of shit."

There was a *crunch.*

It was the sound of the villain's sole coming down on the cell phone the terrorists been using to film, utterly crushing it.

And with that noise, the number-one enemy in Academy City began his battle.

7

Level Five espers were still only human.

Number one or not, it didn't change the fact that he was a primate like the rest of them.

Whatever special powers he had, he would die if he couldn't breathe air; he would starve if he didn't eat food. He had a normal lifespan, too. If you stabbed his internal organs, it should kill him no problem.

Any human who shared these weaknesses could be killed.

No matter how monstrous, if they could still be classified as a human, it was doable.

Spark Signal was originally a special unit with the goal of aggressively eliminating any who threatened to leak Academy City secrets. They had fought many powerful espers during their term of service. That was why Spark Signal could appropriately respond to espers who had strange, unfathomable powers. They could calmly size up the enemy and formulate a means of defeating them.

This was what the masked former members of Spark Signal thought.

They honestly believed it was possible.

However.

Was Academy City's number one really human?

Roar!! A whirling blast wind tore through the air.

The bullets caught in it seemed to scatter every which way, but then every single shot hit one of the former Spark Signal terrorists.

Of course, they hadn't executed this grand design only to wind up being shot like this. Sensing a serious threat to their lives, they mobilized all the prowess and knowledge they'd cultivated in order to stand up to the white-haired Level Five with all their might, hoping to find a way to escape.

One tried to hide behind an obstacle and fire a rifle.

Another tried to take a hostage and convince him to stop.

Yet another tried to use explosives to take out a pillar, aiming to crush him under so many pounds of debris.

But all of it was pointless.

Not ineffective—it simply had no meaning.

The bullets didn't work.

As soon as the rounds made contact with the monster's skin, they bounced straight back and punched right through the shooter.

The hostage didn't work.

Right as the terrorist reached out to grab a child to use as a shield, his arm snapped in an unnatural direction.

The explosives didn't work.

Before he could hit the detonator, his fingers were crushed, along with the transmitter they held, and then blown away.

No...

That isn't all, thought one of the masked former Spark Signal members.

The man, cold sweat thick on his face invisible to the outside, realized the true terror welling up within him was due to something else.

No.

Academy City's number-one Level Five, Accelerator, wasn't arrogant.

He didn't boast needlessly about his overwhelming power. When he saw the terrorists dropping like flies, he didn't slip up. If he had slipped up, they might have still had a chance, but Accelerator wouldn't allow even that slim possibility.

Sometimes using his ability and sometimes relying on his gun, he brandished the least amount of power necessary along the shortest route to obtain the greatest results. This was no longer a "man vs. man" battle, nor a match of "man vs. monster." There was no emotion involved in this violence.

As an analogy:

He was a heat-seeking missile precisely tracking a desperately fleeing jet from behind.

The argument wasn't over who would win. It was whether or not the attack reached its targets. And if it did, death undoubtedly awaited. The calamity Accelerator was causing had already reached such a level.

How much work do you think we put into this plan...?

Using his ability, the Level Five somehow moved in a low arc through the air to attack the former Spark Signal man's teammates. He watched, dumbfounded, trying to make sense of the chaos in his mind.

Spark Signal's abilities are on full display, plus we had several contingency plans prepared in addition to the main one...And yet, and yet...He's crushing us like a pile of dead leaves...?!

And then it happened.

After another one of his teammates went down, their consciousness draining along with their freshly spilled blood, the monster's head swiveled to look at him.

What are we supposed to do...?

The former Spark Signal terrorist locked gazes with those red eyes.

They're almost like a laser sight, he thought.

What are we supposed to—?!

There was no winning or losing.

He'd been locked onto—and the attack was incoming.

The time required had been just three hundred seconds.

Then, silence and peace visited the world's largest particle accelerator, the Hula Hoop, once more.

8

Now the boy knew.

He couldn't see what was going on through the blindfold. But the electricity in the air had gone away. The very world of despair those terrorists had created was gone.

He heard a gasp from nearby.

It was probably one of his classmates or one of the adults with them.

He couldn't sense any relief in their sighs. Maybe the way the situation was resolved had been too violent.

The boy frantically worked his bound hands. Just when he thought he was about to tear his skin on the rope, the loop suddenly fell off one of his hands. He moved his trembling arm and took the blindfold off his face.

The first light he'd seen in some time stunned him at first.

The boy put a hand up to block the fluorescent white light, squinted, and then took a look around. He *had to be somewhere around here.* Thinking that, the boy's head stopped in a certain direction.

Along the wall.

Terrorists, beaten and battered but still barely breathing, lay there. And facing those terrorists was a person with white hair and a crutch. He was facing away from the boy. It wasn't visible what sort of expression this person was making.

...That was the feeling the boy got.

But maybe that wasn't the reality.

After all, a moment later, the white-haired person had disappeared into thin air. Without any announcement, as though two frames of film had been cut together wrong, the white-haired person was no longer anywhere to be found.

The boy stared at the empty space he'd occupied for some time.

A villainous piece of shit.

He thought about who that person could be. The boy had been hoping for a hero, but all he had instead was that unflinching answer.

9

"Nice job out there. Looks like you have a pretty heroic streak, huh?"

When Awaki Musujime spoke to him, Accelerator very nearly pulled the trigger on her.

He'd disappeared so suddenly, of course, because he'd retreated using her Move Point. Now that he'd eliminated Spark Signal, the only things to be done were for the Hula Hoop employees to unlock the doors and elevators and quickly release the children onto the surface. There was no more need for a villain.

Accelerator took a look around.

They were in the basement of the air force building they'd originally arrived at before his assault. On the spacious floor, polished to a shine like a high-class department store, stood not only Musujime, but also Tsuchimikado and Unabara.

"One thing is bugging me," said Accelerator. "It's about what those shithead terrorists were demanding from the higher-ups."

Tsuchimikado's eyebrow arched with a twitch. "...I decided to look into it while you were storming the castle, but their guard is even tighter than I expected. All we know is that it must be something the higher-ups really aren't happy about—"

"I don't want to hear about your incompetence. Shut up and listen to me, you half-wit," spat Accelerator, getting back on topic. "While I was turning those assholes down there into meatballs, I heard a few of their screechings. I think they were crying because they wouldn't be able to achieve their goal at this rate."

"...Are you saying they leaked what their demands were as well?" prompted Unabara.

Accelerator was silent for a moment.

Eventually, he answered, "...Dragon."

The simple six-letter word filled the air with tension.

Even in the hidden nanodevice network Underline, that information was so secret only its name existed. Even Accelerator and the others, who lived in the heart of darkness, didn't know what it was—but perhaps the act of searching for it would be the link they needed to oppose the leadership of the all-powerful Academy City. The term had enough weight and meaning behind it to warrant such speculation.

Accelerator, Motoharu Tsuchimikado, Awaki Musujime, Mitsuki Unabara.

They'd formed a temporary allied front, each searching for what Dragon was, each for their own reasons.

However—

Apparently, they weren't the only ones chasing the Dragon.

Then, as if offering proof, Accelerator said:

"*'Disclose information on Dragon at once.'*...Apparently, that was the only thing those shithead terrorists were demanding. Meaning the higher-ups managed to trick us into destroying a clue without knowing it."

INTERLUDE
ONE

Academy City, District 1.

This district, lined with nothing but facilities presiding over judicature and administration, had none of the vitality of the other normal districts. Residential areas were absent as a matter of course, but restaurants were also few and far between. In exchange for condensing the mechanisms required to maintain a smoothly running megacity into one area, this district held only the bare minimum needed to function as a human settlement.

It was a sprawling, highly mechanical landscape, and yet, mixed within that zone was one extremely peculiar building:

The General Board office building.

Considering how it occupied an entire skyscraper, it went beyond "office building." Combined with the fact that its upkeep costs were 100 percent paid for by taxes, the term *palace* might have been more appropriate. In any case, it was an extremely extravagant building, and it had been prepared for but one of the twelve leaders of Academy City.

That man's name was Thomas Platinaburg.

Thomas—the building's owner—was currently standing in a vast,

gorgeous room within his tower that resembled the audience cham-
bers that could be found often in RPG castles. The space, used for
meetings with visitors, took up one whole floor.

His surroundings were currently absent of subordinates, however.
Given his position, it wouldn't be strange if Thomas brought countless bodyguards with him, but he purposely distanced others from
this expansive room. And right now, this official General Board
member was, in fact, meeting with a guest.

A guest he'd called personally from outside the city.

A guest who was a sniper for hire.

She was a tall woman. Fair-skinned, with long blond hair. Her
beauty could have easily earned her a spot to shine under stage
lights, rather than stand on muddy battlefields. But at her feet, as she
sat on the sofa, was a bag large enough to fit an entire person, most
likely containing her "tool of the trade."

She was relatively famous in the industry—though Thomas didn't
know whether being famous was an honor for their particular line
of work.

"How is Mr. Sunazara doing, Miss Stephanie Gorgeouspalace?"

Thomas named two people.

Stephanie was the sniper's name. And Sunazara was the name of
the man that sniper had looked up to as a master.

The woman nodded straightforwardly in response. "Things are
going well. He hasn't woken up yet, though. Still, it's all possible
because of the Academy City life support equipment you lent us,
and so you have my thanks. Without it, he would have been gone
by now."

"No, no. It pains me quite a lot as well. It seems we had a minor
disagreement and some other minor issues, but your friend was still
harmed by one of Academy City's people."

Once before, five secret organizations—Group, Item, Block, Member,
and School—had fought, and several had fallen apart. Chimitsu Sunazara had been hired by one of them and subsequently lost to someone
from a different organization. The bomb he fell prey to had blasted an
entire building apart, leaving him heavily wounded and comatose.

When Thomas Platinaburg had heard about the news, he had secretly retrieved Chimitsu Sunazara and sent him and a life support-equipped bed out of the city to Stephanie.

Not out of pure kindness, of course. It was to indebt her to him, to bring him business that would be to his benefit.

"If you don't mind me asking, who would you like me to target?"

"Oh, yes. I will prepare the documents separately, but...You may know his name already. Academy City's number one—the Level Five known as Accelerator."

This request wasn't made as a representative of Academy City. On the contrary, it was an extremely personal ambition.

On September 30, Accelerator, who had engaged an Amata Kihara-led Hound Dog force in battle, raided Thomas Platinaburg's personal residence while searching for information and even fired a shotgun at Thomas himself.

And this here was his act of retaliation, pure and simple.

Of course, it was retaliation in two ways—both simple revenge on an emotional front and a clever way of disciplining his subordinates who couldn't keep things under control.

"Can you do it?"

"If you tell me to."

Her answer was what he'd expected. He'd had the "consideration" to distance his subordinates from the actual talks, and above all, Thomas had prepared a trump card.

"When firing on the target, there is no need to worry about collateral damage. No matter who you involve in the process, we will cover it up...Yes, and if you wish to fill Saiai Kinuhata and the other former members of Item with lead the way they did to Mr. Sunazara, that's be fine by me."

"Well, well. This on top of everything you've already done for Mr. Sunazara. Yes, Academy City's technology is truly a wonderful thing. I have never seen healing devices quite like that."

"Ha-ha. There's more than just good technology in this city, but I'm proud when it finds peaceful uses."

"Yes, quite...It is incredible that you managed to place a small transmitter inside Mr. Sunazara's wounded body. It seems slightly different from a basic nanodevice, however. Still, one cannot quite find something so miniaturized inside a body anywhere else."

A moment later.

A chill permeated the room's air, all the way to its corners.

Except…it wasn't the air. Not on close inspection.

It was just Thomas Platinaburg himself, perceiving the world around him again, this time through the filter of terror.

"Please, wait."

Thomas held out a hand to stop her.

"I'm sure you're well aware of how vital the technology that went into that life support machine is. It may be downgraded to an extent for use on the outside, but it still has incredible value as Academy City tech. We wanted to deliver Chimitsu Sunazara to you as swiftly and safely as possible. However, we cannot have our life support technology leaking to external actors. That was why we put *that* in him. Without it, we wouldn't have been able to get Mr. Sunazara, sleeping in his bed, to you this quickly."

"I see."

At this time, Thomas Platinaburg failed to notice something. No one could reasonably blame him, but it was a fatal oversight.

After all…

Stephanie Gorgeouspalace never normally spoke so politely.

And the other fact…

…was that purposely changing her tone like this meant she was suppressing her emotions to an extreme degree.

"Well then, aside from the grain-sized transmitter, he's been fitted with devices that give off shocks, so you could stop his four major organs at any time with one signal…Is that also part of the basic safety precautions?"

A shock of another kind shot through Thomas's body.

An unpleasant sweat dripped down his skin, all over his body.

But it was already too late.

The next thing he knew, Stephanie, who had been sitting on the couch, quickly blurred and appeared directly in front of him. She reached out with her right hand, and with the feather pen she'd gripped in it, stabbed it straight into Thomas's gut.

Thomas didn't feel the pain of his flesh tearing.

There was no time for that.

"I fear I must return the favor."

When Stephanie pulled the feather pen out, there was a small transceiver in her hand. What had she buried in the wound? And the transceiver's frequency—what was it supposed to send a signal to? When Thomas came up with a guess, he felt the fear of death so clearly it paralyzed his most basic sensation of pain.

"Your poor tricks were a mistake. If you had been up-front about returning Mr. Sunazara and making this request of me, I would have been glad to be your pawn."

"…Wa…Wait…"

Thomas Platinaburg, face trembling, glared at the assassin…and more specifically, at her thumb on the transceiver. Abandoning the polite speech he'd been using for show, he made his final attempt at negotiation in a ragged voice.

"…If you…cause a mess here…it could get in the way of your revenge…If you would be up-front…about letting me help you… you could easily…avenge Sunazara…"

"Oh, yes, I forgot to mention one thing," answered Stephanie immediately, without seeming to have particularly given it much thought.

Almost like she was cutting the conversation itself off.

"My revenge is against all of Academy City."

An instant later, she pressed the transceiver button.

The transmitter buried in Thomas's wound responded quickly, executing a special electric shock. It swiftly stopped four of his organs, which put an end to him as well.

His final moments were one long scream.

Without so much as a glance to the fallen corpse, Stephanie pocketed the transceiver, her expression annoyed at the triviality.

She began to hear the pattering of footsteps nearby.

Thomas's black-suited bodyguards had probably heard his screams and were finally coming. Judging from the number of people she noticed on her way to this reception room, she estimated there would be around two hundred of them.

But Stephanie's expression was utterly unconcerned. Humming to herself, she unhitched the fasteners of the giant bag at her feet, then withdrew her "tool of the trade."

It was no sniper rifle.

Her weapon of choice was a light automatic shotgun.

She could carry it around, with effort, but it was a special firearm, based on the high rate of fire of a machine gun and normally used while mounted on a tripod, except its ammunition was purely shotgun rounds. A custom gun, designed just for Stephanie, with enough destructive power that firing at point-blank range would transform an armored car into a crunched-up aluminum can.

The reason Stephanie, who nominally worked as a sniper, had brought a direct weapon like that was very simple.

"Mr. Sunazara took potshots from afar."

At last, mixing in a somehow nostalgic tone, Stephanie Gorgeouspalace finally returned to her usual voice as she spoke to herself.

"But isn't it simpler to get up close and start firing like crazy?"

Bam!!

The massive doors crashed inward.

At the same time, a calamitous storm thundered out from her shotgun.

Her revenge had begun.

CHAPTER 2

A Simple Yet Complex Point
V.S._Calamity.

1

"I see."

The voice of one of the General Board members, Shiokishi, drifted into the camper.

That didn't mean such a prominent city figure had personally visited the vehicle Accelerator and the others were aboard. No, it was simply a live-video call, displayed on a screen.

"Well, I'm glad you could resolve the Hula Hoop issue without much damage…But still, I checked the battle report you sent, and I have to say that you're all incredibly high spec. As always," the man continued, his tone half appalled.

For once, Accelerator and the others were in agreement: This was the last person they wanted to hear that from.

Pictured on the large screen was not a soft old man who would look good in a tuxedo.

Well, maybe he was like that on the inside, but at a glance, you wouldn't be able to tell, because…

He was wearing a powered suit.

It increased the user's physical abilities with highly elastic wires and powerful motors, which in turn was covered by thick armor.

The stocky mech, better described as *weapon* than *armor*, was making Shiokishi's elegant chair creak.

"Is that what's on your mind?"

They didn't know who of the four he'd spoken to, but Shiokishi's tone was casual. He didn't appear unhappy, even though his subordinates looked at him the way someone might regard a crazed person.

"Calmly think it over for a second and you'll understand. This world we live in has no shortage of things that can end a person's life. People often say 'I can't believe that happened to him' or 'He wasn't a person anyone would hate'...But that's absurd. Humans die when their time comes, whether or not there's an apparent reason. And all the more true for someone in my position. I'm of the opinion that anyone who wants to escape the grasp of sudden misfortune has no choice but to be on guard at all times."

With his heavily armored hand, he rapped on the caramel-brown table in front of him.

"That's why I excuse myself from meeting with you all in person, instead using video feeds and the like. Why let others know where I am? One can never be too careful."

"What're you so scared of?" spat Accelerator. "I bet you're just holed up in some nuke shelter."

"Are you saying I should stop worrying if that's true? Perish the thought. We're in Academy City. Let's see—Musujime, was it?— the thickness of the walls doesn't mean much if you have an ability like hers. Even now, I'm scared someone might throw a bomb inside this room."

"...You may be on the General Board as well, but you seem quite different from others on it, for instance, Monaka Oyafune."

The one who said that was Mitsuki Unabara. It was probably because he'd been in contact with said board member during the Hula Hoop incident.

In contrast to Shiokishi, Oyafune started by trusting others, then trying to advance matters through compromise and cooperation—a rare sight in the General Board, which was mostly a collection of blackhearted men and women of authority— But...

"*No, that's simply how she defends herself.*"

...Shiokishi saw it differently.

"*It's rather like the Self-Defense Forces. She makes an appeal to her harmlessness on the basis that she doesn't possess any apparent offensive capability, denying others any excuse to attack her. It's a high-level technique in its own right, and one I certainly can't imitate...In the past, though, she used to be quite the aggressive negotiator. Her daughter must be the main reason that she...*"

"*Still, even with this, I feel uneasy,*" noted Shiokishi, wrapping his hands around his stumpy powered suit. "*I would be slightly more reassured if there were cyborg technology that let me change out pieces of my very body instead of having to equip a machine like this. But it seems there are many problems on that front as well. Understandable, too—precision equipment starts to die after around five years, and having major surgery each time to exchange artificial organs would be too much of a strain. It would be less taxing to take those artificial organs and consolidate them all into a life support machine, put that into a powered suit, then wear it on the outside. And while cyborgs still have bodies with limited capacity, you can add as much machinery to a powered suit as needed. I will admit that as a development of the hospital bed and the portable oxygen tank, it is nice, but if you asked me, I—*"

"Mr. Shiokishi," cut in Tsuchimikado. He knew that once this board member started rambling about his stupid obsessions, they'd never hear the end of it. "I assume you went through the trouble of contacting us for more than a basic combat report. It would have been faster to go through The Voice on the Phone if that was all you wanted."

"*I'm sure you had a faint idea, but I have the agent that normally commands you elsewhere at the moment. More than one incident is occurring in the city, after all...I thought he'd stop before things got out of hand, but to think that youngster at our table would be taken out.*"

"..."

"There's no reason to be distrustful. No need to fret over undisclosed information—everything is connected. If you all do what you need to do, everything will become clear sooner or later."

The camera wobbled. "Sugitani? Minobe?" said Shiokishi shortly before someone outside the video frame grabbed the camera and restabilized it.

"On that note, I'd like to request another job of you."

"...Are you saying that we're looking at back-to-back crises?" asked Tsuchimikado again, remembering the past death matches between the five organizations of Group, School, Member, Item, and Block.

Shiokishi, however, shook his powered suit helmet. *"It's nothing that serious. Essentially, I want you to mop up the leftovers. Associates of what used to be Spark Signal, the ones who attacked the Hula Hoop, still seem to be hiding in Academy City. If we leave them to their own devices, they may come up with strange contingency plans."*

Their associates.

Ones who sought information about Dragon, one of Academy City's deepest, darkest secrets.

"I'll forward you the target details, but this should be easier than the Hula Hoop incident...At least, easy enough that you won't need too much time to prepare. After surviving something like that, I'm sure you'll have no trouble dealing with them. That's about it."

Shiokishi moved to hang up, but suddenly, Accelerator asked:

"...Ever heard the word *dragon* before?"

"A famous word. I believe it's in the title of one of our video games beloved the world over."

Accelerator clicked his tongue. If Shiokishi had said he didn't know, Accelerator could have pressed the issue, but a reply like that left him no room to maneuver. If he pursued the subject any further, Shiokishi would just evade it.

Whether he knew about Accelerator's intent or not, Shiokishi clapped his thick steel palms together a couple times and wrapped things up by saying, *"You're all students, too. Get this trivial stuff out of the way, and you can go back to leading your own lives."*

2

Tonight was Rikou Takitsubo's welcome-home party.

Having suddenly ended up in a position to prepare for it, Shiage Hamazura and Saiai Kinuhata had bought a large amount of silly party favors in a District 7 shopping area.

"...Hey, I don't get this. Why am I in a movie theater, and why are we the only ones in here two minutes before the show starts?"

"I'm a short-film expert, so it's super-okay. And these are the ten-minute-long kind so you can watch a bunch of in a row with five minute breaks in between. If you do the math, we can watch two and still totally make it in time to meet up with Takitsubo."

"Wait a second—none of that explains why it's empty except for us two."

"You're being too loud and I'm like totally holding it in right now, so please don't talk to me, Hamazura."

You want to watch that badly, huh? he thought, shoulders drooping.

Kinuhata's hobby was watching movies, but she didn't seem very interested in blockbuster Hollywood films or the like. But when it came to B movies, or anything bad enough that it could be called a C movie, she couldn't seem to pass it up.

"Gwah, this is awful. It only just started, but I can already tell from the first two minutes that this movie is totally gonna suck..."

"Well, that's usually how it goes when you get me involved!!" shouted Hamazura at the top of his lungs in the dark, since there was nobody else in the seats anyway. "You were the one who dragged me into this theater!!"

But Kinuhata, not caring one bit about what Hamazura had to say, shook her head, expression downcast. "No, no. That's totally not it. I don't want to watch C movies that are self-aware, where they're like *Yippee, let's all make a really dumb C movie!!*— I want to see the natural ones, the ones where they were super-serious about taking on Hollywood but had so many problems they ended up being C reels."

"Yeah? The fact that the setting of this one is supposed to be the near future but the heroine is wearing a dress straight from the

Middle Ages with no explanation. I can put that down to the world building, but...Doesn't this story take place in the middle of winter? Did they film it during the summer or something? Everyone's sweating, and now I can't think of anything else."

"Hamazura. Look at the left side of the screen. You can totally see a smokestack from a thermal power plant on the opposite shore..."

"Are you serious? That completely ruins all the SF atmosphere they worked so hard for! I heard about bad shots where planes fly over while filming, but the least you can do is make sure ahead of time that none of the buildings are wrong!!"

Even Hamazura, who didn't particularly have a thing for movies, had his head in his hands at this one. For a short while, Kinuhata was fidgeting, thighs rubbing against each other, but finally she said, "I can't hold it in any longer. I totally don't have it in me to stick this one out. I'm going to the bathroom. I'll put all my eggs in the next short-film basket."

"What? I have to go it alone?!" cried Hamazura in a fluster, but Kinuhata had already swiftly left the screening room.

With nothing else to do, he looked back at the screen, intending to kill time rather than seriously enjoy the movie, then noticed that they were having some kind of strategy meeting that was leading right into the climax.

...What? The map behind that noble girl...

Hamazura, whose eyes had become like a dead fish's, abruptly started paying attention again.

...A map of Martian craters and mountain ranges? Why isn't it a regular world map? Why would they go through the trouble of hanging a map like...Waaaaaaahhhhh?!

Then, like he'd been hit by lightning, his eyes ballooned.

They said it was a midwinter story, but it wasn't an Earth winter at all!! They pretended like it was, but it was actually a "what if" set in modern times—and on a bizarrely developed Mars!! So when the cast was looking all hot, it could have been natural depending on how they did the terraforming. That smokestack before wasn't a filming slipup...Gwaahhhh!! It got me!!

The story had suddenly gotten a thousand times better in the last five minutes. The boring first half had been planned all along. The filmmakers wanted these five minutes to really shine, so they purposely left viewers in the dark earlier. Like giving someone a cup of water after a difficult marathon.

If anyone used this method in a hundred-minute feature-length film, the viewers would simply hoist the white flag long before the end. But this was a short film. It was over so quickly that even if the beginning was incredibly boring, the audience would just idly keep watching along. It'd all been calculated.

Uwaaahhh! Uwaaahhh!! Uwaaahhh!!!!! What is this? This isn't a C movie. They're seriously filming like they 100 percent wanted to compete with Hollywood!! You've gotta be shitting me. This thing is only ten minutes long. How'd they manage to do more world building than some trilogies that are just going through the motions?! How did they cram so much in it and still disguise it so you wouldn't be able to realize earlier?!

"Ha-ha-ha-ha-ha-ha-ha-ha!!" At this point, Shiage Hamazura couldn't help laughing. He seriously considered kissing Saiai Kinuhata's feet at this point. Yes, he understood now—the point of wading through so many terrible low-budget short films was to hunt for new talent like this. The overwhelming feeling of discovery made Hamazura keep laughing, but...

Suddenly, a chill ran down his spine.

He felt someone's eyes on him.

Nervously, he turned around...

There was the girl, the peerless lover of movies, who had only just returned from the bathroom.

With a face that screamed "Damn it!! How could I have walked out on such an interesting work?!" she was peeking into the screening room from the slightly ajar door and trembling all over.

After the screenings ended...

I see, so the director's name is Beverley Seathrough. I've gotta look her up...thought Hamazura, mentally taking notes as Kinuhata walked next to him.

At the moment, Kinuhata was walking like a limp fish, with no energy and a pitch-black, thunderhead-like aura around her, wearing a face like it was the end of the world.

"Kinuhata? Hey, Kinuhata. Don't worry. You're a winner at life. I would never, ever have seen that work of art by myself. There are as many movies out there as stars in the sky—but you found that one. Your antenna is the real thing."

"...And now Hamazura is totally pitying with me. C movies are all about luck. Maybe this is totally a sign my senses aren't what they used to be...," Kinuhata muttered.

Right as they were thinking they'd go back to the hospital to meet up with Takitsubo after wrapping up their side-adventure, Kinuhata's cell phone suddenly went off.

For a few moments, the flaccid, dark-eyed Kinuhata didn't react, but eventually, she took out her phone with strangely delayed movements and put it to her ear.

After a short exchange, she eventually hung up and looked at Hamazura.

"Hamazura, please, like, go pick up Takitsubo without me. You totes know where to go, right? If you just go to the booth in District 3 and wait for me there, it would be cool."

"Eh?"

"It's a job. The higher-ups are finally starting up a new team, so they want us all to, like, get together and slaughter a bunch of terrorists threatening the city. I guess they're some people who used to be called Spark Signal."

3

"...Wasn't *Saiai Kinuhata* supposed to be going to her secret meeting place?"

"...*Saiai Kinuhata* went to her secret meeting place, totally got fed up within five minutes, and came right back."

As soon as they ran into each other again, they began to argue.

They'd split up earlier, but before Hamazura reached the hospital, he'd been accosted by the returning Kinuhata...He wondered if there was some kind of transmitter on him, but it didn't seem particularly like it.

As they walked on foot toward the hospital (final closing time was past for schools, and so the last trains and buses had already left), Hamazura asked, appalled, "What the hell happened? Weren't they making a new team so you could fight some terrorists?"

"Yes, but listen to this."

Kinuhata began relating some of the events she'd just experienced.

After coming to the dimly lit underground area, Saiai Kinuhata looked around at the faces waiting there. She frowned, and then with perfect timing, her cell phone went off, and she heard these words through it:

"Heya, thanks for coming. Item, School, Block, and Member got destroyed in the last battle, right? And so, I have for you......Ta-daa! A new team made up of their survivors! I know you were killing one another before, but I hope you get along great!"

"Hey, wait, no, you're yanking my chain!! Something weird made its way into your story right off the bat!"

"At first, I thought it was a joke, too, but it was super-serious. I totes couldn't put up with them, so, like, I ran away and came back. Oh, right—the Heart Measure girl in the dress totally told me to say hi to you, though."

"...Great. I've got a sinking feeling I know exactly who that is." This made Hamazura literally droop, but then he looked up again. "Wait, then will you be all right? Those phone people seem to have a lot of authority. They gonna let you off batting away their orders?"

"Well, probably not. That's why I want you to help me with

something. If I can do the whole thing by myself, they won't be able to complain."

"Huh?" The boy's eyes went wide.

Kinuhata put it plain and simple. "Steal a car from around here and, you know, get us transportation like you always do. We'll use it to chase the so-called friends of Spark Signal, the guys who attacked the Hula Hoop, and mop them up real nice. We can't afford to let Takitsubo wait much longer. Let's get this over and done with, lickety-split."

"Just you wait. Weren't you just going on about how I didn't need to answer to Item anymore? Did you think I wasn't serious when I said I want to wash my hands of this shady business and support my beloved Takitsubo—"

"Then you can just go by yourself with Takitsubo and totes leave me behind even though she'll probably be super-worried when I never come no matter how much time passes but just as long as you have fun and everything, it's fine I guess."

"Damn it!! We worked so hard on this welcome-home party, and you're just gonna leave an unpleasant aftertaste?!"

"If you don't like it then get moving and get us a car please so we can bust some Spark Signal terrorist skulls and then celebrate our girl getting discharged from the hospital come on Hamazura come on!"

With her even using a soft, coaxing voice near the end, Hamazura, teary-eyed, swore and shoved his hand into his pocket. Out came what looked like lock-picking tools.

Keeping one eye on Kinuhata as she used her cell phone to get in touch with Takitsubo and tell her to go ahead of them to the nearby District 3 private salon on her own, Hamazura easily unlocked the door of a family car parked on the road.

"Man, you're really the type to rely on acquaintances, huh?"

"Did you, like, say something, Underling Hamazura?"

4

The camper with Accelerator, Motoharu Tsuchimikado, Awaki Musujime, and Mitsuki Unabara in it had arrived at District 3, a gathering place of celebrities and rich socialites.

As Tsuchimikado displayed the orders sent by Shiokishi on their big screen, he said, "There are twenty holdouts. With as many submachine guns and grenades, evidently...So yeah, it does seem like an easy job, like the boss man said. Apparently, their main job was to support the guys who messed things up at the Hula Hoop."

"Sure, killing them would be simple," said Accelerator from the simple bed he sat on, rolling his eyes over to Tsuchimikado in a glare, "but are we just gonna keep doing everything those General Board shitheads tell us to? Depending on how we play this, we could be close to a chance at getting a glimpse of Dragon."

"Are you suggesting we fight alongside those former Spark Signal terrorists? With the ones who would take over the Hula Hoop and kidnap children to use as negotiation tools?"

"..."

"From our perspective, it only makes sense to investigate Dragon. But we can't do it the wrong way. These former Spark people are all garbage human beings. If we leave them be, they could take over some random building...But if you're willing to get innocent people involved while investigating the mystery, then the four of us would be finished."

Accelerator sucked his teeth in annoyance.

He was the epitome of evil, a Level Five treated as a living strategic weapon. He was even dropped out of a bomber once. However, he had a strong aversion to harming civilians—more specifically, harming the world where a certain young girl lived peacefully.

After Accelerator fell silent, Musujime was the next one to speak. "These holdouts—where on earth are they hiding?"

"They're moving through the underground mall that's beneath the station. It's closed up already, so no civilians are there, but if they went all the way up there, they must be thinking it won't be very hard to break through security."

Most open-air markets stayed active until late at night, but the ones attached to stations were an exception. Because the last train was scheduled to match up with the school's closing time, stores in the underground mall closed up early, too.

Using the remote, Tsuchimikado pulled up a map of the mall. "They probably know by now that their main force at the Hula Hoop is gone. They seem to be going through the mall to reach vehicles parked elsewhere, and from there, they'll make their next move. Still, we're not sure whether they're simply running or trying to shift to a Plan B that involves high-powered weapons."

"Where exactly do they have their getaway cars?" asked Unabara.

Tsuchimikado idly pointed beyond a wall of the camper. "There."

"...I'm sorry?"

"I gave the driver instructions to cut them off. If we wreck their cars first and have one of us wait here, Spark Signal won't get their way, at least for a while.

"Of course, we won't be stopping there," added Tsuchimikado. "We'll leave our anchor here, and the other three will do mop-up at the mall. It's fine—Musujime can do pinpoint sniping with her ability, while Unabara and I can pretty quickly crush them in the confusion."

Accelerator, of all of them, was the one who suddenly frowned.

As Number One glared at him, Tsuchimikado grinned thinly and tapped his own neck. "You just came from fighting back at the Hula Hoop as well as dealing with Department Store, right? Save your electrode battery."

"Tsk."

Accelerator didn't have any particular responsibility to obey, but he also didn't need to be the one to offer them assistance. If those idiots would take care of the small tacks, he decided, he could just leave them be.

At that point, the camper stopped moving.

As Tsuchimikado reached for the rear door leading outside, he said, "Let's go give 'em the usual fight to the death."

5

When it came to one's wallet, the underground mall in front of the District 3 station was the kind of place a person needed some courage.

The area the former Spark Signal members were proceeding through was already closed and unpopulated. This section dealt in various kinds of sports brand clothing; uniforms from world-famous soccer leagues were lined up in year order. Those who knew their value would be okay with the cost, but for those who didn't, the price tags this place was buried in were completely inexplicable.

"(…Over there. Low-recoil submachine guns are made to be used in one hand, but attaching a heavy grenade on it defeats the purpose. Fortunately, it looks like this will be easier than we thought.)"

"(…Shouldn't we still consider the dangers of grenades being used in an enclosed space?)"

Tsuchimikado and Unabara were discussing their plan in hushed voices as they peered around a corner of the hallway.

Cell phone in hand, Tsuchimikado got in touch with Musujime, who was waiting slightly farther afield.

"Targets sighted at point BBE. Can you see them?"

"I'd like to tear them all a new one now. Would you mind giving the signal?"

"Count down from five. Start at the edges and move in."

Tsuchimikado hung up and gripped his handgun in both hands.

Twenty terrorists, formerly of Spark Signal, ventured through the dark, closer and closer to their position.

Exactly five seconds after hanging up:

Tap.

Almost without any noise, a corkscrew had penetrated one of the armed terrorists.

*   *   *

Normally, Awaki Musujime's Move Point didn't make a sound. The soft tap was likely made by the flesh near the wound as it was pressed inward by the corkscrew that had suddenly appeared, ignoring three-dimensional space.

A scream rang out.

But at first, the armed band didn't realize they'd been attacked.

Continuing further, corkscrews attacked a third person, then a fourth.

The terrorists were grouped together in one cluster as they watched their comrades in the front, back, left, and right all fall down at once, writhing in pain. That was when they finally realized the situation they were in, but since all four victims had fallen together, the ones still on their feet couldn't figure out which direction was safe to escape toward and instead ended up staying rooted in place.

They could expect their prey to be frozen in confusion for only two, maybe three seconds.

And Tsuchimikado didn't let that slip.

"Here we go," he said quietly to Unabara, before bringing his gun up from around the corner.

Without hesitation, he pulled the trigger.

Bang!!

A gunshot and a flash—clear as day this time—and another terrorist fell. Now that there was a clear enemy, the remaining units began to counterattack with their submachine guns as they retreated, firing in Tsuchimikado's direction while looking for anything they could use as shields.

As he and Unabara attacked with pistols from the front, Musujime, who had gone even farther around them, used Move Point and shot through one Spark Signal supporter after another.

In the blink of an eye, the group was down to half its original number.

But then:

"(…Crap, the grenades!!)"

Seeing his opponents' fingers reach away from their the triggers on their firearms to another one close by on the gun, Tsuchimikado focused on those points and fired.

But they got the better of him.

All of them, about ten now, completely synchronized, aimed their grenades at Tsuchimikado and Unabara. Ten explosives fired off at the same time, arcing toward them while revolving through the air like soda cans.

"...*Jump!!*" hissed Tsuchimikado, leaping through the glass window next to them in the passage. It shattered as he landed inside the store.

But Unabara didn't follow.

He reached out for a large button on the wall. It was for the shutters, which were for both crime and fire prevention.

After he slapped it with his palm, a thick metal wall slammed down right before the grenades got there.

It blocked the explosives.

Boom, boom!! Enormous blasts rattled from beyond the wall, wrenching the shutter inward toward them. Still, any fire-hot gales and fragments that made it through wouldn't be able to hurt Unabara.

"You idiot!!"

However, Tsuchimikado was furious.

"Why'd you reduce our chances to attack?! If we give them time, it'll only make their counterattacks stronger!!"

To get around the shutter, the pair tried going through the broken window and the store, but the seconds it took drastically affected what happened next.

Whoom!! A new blast split the air.

It hadn't been to attack Tsuchimikado or Musujime or Unabara.

"!!" Tsuchimikado hastily checked the passage and saw, past the dust cloud, a large hole in the ceiling. That was right where Spark Signal had just been. The wreckage that had fallen was piled up just like a staircase, giving them a perfect route up to the surface.

And now, the former Spark Signal members were nowhere to be found.

They'd made a clean getaway.

"Damn it!!" swore Tsuchimikado loudly, grabbing his cell phone. He called up Accelerator, who was waiting aboveground. "They got out of the mall!! About ten! We'll get up there with Musujime's Move Point, but leave your position and pursue them!! They probably aren't going back there anyway!!"

6

Even Accelerator, who was waiting behind the front lines, managed to get a good view of the explosion.

White stuff was billowing up; he didn't know if it was smoke or disintegrated building particulate. As he made his way in that direction on his crutch, he received even more information:

The asphalt had been blown away, as if something had erupted from below.

Debris was scattered everywhere, while nearby car and restaurant windows had been shattered.

Was that girl crouching and holding her head…bleeding?

He heard groaning and crying from around him, mixed with the sounds of approaching ambulance sirens.

The Spark Signal troops must have already fled.

"(…Villains.)"

As Accelerator watched those caught in the cross fire moaning indecipherably and the curious onlookers who had come to see what was happening lollygagging their best, he slightly, ever-so-slightly, clenched his teeth.

"(…A bunch of piece-of-shit villains go charging in, and this is what they pulled out?)"

Tsuchimikado and the others were probably chasing Spark Signal like honest idiots, but Accelerator didn't really feel like going along with the whole thing. He'd honestly started to consider just shooting them alongside the targets.

His fingertips had just begun to crawl slowly up toward the switch of the choker-style electrode at his neck when it happened—

A much louder wail drifted to him.

There were a lot of people confused by the sudden incident, but this voice went beyond that. Reflexively, he looked toward the source and got a little closer. He saw a boy, about high school age, yelling at an ambulance crew. The crew member seemed to be trying to give medical aid to a woman the boy knew, and the boy was desperately trying to stop him.

"...?"

The woman looked like she was in college, or maybe older. Somewhere around there. The papers that had fallen out of her bag were school-related, so maybe she was a teacher. She seemed more gravely wounded than the youth, who had a line of blood trickling down from his forehead. She was unconscious, lying limp. Normally, you'd think she needed medical attention at once, but...

"Just stop!! Stop!! Don't give her that medicine; you can't give it to her!! If you do, it'll have the opposite effect!!"

"But if I don't give it to her, she won't make it to the hospital! Do you know what her heart rate is right now?! And she doesn't have any allergies to this medication. Why on earth are you refusing her treatment?!"

The high schooler and the paramedic both seemed worked up about an urgent problem.

"...Look, you just can't," said the boy, clinging to the paramedic's arm, his voice sounding squeezed from his throat.

"She's...She's pregnant."

The crew member's face turned to blank surprise at the word. There was no need to question why and who it had been.

The high school boy looked away but continued frantically working his trembling lips.

"You hear all the time about how drugs that are fine for normal people have bad effects on the baby, don't you?! What about those meds? Is it really safe?! She could die, you know!!"

"That's...I..."

It was a delicate problem. A great deal of medicine was developed on the premise that it wouldn't be used on very small children or pregnant women, so they probably hadn't done any real testing to check how safe it would be for a pregnant patient. Theory was one thing, but even a medical professional wouldn't know exactly how things would turn out in practice.

"I'll be honest. When I heard she was pregnant, everything went black. I had no idea what to do. I wished the whole problem would disappear, like fog. Actually, I still do. Really. Why did this have to happen?"

The high schooler bit his lip after his rambling, then continued.

"We were walking around here, and it would sound good if I said it was for a date, but she was trying to calm me down because I was so panicked. I kept asking myself what I should do, but I had no idea. But this isn't fair. It can't end like this. What did I want to do? Did I want to break up? Then why am I still clinging to her now...?"

For a moment, he fell quiet.

Moving his lips furiously, he continued, his voice scraping.

"I don't want to lose her..."

The shaking high school kid finally had tears in his eyes, and he shouted with all his might.

"Maybe I have to make a decision, but this is bullshit!! I don't have a clue what I should do, but I don't want to let things get decided for me like this!! Please, do something!! You're an expert at saving lives, aren't you?! Please, save them both!!"

The ambulance crew member faltered. But think about it as he might, there was only one thing he could do.

One possibility was to not save either of them, and the other was to definitely save at least one.

He was a professional, and if someone had asked him to choose, he already knew which it would be.

"...I'm using the tonic. At this rate, they'll both just die."

"But...!!"

As the scrupulous tirade continued, both men heard the clatter of a crutch on the ground.

"Move."

It was Accelerator.

"Huh…? H-hey, wait! This is for professionals to hand—!"

Without waiting for an answer, Accelerator shoved the para-medic aside with one hand and took his spot. He crouched there, then reached for his choker electrode switch. After that, he slowly reached for the pregnant woman's belly.

Once before, to save a certain little girl, he had reverse calculated from skin-level electrical signals to completely analyze her entire brain structure.

From his point of view, gathering precise information on a baby by touching the mother's skin was a piece of cake.

…Sex, female. Weight, 244 grams. Nourishment supply level, 3,825. Mental activity rate, 3.8. Heartbeat, 60. Stimulation response rate, 5.52. Cytodifferentiation, 88…

After closing his eyes for only a few seconds, he finally turned off the electrode.

To the paramedic, who was on his butt on the ground, he said, "The tonic. Two and a half grams of Ectorin. Attach a coating-type chip to the carotid and inject it over five doses, ten seconds each with a short break of twenty seconds in between. If you do that, you'll save them both."

"Wait!!"

It was not the crew member but the high school boy who argued.

"What'll happen to the baby if we do?!"

"That's what I just did those goddamn calculations for, shithead!!" shouted Accelerator in return.

The kid, overwhelmed, fell silent in spite of himself.

Ignoring him, Accelerator continued, "If you really don't want them to die, do what I said. If you medicate with the values I gave you, it won't harm the mother or the child. You don't want both of them to die because you're fussing over the details, do you?"

Having said as much as he intended to, and without waiting for a reply, he looked at the paramedic.

"You've only got five minutes to decide if you want to start. You want to save them both if you can, don't you? Give my method a shot. You're using the damn tonic anyway. No reason to refuse, right?"

The paramedic shook his head, then eventually took a strip out of a handbag. It looked like a stick of gum. He put the thing on the woman's neck, like Accelerator said, and then peeled it off again after a short time before repeating the process.

Finally, he'd done it five times, just as Accelerator had told him to.

"...*Uughn...*"

They heard a quiet groan.

At first, her companion didn't know whose it was.

But then, the moment the unconscious woman opened her eyes a crack—

He honestly felt like he was going to collapse on the spot.

"...No effect on the baby, either. Cell division rate looks fine, too," said Accelerator, turning his electrode on for a short time and doing a quick examination with his fingertip. "Get her to the hospital," he said to the paramedic. "And also, take it outside District 3's jurisdiction and into District 7. It's a little longer to get there, but their hospital would never turn someone down. With a delicate patient like this, not every place will accept her, even if you request it normally. In the end, it'll be quicker to bring her somewhere that will take her no matter what."

Finished, Accelerator turned his back to them.

He couldn't afford to stay here forever. He needed to be sure he wiped out all his targets, now also to make sure this situation didn't happen again.

But—

"Hey!! Wait up— Hey!!"

It was the high schooler from before. Accelerator didn't turn around to his shouting, but he did stop rather than leave.

The boy rambled to his back. "Thank you. If you hadn't done something back there, I would have lived the rest of my life an empty shell."

"...Get lost already."

He'd muttered that, but maybe the high schooler hadn't heard him.

He continued. "I won't forget what you've done. I'll never forget that you saved something more important than my own life!! At some point, I want to make it up to you. So—"

The boy's words cut off.

The cause was a sharp *clack* and a dull impact to his cheek.

Something hard and black was pushed up against his forehead before he knew what was happening. It was a small gun. Accelerator had pulled it from his pants belt and hit the kid's cheek with the grip, then pressed the muzzle against his brow. Maybe it would cause a new commotion, but Number One wasn't the kind to care about that.

"Get lost," he repeated.

For a few moments, the teenager was speechless. He backed away a few steps. Finally, he bowed his head to Accelerator. Very deeply. Then, he turned around and ran in a straight line to the ambulance with his acquaintance on it.

After the vehicle drove off, Accelerator returned the gun to his belt and took a slow look around.

"…"

He mumbled something.

But no one heard it.

Eventually, his slender finger reached for his electrode's switch.

Gra-bam!! An explosion rang out.

Neither the victims nor the curious onlookers at the scene saw anything of Accelerator after that.

However.

They would say they saw giant new cracks in the asphalt, as though they were the traces of a monster's wrath.

7

The family sedan Shiage Hamazura drove (after stealing it) was on its way from District 7 to District 3. They were on an elevated road bypass. Currently, he was chasing some terrorists to help with Kinuhata's job, but…

"Hey, what is this? Hey!! What is that crazy thing following us?!" cried Hamazura after glancing in the rearview mirror, then turning his head to check behind them. He was baffled.

No one could really blame him, though.

"An HsAFH-11 Hexawing—an unmanned attack helicopter, by the looks of it," said Kinuhata with the kind of mild irritation someone might get from being stuck in traffic.

It resembled an Apache or something, clearly a military helicopter since it had wings with missiles and stuff attached to it. But it wasn't that brand specifically; its jumbled wings each split in three, and with a loud cracking noise, it now had six wings. They moved and rotated as though they were human arms with joints, lining themselves up with their target.

And all six had the hots for the car Hamazura was driving.

At least it was polite enough to match their speed. As he stared at the low-flying helicopter in the mirror, he felt his throat dry up.

"This is horseshit!! Okay, fine, I stole a car so we'd have transportation! But that's all I did! And they sent *that* after us?! Is that normal?!"

"Does that look like one of Anti-Skill's toys to you, Hamazura?! They're totally not the ones who sent that!!"

"Then what? Are those terrorists you're chasing intercepting us? You're telling me they have stuff like this?!"

"No. Hexawings are unmanned weapons belonging to Academy City's air defense forces, right? Some rando dregs would never be using it for combat."

"So it really is Academy City?! The leadership is after us?! There's only one reason I can think of! It's because you ignored the instructions you received on the phone and went home!!"

"…Hmm. But are they really that, like, short-tempered?"

"Why are you so calm about this?! Do you understand our situation?! How fast do you think a military helicopter can fly?!"

"Hmm? Well, it's, like, an HsAFH-11, so about three thousand kilometers per hour max, right?"

"Mach 2.5?! How is it still classified as a helicopter?!"

"Relax, they can't use the rocket engines while the wings are deployed. The wind pressure could, like, damage the joints. Right now, it can only go three, maybe four hundred kilometers per hour."

"Considering we're in a car, I don't think the difference matters!!"

As they argued, the Hexawing aligned its movements with the car's, and in relation to them, it practically seemed like it had stopped dead. Hamazura didn't know the specifics, but it appeared as though it had finished locking onto them.

"Now what?! If it hits us with a missile or something, it'll take us out in one shot!!"

"We'll have to pray it uses short-range antitank missiles," said Kinuhata with a ridiculous notion, while leaning down and squirming around as she tied some kind of rope to herself.

"That would *definitely* take us out in one shot!!"

"No, no," said Kinuhata, sitting back up. "The short-range anti-armor missiles used by the Hexawings totally seem to be SRM21s. So they must be using, like, infrared sensors to lock onto us."

"And?! Who cares if it's ultra-shortwave radar or infrared or ultraviolet?! Now that it's after us, we can't get away!! Do you have any idea how fast those missiles will fly at us?!"

"Oh, calm yourself. Have a smoke or something, dude."

Hamazura hacked and coughed. "A road flare?! You can't light one of those *in* the vehicle!!"

"I can't? But I can totally use it like this, see?" said Kinuhata, sticking out a tongue. She opened the passenger seat window and hurled the flare outside.

A second later, a relatively short-looking missile blasted out of one of the Hexawing's armlike wings.

Hamazura thought his heart would stop for a moment. But as it turned out, the missile didn't hit the car and send it flying away in roiling flames.

The reason: the road flare.

By tossing out a dummy heat source, they'd gotten the short-range missile to veer off course.

"Hawt," noted Kinuhata casually.

The threat, though, wasn't gone yet.

Ka-bam!! The missile, diverted toward the smoking flare thrown above the road, exploded. They'd avoided a direct hit, but the intense blastwave was coming straight for the car. Its window glass shattered, and the car's body shook around unnaturally. As the car threatened to spin out, Hamazura desperately fought to keep it under control, lest the wheel be taken from him.

On top of that, as the Hexawing fanned away its own flames with its gusting rotors, it continued to pursue Hamazura's car.

He could floor it, since there were few cars around, but a casual commuter vehicle would never be able to use its speed to shake an attack chopper.

"Now what? You probably only had one of those things, and if that thing's predictive function learns our response and switches weapons to a machine gun, flares aren't going to work as defense anymore."

"Hamazura, just hush and take a left at the next fork."

"Huh? What did you say? The wind is blowing too loud for me to—"

"*Hhnnnn!!*"

Without saying any more, Kinuhata suddenly shoved the hand brake lever up from the passenger seat.

Ga-clunk!! The car rapidly decelerated and began to slide sideways in a drift.

The abrupt diagonal movement caused the car to charge straight into the left-hand side of the road.

"*Uwwwoaaaaaaaaaaaahhhhhhhhhhhhhhhhhh?!*"

Panicking, he put the hand brake back and moved the wheel. If he was careless enough to step on the brakes, the car was sure to spin out. Instead, he purposely used only slick steering ability and didn't decelerate, bringing the car's motion back on its original vector.

"What's the big idea?!"

"You, like, want to survive this, right, bro? After this, go straight on this big road. It's super-big, three lanes on each side, but keep the car from swerving as much as possible and keep going straight."

"Did I get myself into a terrible mess without realizing it?"

"That's par for the course, isn't it? Anyway, just go totally straight."

"Are you sure about this? I know it might not work, but shouldn't I try to weave to throw off their aim…?"

Hamazura drove the car as Kinuhata directed, even while grumbling to himself. He looked around, foot depressing the accelerator. This area had a lot of high-rise buildings, meaning the Hexawing would also naturally go straight if it was following the car. If the helicopter moved around without care, it'd probably crash into a building wall.

Plus, there was the occasional signboard sticking out from a building, and other paths crisscrossing above the elevated highway, meaning the Hexawing lowered its altitude as it chased the car. Within moments, it had sunk to a point just over the ground, about the same height as the car or a little higher.

"Hey, Kinuhata, are we—? *Pfft?!*"

When Hamazura glanced at the passenger seat, he sputtered in spite of himself.

Saiai Kinuhata was leaning out of the passenger-seat window—well, no, she was doing far more than that. Almost her entire body, save for her legs, was outside the window. With her slender feet parked on the seat to keep her stable, she was pointing the gun in her hand behind the car.

But the car, moving forward, was obviously creating a massive stream of wind.

"Wow! Ow-wow!! Ow-wow-wow, those dainty bits!! Kinuhata, that's way beyond a panty flash but *panties* what are you *panties* going to *panties*?!"

Kinuhata fired a bullet through the car into the driver's side door, then said, "…Keep your eyes on the road and, just like, focus, please."

"Yes ma'am!! But *panties*!!"

Ignoring the weirdly excited boy, Kinuhata took aim at a point behind the car again. Almost as if in tandem, the Hexawing's machine gun barrel moved with it.

"Kinuhata, that won't work!! Maybe if you had a high-caliber cannon, but some 9mm gun can't bust through a military copter's armor, can it?!"

"...I'm using self-destroying bullet tips, duh. They're made of clay-like paper material, so if I shoot it indoors, it totes won't hurt any allies. They're designed to break up super-easy."

"Then it should be even worse against armor!!"

"Who said I was trying to penetrate the armor?" sighed Kinuhata.

"I'm trying to shoot out the air intake for its engine, obvs."

Bang-bang! Bam-bam!! Gunshots repeatedly rang out. They converged on what looked like a hole right underneath the helicopter's rotor.

Like cars, helicopters obtained energy from reactions between fuel and oxygen, so when building one, the designers had to include a hole to suck in the air. If an impurity became lodged inside, it would stop the engine—and probably bring the helicopter down.

In general, though, the air intake would have several countermeasures in place to prevent issues like that from happening. Normally, it would block the entry of dust from the downward air the rotors created and had a fine net that stopped impurities from getting inside. Something nine millimeters in size probably wouldn't get sucked in.

However.

This point came with an important footnote.

Saiai Kinuhata's bullet tips were designed to break apart. They were created from a papier-mâché-like material. To prevent ricochets in cramped areas, they broke into pieces the moment they impacted with the target.

Yes.

Into pieces—pieces like the ones you get from breaking dry papier-mâché.

The bullet-tip fragments, now mere particles finer than sand, rushed mercilessly between the metal grating's tiny holes that protected the air intake. And with the impurities now inside the engine, they immediately caught fire and made the engine break down. This led to the entire Hexawing's available lift decreasing dramatically.

With a boom, smoke rose from the helicopter's engine.

The Hexawing's nose veered ever so slightly from the road's direction—and not a moment later, its side began scraping against the asphalt.

The machine was loaded with a large amount of aviation fuel for the rotors, special combustion agents for the rocket engines, and explosives like missiles and gunpowder. The explosion was fantastic.

"Freaking sweet—I did it!!"

Kinuhata wriggled back into the passenger seat like a snake, but Hamazura didn't have time to watch.

A massive shock wave, the likes of which were incomparably larger than what the short-range missile caused earlier, was heading for the car. In the blink of an eye, Hamazura lost control of the steering wheel, and this time, the car actually did start to spin out.

"Shit! Kinuhata, use Nitrogen Armor!! If it can block sniper-rifle rounds, you should manage!!"

"Wait, what about—?"

Kinuhata tried to yell at him in opposition, but there was no time to listen.

The car, completely out of control, slammed hard into the elevated highway's side wall.

"Guh…"

After losing consciousness for a moment, Hamazura sat up slowly. He'd been launched outside the vehicle, but he'd avoided injury by hitting a synthetic fiber balloon filled with a lot of water. They were lined up on the sides of the road to soften impacts during accidents.

Where's Kinuhata…?

He glanced around, looked at the busted sedan, but he couldn't

find any sign of her. He didn't know how long he'd been out for, but she'd probably woken up before him. Maybe she couldn't find him and went off to do her own thing.

Could this day get any worse?

He sat up and checked his limbs. None seemed to be broken.

From what he could tell from a nearby sign, they'd gotten into District 3 while fleeing from the helicopter by car.

Should he search for Kinuhata and keep helping her or meet up with Takitsubo first? He began considering his next move, but soon it would be in vain.

Because his cell phone went off.

The number was suspiciously listed as private, but Hamazura felt a chill at someone contacting him with this timing. On a hunch, he picked up.

"*Oh, hello there. If I said Heart Measure, would you remember my face, at least?*"

"…How do you know my number…?"

"*You want me to explain everything? No, that would be a pain, sorry. More importantly, I have a question. Is Saiai Kinuhata with you? I tried to call her, but she won't pick up.*"

"…" Shiage Hamazura looked at the shot-down Hexawing. "*I thought so. You guys were behind that, hmm?*"

"?" Rather than words, he heard a strange intake of breath. It sounded like the caller was surprised at something. "*I'm not sure what you mean, but whatever the case, tell her to get in touch with me. She should know that we left her alone since she said she'd do it herself, but now the Spark Signal terrorists have taken over a private salon facility in District 3. Could you get her to give up and leave it to us?*"

"A private salon…in District 3…?" groaned Shiage Hamazura. That…

Wasn't that the place where Rikou Takitsubo was waiting after just having gotten out of the hospital?

8

Shiage Hamazura was running through District 3 that night.

While praying, over and over, that it had to be a lie.

But the situation was severe.

All around the high-rise Takitsubo waited within were Anti-Skill officers. He couldn't get inside. The yellow tape marking the scene was a warning signal that beat at Hamazura's heart.

Bang!! A dry crack echoed.

When he heard it from the upper floors of the high-rise, sounding like a gunshot...Shiage Hamazura took a deep breath and made up his mind.

The terrorists were occupying the building that held the rentable salons, which meant Takitsubo probably couldn't get out, either.

Which meant there was only one thing to do.

"Shit..."

Hamazura, who didn't much want to get involved in this kind of incident, swore, angry from the bottom of his heart.

Eventually, he said the same word, over and over, shouting it.

"Shit! Shit!! Shit!!!!!! Why, *why*, of all the buildings you could have chosen! Why'd you have to pick this exact one?!"

After shouting himself hoarse, Hamazura turned his back to the private salon building once. He looked around, then spotted an unnatural cleaning van. He drew up to it without hesitation, then pulled the passenger door open and climbed inside.

The driver was the surprised one.

"Uwaaaah?! Wh-who are you? A carjacker?!"

"Let's cut to the chase. You're a peon for some shady side business, just like me, yeah?" asked Hamazura in a low voice, keeping his hand in his pants pocket. As the uniformed cleaning worker's face drew back, he continued. "Doing some early preparations to help out the big boss, understand? ...Take out any spare guns you have. Or I could just kill you and take them."

Thinking about it calmly, someone who already had a weapon wouldn't demand one. But the cleaner hadn't realized that. He reached into his cheap bag and took out a small handgun and several magazines, then gave them to Hamazura.

"Wh-which department are you with anyway? If you wanted a weapon, you should go through the proper routes—"

The man was off the mark, but Hamazura averted his face slightly. What was he doing?

He was nothing but a Level Zero. He couldn't mow down all the enemies in his path with a crazy special power like Saiai Kinuhata could. He was a weakling. He could easily die in fights with other delinquents if he messed up.

"Not with any of them. I'm retired," he said after a short moment's thought.

But there were things he knew specifically because he was weak. This world wasn't kind. Even the leader of a delinquent gang like Ritoku Komaba had died easily. He didn't want to think about it, but the same probably applied to Rikou Takitsubo as well. That was why Hamazura took up a weapon. It didn't matter whether he was a Level Zero or not.

"...But a friend of mine is captive in that building. I have to go, don't I?"

After saying his piece, Hamazura got out of the cleaning van's passenger seat. He'd obtained a weapon, but he couldn't charge into the private salon like this. No matter what his angle was, the Anti-Skill officers on the perimeter would grab him.

...No blind spots in any direction, he thought. *Anti-Skill isn't stupid enough to leave any obvious routes the criminals could escape by. Which also means there's no way for me to get past them, either.*

He looked up into the starry sky.

...If I can't go by ground, I'll have to go by air.

Yes.

Even though Shiage Hamazura had just been attacked by a helicopter moments ago.

After a look around, he went not to the private salon, but to the high-rise hotel right next to it. Using the elevator, he moved to its roof, and as he predicted, there was a heliport. It was probably waiting for someone who wanted to enjoy the nightscape. A small helicopter was parked there as well, round like an egg.

He went straight for it and opened the door.

Thrusting his gun at the female pilot doing instrument checks, he said, "Sorry, but you're taking off now. Three streets over, to the private salon."

The pilot, gun aimed at her head, was silent for a few seconds.

Eventually, without removing her headset, she said, "Unfortunately, I used to be part of the department overseeing air defense for Academy City."

When Hamazura frowned at her quiet words, he noticed it.

At some point, the female pilot was holding a box cutter in her hand.

"Did you think a pilot wouldn't be skilled at using weapons? If we're shot down over enemy territory, we have to take independent action. We train far more rigorously than the army grunts who always have ample access to firearms and move together in large groups."

...Wait a minute. When did she grab that thing?

If he remembered right, when he got into the cockpit, the woman had been using all her svelte fingers on both hands to check her instruments. Without him noticing, she'd grabbed a hidden blade. He understood that, but he couldn't get anything close to a concrete image of her doing it.

If he didn't focus, it would turn out badly.

Despite the gun in his hand, it was his turn to feel a chill down his spine.

But then it happened.

His cell phone, in his pocket, suddenly rang. He scowled. At a time like this? In contrast, the female pilot remained seated. She gave a thin smile and provoked him. "Shouldn't you answer? You can still use your phone before liftoff."

"..."

Without moving his head, he used his hand not holding the gun and reached slowly for his pocket. Carefully, taking almost thirty whole seconds. The scariest moment would be the one where he glanced at the phone screen…but as soon as he saw the name there, it was like he'd been struck by lightning. He hit the call button and put it to his ear.

"…*Hama…zura…*"

"Takitsubo, are you safe?! Where are you?!"

"…*The meeting…place. The private salon…*"

The fond voice almost let him feel relieved, but his doubts quickly stole away the warmth. Why did her voice sound so raspy?

"I heard what happened. Terrorists busted into the private salon. Are you all right? You didn't get hit by any stray bullets or anything, did you?!"

"*I'm…okay…*"

Just as she said the word *okay*, there was a *bang* over the phone, interrupting her. Then he heard what sounded like hasty pattering footsteps.

"Takitsubo!!"

"*I'm really…okay…I'm hiding right now. I don't think…they noticed me yet.*"

He heard a soft bump over the line.

It sounded like her leaning against the wall.

"Wait. Then why are you on the floor like that?!"

"*I just…started not feeling so good. It's not…enough to worry about.*"

"Shit!!" he swore without thinking.

Rikou Takitsubo had just gotten out of the hospital. She could lead a normal life, but she might harm her body if she attempted any heavy labor or came under extreme strain. Plus, the whole reason she was in the hospital was because of those Crystal things he didn't understand. He couldn't imagine how much damage had built up.

"*Hama…zura…*"

"All right. It's fine. Let me do the talking. You'll be fine, all right? I'm on my way there. I'm going to save you. Just hold out a little longer. Can you do that?"

"*No, that's not…*"

Hamazura worked his lips frantically, but Takitsubo's reaction was the direct opposite.

"Hamazura, don't come. Don't come here. There are ten terrorists. I think they all have automatic weapons and grenades. Hamazura, you might know how to use handguns, but not rifles, right? If you jump in and they focus on you, you won't be able to deal with them. So don't come here."

"...Don't give me that...," said Hamazura in spite of himself, trembling.

It was a different trembling than before. It wasn't fear—it was anger.

"I'm going. Why the hell shouldn't I?! I can't leave you there! I don't care what I have to do, I'm going to rescue you. Wait for me. And don't give up!! Maybe this is all totally beyond me, but I'm going anyway!!"

There was no answer from Takitsubo.

The call had suddenly ended. Maybe they'd destroyed the private salon's cell phone relay antenna. For a few moments, Hamazura gazed at his disconnected cell phone, and then his trembling reached a peak. A cry exploded from his throat.

The pilot sitting in the cockpit watched him, one eyebrow moving slightly.

"Please..." While holding her at gunpoint with a trembling hand, while she toyed with the box cutter in her hand that she could attack with at any time, he spoke, his face broken down into tears and snot. "You can charge me with whatever you want. Drop me into the bottom of hell if you need to, I won't complain. So please, just this once, help me rescue her..."

Only his wrung-out words resounded in the helicopter.

A few seconds passed.

All that continued was the silence, but eventually, the woman heaved a sigh. Then, in an almost inaudible voice, she said, "Say something next time."

"?" Hamazura, not hearing her, was about to tilt his head when a roaring noise pounded on his eardrums. The helicopter's rotor had rapidly increased its rotation frequency. Looking overhead, toward where the noise came from, he felt the sensation at his feet suddenly disappear. They were in the air.

The pilot tossed her box cutter aside and grabbed her can of coffee, which apparently still had some left in it. She keyed in some numbers on a number pad, and after what looked like a small door right next to the flight yoke popped open, she dumped the coffee into it.

...The flight recorder...?

The device recorded conversations inside the helicopter in order to find out what happened during crashes. By pouring coffee inside its heatproof, waterproof, shockproof casing, she'd erased everything they'd said—everything that could incriminate Hamazura or Takitsubo.

The woman sped the helicopter up and spoke through her headset microphone without looking at him.

"Hijack on flight H3389. I repeat, hijack on flight H3389!! The culprit has a gun and a small canister of liquid. Its volume appears to be ten liters! If his words are to be believed, it's liquid explosive, and he's threatening to pour it all out of the helicopter along with igniters. I will follow his instructions for now to prioritize the lives of local citizens!!"

A frantic man's voice, probably the airport controller, came back over the headset's earpieces. Then, the pilot proceeded to speak to him in code:

"Tee-ay, tee-ay. Code black. Direction two zero two, cruising speed eighty, your permission! Bee-eye-elle, time unit thirty-five to forty. Large. I'm going now, do you understand?!"

At first, Hamazura thought it was special air radio lingo or something. But when he thought about it, he realized it didn't mean anything. She was listing the criminal's characteristics. She was probably saying he was somewhere from thirty-five to forty years old, 202 centimeters tall, about eighty kilograms, and his skin color was black...That's probably what she wanted to tell them.

Of course, none was anywhere near Hamazura's physical traits.

The woman hung up completely, then looked at her surprised

passenger. "Can't exactly launch because a kid's being selfish. Sorry, but I'll have to make it big."

"You..."

Hamazura didn't know what to say, and as he was thinking about it, the helicopter flew on. The private salon building was a mere three streets away from the high-rise hotel they'd taken off from. They reached it very quickly.

This building was extravagantly constructed, its style rivaling the hotel they had taken off from.

Several figures were standing in the lit-up heliport. They weren't customers seeking aid. Submachine guns rested in their hands.

Hamazura felt as though someone had clutched his heart, but they didn't attack when they saw the helicopter flying overhead.

He bent his head to the side. "What's going on?"

"...I don't know who they're in contact with, but maybe one of their demands was a way to escape. They might be mistaking our helicopter for us giving in to their demands," she said, circling around the building. "...But that doesn't mean they're not still cautious of us. We still won't be able to land on the heliport. We want to avoid the terrorists actually seizing this helicopter."

"I got it. I don't want to make you do all that anyway." Hamazura glared at the heliport spread out below them, then pointed at something. "What's that?"

"...An artificial tree, I assume. A little early for that. They pull a bunch of white cloths taut like a yacht sail, then overlap them into a tree shape and decorate it with multicolored lights. If they used a real tree, the wind could break branches off and cause problems for helicopters trying to land."

"Oh."

Hamazura thought for a moment.

Then, without hesitation, he opened the helicopter door.

"Thanks for the good info."

"?!"

Even the female pilot had to gasp.

Shiage Hamazura had just leaped out into the night sky.

It was around twenty meters down to the heliport. His body fell freely before smashing into the tree formed by overlapping cloths. The sail-like decorations cracked and broke, but they softened the impact enough so it wasn't fatal, and then Hamazura was on his feet on the heliport floor.

At first, the three terrorists, armed like the others, were shocked. They'd thought the helicopter had arrived in accordance with their demands, but then a strange man had fallen on them.

And Hamazura didn't wait for them to catch up.

Without mercy, he pointed his gun and pulled the trigger in succession.

Bang-bang-bam!! Dry gunshots ripped through the sky, mowing down the terrorists before they had a chance to show their real power.

He gave a wave to the helicopter circling overhead, then gestured for it to leave the area before turning back to face the door leading inside the building.

His lips moved slightly.

"...I've arrived, partner. All the way to the pit of hell."

Even Shiage Hamazura himself probably didn't realize it.

He may have been a worthless, third-rate minion. There wouldn't be any surprise twists, like he actually had a crazy hidden power all along or anything. He really was, as his appearance implied, nothing more than a frail Level Zero.

However.

At this time alone, as he risked his life to protect a certain girl, he'd become a true protagonist.

9

Those among the terrorists formerly known as Spark Signal occupying the private salon looked up unconsciously.

Gunshots.

But the crack and report didn't sound like the bullets they'd prepared. The caliber was probably the same, but the type of gunpowder was different.

"Wasn't there a team who went to the roof to see if they gave us that helicopter we demanded?"

"When do we meet up with Stephanie? Depending on how she made her move—"

"Or maybe we should consider a teleport-type esper?"

But they weren't simpleminded enough to all go up to where they heard the sound right away. They'd brought almost everyone in the building under their control, but they continued to require a certain amount of people to still be able to act as needed.

Plus, if the gunshots themselves were a trap, if there were bombs or something set up for anyone who rushed to respond, they ran the risk of everyone getting taken out in one fell swoop.

The seven former Spark Signal members considered all this in an instant, then decided to split into three teams.

They probably thought theirs had been a swift decision.

However.

Calamity always ignores such rules. It simply comes out of the blue.

And this calamity came to them from the window.

Wham!!

A deep bursting sound, like the main guns of a battleship firing, rang out. The windows covering one wall, a panorama of the nighttime cityscape beyond them, shattered all at once. But what flew in was not a fireball or anything of the sort.

It was a person.

Someone with white hair, red eyes, and a smile that split his face.

It was Academy City's strongest Level Five: Accelerator.

…This…This is the twenty-eighth floor!!

Despite how out of the ordinary this was, the thoughts of Spark Signal still turned into something cliché. And when facing Accelerator, that little loss of time would be fatal.

The Level Five's action was simple.

He grabbed the nearest Spark Signal member with one hand, then threw him toward another. He moved like a child throwing a tantrum, but when it involved his ability to focus control of every possible vector, it created destructive force comparable to a cannonball.

Whomp!! came the blast.

Three former Spark Signal members were caught in it, blown away without much of a say in the matter.

Without stopping to listen to the sounds of tearing flesh and bone, Accelerator turned his red eyes to the next target.

The terrorists had finally found cover and were starting to position their weapons.

However.

Gunshots suddenly rang out, one after another, from an unexpected place.

"…!"

Rat-tat-tat-tat!! Gunshots echoed from the floor's exit. The terrorists, preoccupied with Accelerator, weren't able to respond to the flurry of shots. Blood splattered over the floor, and they fell in turn. Each received a single bullet right to the middle of the gut. There was no doubt they'd died instantly. Not one of them even cried out.

Accelerator turned around to where the gunshots came from.

A man he'd never seen before was standing there in a suit. He looked around thirty or so. Judging by the column of smoke coming from the gun in his hand, he must have been the shooter.

"Who're you?!"

"It doesn't matter," said the man in the suit, aiming the pistol elsewhere. He fired at the terrorists who Accelerator had already mowed down using his vector ability, right in the gut, just in case. The shots were loud, as if in proportion to the barrel's size. It probably wasn't a standard 9mm. He was using bullets of a larger caliber.

As he exchanged magazines, the man in the suit said to Accelerator, "If you really want to protect this city, you should do things more cleanly."

"Who do you think you are? You wanna die right now?"

"I'm Sugitani," said the man casually without batting an eyebrow. He kicked at each of the corpses, making sure they didn't respond. "I pray we never meet again. Do your best to make sure of it."

With only that, the man in the suit put his gun away and headed for the floor exit. Accelerator, after glaring at his receding back, eventually switched his electrode back to normal mode as well. However it happened, the threat to the private salon was gone for now.

Accelerator took out his cell phone.

He detested having to seek help from people who had messed up so badly, but doing the more trivial parts himself would be painful.

"...Hey, Tsuchimikado. I cleaned up the guys you let escape in the private salon building. Get up here and check for injured people and traps. And if you say you can't do that, I'll put a bullet right between your eyes for real this time."

He put away his phone and walked through the rooms on this floor.

There was an open door, and inside was a large space, like the kind used for parties. People were gathered there, probably hostages, around three hundred at a glance. A few eerie cries came from within the group, but not the kind that would imply anyone was dying.

Then he heard a thump from another direction.

Accelerator stopped right before entering the large hall. On his modern-design crutch, he walked down the hallway, then found something lying there behind a pillar.

It was a girl who looked high school age, wearing a pink tracksuit.

She seemed to have no energy, and she was sweating all over. It made Accelerator inadvertently think of Last Order, whose mind had once been violated by a virus.

The girl in the tracksuit seemed to be barely conscious, and despite her eyelids opening and closing faintly, she didn't try to get up even when she saw Accelerator approaching.

He stooped down to check on her, then arched an eyebrow.

No noticeable loss of blood. She must not have been shot. A sudden illness or something? he wondered. *Don't tell me she's pregnant, too...?*

For now, though, he decided he'd better get her to the hospital right away and took out his cell phone.

That was when it happened:

"...What the hell are you doing?"

He heard a young man growl.

Accelerator immediately looked and found one man walking toward him from farther down the hallway.

And it was—

Shiage Hamazura.

He was glaring at Accelerator and the limp, unmoving girl in the tracksuit, squeezing the words from his throat as he spoke.

"I asked you what the hell you're doing to Takitsubo!"

10

Hamazura had lost his cool.

He'd come from the roof to slip into the building but, obviously, he couldn't use something as simple as the elevator; that would be idiotic. Instead, he'd climbed down and down the fire escape, but even those stairs were basically a straight line. If he encountered any hostile terrorists, he wouldn't be able to avoid a disadvantageous shoot-out.

His tension was maxed out the entire time. Once he'd descended to a certain floor, he'd heard gunshots. He'd shot down the rest of the way to the twenty-eighth floor, and there, he had witnessed it:

Academy City's strongest Level Five, Accelerator, crouched right next to an unconscious Rikou Takitsubo, trying to do something to her.

If he'd been able to examine the situation from an objective, impartial perspective, maybe he could've concluded that Accelerator was trying to do some sort of first aid.

But he couldn't.

The reason was simple.

Shiage Hamazura had once belonged to a gang of delinquents called Skill-Out. At the time, someone named Ritoku Komaba had been its leader. But then the city's leaders decided they were inexpedient for the city.

As a result, they'd dispatched Accelerator.

He'd shot their leader, Ritoku Komaba, temporarily driving Skill-Out to the brink of destruction.

"…You were behind this, too?"

That person, that General Board's lapdog, had appeared before him once again—and not only that, he had made contact with Rikou Takitsubo and was attempting to do something to her.

"Are you the head of these terrorists—and survived on your own? Or did you have a falling-out and kill all the rest? You know what— it doesn't matter. You're still plotting evil in the darkness."

If you considered how this was right after he'd been attacked by an Academy City Hexawing, you'd probably understand right away what conclusion Hamazura had reached.

"When Skill-Out went down, part of that was our fault. Even our leader Komaba knew his fight against you would be his last, so I won't say anything more about that. I really, really want to, but for his sake, I'll stay quiet."

An impartial observer likely wouldn't have understood him.

But Hamazura wasn't speaking in the hope that someone would understand.

His mouth was simply moving on its own.

"…But if you're gonna try to take something important away from me again, if you're going to take Takitsubo's life even though she's not prepared like Komaba, when all she wanted to do was live a normal life from now on…"

Tremble.

Without caring a single iota about tiny differences like Level Zeroes and Level Fives, in order to protect the incapacitated girl, Shiage Hamazura pointed his handgun at Accelerator.

"It's time to accept your fate, Number One!!"

In contrast:

Accelerator had already realized what was happening, essentially.

But even knowing he was being misunderstood, he didn't try to deny it.

"...I like you." He grinned, a face-splitting smirk, as he stood up slowly and reached for his choker.

And then, Accelerator gave the most evil smile as he made a declaration.

"You're a good villain."

The line wouldn't have made any sense at first, but he almost never rated anyone this highly.

And yet, before Hamazura could realize that fact, Accelerator controlled the vectors of his legs and rushed straight up to him.

Whoom!! echoed the roar a moment later.

As Accelerator flew at him in a super-low arc, Shiage Hamazura tried to back away, his gun still raised.

...He might be a Level Five, but he's still human!! I should be able to kill him with one bullet. Come to think of it, he uses a trick to make sure the bullet doesn't hit him. If I start by lowering him to a situation where that one bullet has to hit...!

The answer he came to was a direct result of having shot and killed the fourth-ranked Level Five, Shizuri Mugino, the Meltdown.

Except—

Hamazura knew of one other Level Zero who could think that way. Once, his leader Ritoku Komaba had observed Accelerator's actions and, by studying their characteristics, had arrived at the answer by himself: that by causing electromagnetic interference, he could temporarily shut his ability down.

In that case.

...I'll make that choker malfunction. But how?! Leader used a chaff to cause interference, but...?!

Hamazura knew where he needed to go, but didn't know how to get there.

And in the meantime, Accelerator spun himself and whipped around his clenched fist.

Using his arm, which was rumored to kill people just by touching them.

"???!!!"

Hamazura instantly swung to the side in an effort to evade.

The arm didn't end up making contact. However, there was a strange blast of hot wind, and the wake of its passing alone was enough to send Hamazura flying. He flew over two meters clear through the air, then slammed into the hallway's wall. An unnatural strength activated in his trigger finger, and he shot a meaningless bullet into the ceiling.

Accelerator's head turned his way again.

Hamazura knew he'd be killed at this rate.

Then he saw a security robot trailing down the hallway toward them. The terrorists had probably locked them all in one room, and now that they were liberated, they'd begun tracking their normal routes.

He put everything into that bullet he shot in the robot.

Despite all its durability, the armor shattered, and the bullet made a complete mess of its internals. Hamazura shoved a hand inside. The awful numbing sensation from an electric shock went up from his fingers to his shoulder, then to his chest, but he ignored it and tore the thing out.

It was the giant motor piece the robot used to move.

Having torn the cord off, Hamazura took the permanent magnet used in the motor and hurled it at Accelerator.

Security and cleaning robots were designed to be heavy on purpose to prevent theft. To let the machines climb smoothly up hills, their motor had to be equally large, with output to match.

Certainly large enough to induce malfunctions when he pushed one's permanent magnet against an electronic device.

...*Will this work?!*

He had two bullets left in his gun and no time to replace magazines. But if he could weaken Accelerator to the point where he'd die if bullets struck him, he could end it right now.

However.

There was never any panic on Accelerator's face.

A strange wave shoved the giant magnet in a different direction.

"Crap...?!"

He tried to avoid it, but his legs hadn't completely recovered from slamming against the wall. He was late to react—and Accelerator grabbed his collar ruthlessly.

With his arm that spread death and fresh blood.

Victory had been determined.

Accelerator pulled him in by his collar, then tossed him to the side almost lazily. It was an incredibly casual act, but Hamazura's body shot away like a cannonball. He hit the hard floor several times before finally coming to a stop. The dull agony permeated the gaps between his bones and dove down to the core of his innards. He couldn't get up anymore. He'd never thought it so unnatural that he wasn't coughing up blood.

"*Gah...hah...!!*"

He clenched his teeth against the intense pain but still clutched at the floor with his fingertips.

Accelerator watched, switching off his electrode. He didn't drop his guard, and as he extended his crutch, he took aim with his gun.

To kill Hamazura instantly, in one shot.

"It's over. Stay down, and I'll let you go—try to get up, and you're dead on the spot. But it's your life. I'll let you choose."

"...You...know the answer...," said Hamazura through coughs, still glaring at Accelerator. "...You don't...even have any...reason to leave..."

"Guess not. I wouldn't mind quietly adding a bullet to your body. Not like killing you'd give me a bad aftertaste. Don't have an obligation to let you go knowing you could take revenge later, either. It would be easier just to kill you and get it over with.

"But," added Accelerator, sounding fed up with the situation.

"Having the sick one stand up and protect you is breaking the rules, isn't it?"

At those words, Hamazura looked away from Accelerator for the first time.

In surprise and still on the floor, he turned his head just as Rikou Takitsubo, consciousness hazy and sweating all over, one hand desperately clinging to the wall, approached him.

To protect him.

To save him.

Using every ounce of energy she could, with a body that was probably wrecked worse than his.

"What're you gonna do? If you want to use this brat as a shield and come at me two on one, I'll answer your request and turn you into a blood puddle. But if that brat is still gonna get in the way of the fight, then we'll start over. I'll leave for now, loath though I may be to say it. Think of it as a villain's sense of aesthetics."

The question caused Hamazura to finally relax the arm trying to reach for his gun that had fallen on the floor.

And finally, he asked himself *why*.

Why was Accelerator, who was trying to harm Takitsubo, apprehensive about getting her involved in their fight? If he wanted to, it would have been much easier to kill them both at once.

…Wait, he thought in his daze. *…Wait, have I…misunderstood something…?*

But before he could turn back toward Accelerator, he heard a soft tapping noise.

And then, Academy City's number one, who Hamazura knew had him cornered, was suddenly nowhere to be found. He must have manipulated his leg-force vectors somehow. Now Hamazura only heard a soft, regular tapping from the other side of the floor.

"Hamazura…"

After looking on in a daze for a few moments, he heard a girl's voice call his name.

Rikou Takitsubo.

The girl he most wanted to protect was dragging herself over to him. She lifted his unmoving body, every bit of it wounded, and embraced it.

"Hamazura!!"

"I'm so pathetic…," he muttered thoughtlessly, still with no energy in his limbs. "I said all that about saving you, and in the end…this was all I could do. Hah, pathetic. And the worst part is I attacked the guy who might have been saving your life. Could I possibly be any more pathetic…?"

"That's not true."

Takitsubo shook her head vehemently, despite it likely causing her considerable pain.

Her lips trembling, she denied Hamazura's statement.

"Hamazura, you came all this way by yourself. Even Anti-Skill didn't know what to do, but you jumped right into the building. You're not pathetic at all."

"Really…?"

Hamazura smiled a little but, in the meantime, took a moment to think to himself, while trying not to let the girl near him notice he was clenching his teeth.

…In that case…

…In that case, why are you crying?

It wasn't like Hamazura had been beaten up because Academy City's strongest Level Five had shown up. Even if that monster hadn't, even if he'd had to fight the terrorists like he'd planned—would he really have been able to rescue Rikou Takitsubo? No, on an even more basic level. Even if the enemy had been just a gang of delinquents, could he say for sure he'd have succeeded?

He couldn't.

In fact, the chances were low. Hamazura was no professional, with all sorts of special training. He didn't have a natural talent for fighting, and he didn't wield rare, powerful abilities. If it came down to a large-scale brawl, a war between one gang and another, he was just the third-rate street thug who would suddenly collapse in a corner of the alley.

Even if he risked his life, if he sacrificed everything and challenged everything head-on, he couldn't guarantee even something that simple. If he'd been a main character since birth, blessed with amazing abilities, then maybe he could have saved his friend more skillfully. He wouldn't have needed to make her worry about him like this. Hamazura felt an acute sense of loss, then realized what it was and clenched his teeth, his body ruined.

It wasn't that something he'd accumulated had fallen apart.

It was the opposite. He felt keenly now, once again, that even though he'd won against Shizuri Mugino in a fierce battle in the past, he hadn't actually gained anything from it.

...So much for the man who beat a Level Five. The man who brought down Number Four by himself. What's the point of getting so full of myself over a stroke of luck? In the end, I'm nothing but the same old Shiage Hamazura. My story didn't dramatically change after that. Nothing's that convenient.

He wanted to swear.

He didn't want to worry Takitsubo anymore, but he still harbored intense feelings about this.

He didn't have to turn into an evil, charismatic figure like Number One.

He could accept staying a third-rate street thug.

But at the very least...

As nothing but Shiage Hamazura, he wanted to become a man who could protect this girl's smile.

11

Looks like they're really going at it...

Saiai Kinuhata was observing, from a slight distance, the building at the center of the incident. It seemed like the former Spark Signal members had been mopped up already; the Anti-Skill officers blockading the building had decided to head inside, despite their apprehension at the sudden change in the situation.

The Heart Measure girl had reported that Shiage Hamazura had charged into the private salon building with a gun in order to save Rikou Takitsubo.

Hamazura didn't seem good enough to face almost ten Spark Signal members on his own, but apparently the two of them were safe. The problems, though, didn't end there.

Hamazura and Takitsubo weren't currently active in any shady side businesses. Academy City had several mechanisms to cover up incidents, but that service wouldn't cover the two of them—which meant that if Anti-Skill discovered he possessed a weapon, things would be bad.

If it was going to come to this, I suppose I should have gotten moving, like, right away.

There was a simple reason Kinuhata hadn't made it to the private salon building. She'd been looking into the Hexawing helicopter that had attacked their car. The voice on the phone, at least, had insisted she had nothing to do with it, but it was also difficult to imagine Spark Signal somehow being in control of it.

Her efforts had eventually proven fruitless.

…I'm totally gonna have to apologize for being late. And debts like this are best paid off superfast. Looks like I'll give them a hand busting out of there.

That was what she thought anyway, but in reality, she would never execute that plan.

Ga-boom!!

All of a sudden, there was a shotgun blast from the side, and it knocked her small body flying.

The girl's petite body, clad in a white woolen dress, bounced on the road twice, then a third time. The curious onlookers nearby began to panic after hearing the gunshot out of nowhere, but Kinuhata was calm even as she rolled along. The pellets had struck her from her right cheek to her chest, but thanks to her Nitrogen Armor, she wasn't bleeding.

…A twenty-pellet buckshot from a single sound. Single shot size of over five millimeters. I totally don't need to use my ability—I should be able to just hide behind that over there!!

Reverse calculating the attack's power, Kinuhata bounded behind a car parked nearby on the road.

But her assailant kept precise aim with the muzzle.

The next shot was not the single discharge sound normally associated with shotguns.

Ba-gha-gha-gha-gha-gha-gha!! It was the sound of automatic fire.

"What—? That's no ordinary shotgun?!"

The car's frame didn't even last two seconds.

This was beyond opening a few air holes. Its metal body inflated from within like a popping balloon, and the torrent of pellets that pierced it slammed straight into Kinuhata's body. Despite having made a thin wall of nitrogen, an overwhelming number of lethal weapons shot at her, meaning to tear through both her and her wall.

It knocked her over ten meters away.

When she quickly rose to her feet, she noticed a rivulet of blood trickling down her cheek.

It hadn't been fatal, but her armor had certainly been penetrated.

As the thought made her shudder, a voice called out, its cheerfulness standing in stark contrast to the situation.

"Heya! You're Saiai Kinuhata, right? Boy, I thought I'd have a hard time since your defenses looked relatively tough. Those *unrelated Spark Signal guys* happened to be moving at the same time as me, though. I seem to have made the right choice using them as decoys. While you were focused on them, I seized the chance to take a nice big chomp out of your soft flank.

"Still, these supernatural abilities of Academy City's are quite the trouble, aren't they?" she continued, moving her giant, beach parasol–sized gun.

Kinuhata heard a clanking of machinery.

The woman came closer, parting the gunpowder-smoke-laden air. She was tall and blond.

In her hands she held—a light machine gun with an incredibly high firing rate?

It was over a meter long. Assault rifles were designed to let infantry carry them on foot for long periods of time without causing issues, but this was different, an even larger gun. It had a box magazine attached that looked big enough to hold anywhere from fifty to two hundred rounds. Its intended usage appeared to be for suppressing entire areas, not individual targets.

The bullets she was using, though, were clearly custom shotgun shells. Real armies would rule out firearms of such bad taste right away. The combination was awful—shotguns were meant to be used up close, but its weight made it unsuited for melee combat. On the other hand, that probably meant this woman had the speed and technique to make it work anyway.

The woman wielding the automatic shotgun smiled sweetly at her. "If I said Chimitsu Sunazara, would you understand? You tried to kill him with explosives." She made a cute pose to garner agreement, one which probably would have made someone like Hamazura break out in a nosebleed. "I'm Stephanie Gorgeouspalace. I came here to avenge Mr. Sunazara. I think you should prepare yourself, don't you?"

She pointed her monstrously sized gun at Kinuhata and proclaimed her death with a smile.

INTERLUDE
TWO

Stephanie lived in a hopelessly peaceful nation, and she wanted for nothing in her life. The tepid, safe environment was exactly what made her start questioning things (or what gave her the time to do so), and that made her decide to fly out into the world. She was a civilian, and her motive for going to the battlefield as a mercenary was an extremely puerile one: She was concerned, as many are, about the distortions in society. She was at an age where she couldn't allow people to go on suffering the way they did. An age where she wouldn't be satisfied if she didn't do things herself.

And then.

The civil war in Costa Rica became the first hell she'd ever experienced.

A baptism—not for an official soldier, but the kind reserved for mercenaries. The new recruit was assaulted by incomplete intelligence. They'd been told there would be attack helicopters, but not that the helicopters were equipped with extra electronic devices and machines linked up with swift antipersonnel ambush radar setups on the ground. It had found Stephanie and the rest of her mercenary unit's hiding place in the underbrush, and a rain of rocket fire had descended upon them from above.

Their patchwork unit was annihilated that very day.

All of her comrades ended up in worse shape than mere corpses. None of their dog tags even remained, supplied on loan from their client. In Stephanie's case, it was nothing short of a miracle that her head and limbs were all still attached. But being the sole survivor hadn't been something she'd achieved on her own merits.

A large-bore antitank rifle had penetrated an attack helicopter's fuel tank from very far away.

That was when she'd first come across Chimitsu Sunazara.

Unlike Stephanie, he went to battles alone, without particularly forming any teams—a rare type of mercenary. He'd picked her up after she had been wounded and saved her life. No, it wasn't just that. Stephanie had come to this battlefield with half-assed, biased knowledge. Without Sunazara reteaching her all the skills she'd need, she would have ended up on some other battlefield in the same exact situation and died a dog's death.

Stephanie decided to stick with Sunazara even after the civil war ended. It was partly because she looked up to him, but she couldn't deny that she'd done it for a shrewder reason—staying by someone strong was a surefire way to survive as a mercenary.

And as they traveled to more and more battlefields, Stephanie suddenly realized something.

She knew what she got out of this relationship, but what was Sunazara getting out of it?

He was a sniper, a mercenary who acted alone. He'd never formed teams before. Apparently, it was because allies had held him back and dragged him into a desperate situation before, but then why would he want to take a newbie like Stephanie along? She was pretty sure his motive wasn't that he just wanted to have a young woman wait on him hand and foot.

She'd never directly asked Sunazara the reason, but she eventually built up a general idea from the things he'd casually do and say.

Maybe Sunazara was tired of the life.

Because of his job, he was almost guaranteed to kill others. Even if he avoided vital spots and aimed for arms or legs, his high-speed, high-powered rifle bullets would tear limbs right off and cause them to die of blood loss, agony, and shock. Snipers pinpointed their targets from far away—he'd never be able to use less powerful rounds.

On the other hand, Stephanie's realm of expertise was not long-range sniping.

She'd fooled around with sniper rifles, taking after Sunazara, but she knew they didn't match her personality on a fundamental level. She was best in high-speed combat after closing to extremely close ranges.

And there was no rule that said she absolutely had to kill her hostiles.

She fought her enemies inside ten meters, five meters, and occasionally one meter. If she used low-powered handguns, she could shoot their limbs and end the fight without killing them. And if she didn't know if someone was an enemy or not, she could also opt to use martial arts to disable them.

Maybe Sunazara, who only ever killed, envied her options and flexibility. And maybe it was crying for the moon, but perhaps Sunazara had viewed those choices—and her—as valuable.

As he put his sniper's skills to good use, he analyzed Stephanie's movement patterns and gained the ability to close in to middle and close range without making a noise.

Maybe then, if he did that, he could use low-powered rounds and shoot his opponents in the limbs, creating tactics that could end conflicts without killing.

Of course, doing things you aren't used to on a battlefield brings mortal danger with it.

However.

If he could use those tactics, then it would be fine.

If those tactics failed, then at least it would decrease the number of people who died at his hands.

…Maybe that was what the taciturn man had been thinking.

When she considered that, she decided she wanted to save him.

Using a method other than the worst one, the one that Sunazara himself unconsciously longed for.

*   *   *

In spite of all that, Stephanie's determination would, in the end, come to naught.

Group, School, Item, Member, Block. Sunazara had participated as a mercenary in the conflict between five organizations in the darkest parts of Academy City and had been beaten instead, leaving him a comatose patient in critical condition.

And by curious coincidence, in a situation Sunazara himself would probably have described as "the meagerest salvation born of a worst-case scenario," Stephanie Gorgeouspalace now swore vengeance.

Even knowing he hadn't asked for it.

But she did anyway, against the one person who had granted him a path to salvation through the utterly banal, trivial method of death and violence when it *should* have been more complex, more nuanced—she vowed vengeance against Saiai Kinuhata.

CHAPTER 3

Destruction Opens Yet Another Path

Battle_to_Die.

1

Accelerator and the others had returned to the camper.

The air was heavy.

There was normally no festive, jovial mood when the four were together, but this was far worse. The camper interior was tense beyond the breaking point. The stress could have killed small animals.

"…And so, everything goes the way Shiokishi wanted it," spat Accelerator. "Anyone who tries to learn about Dragon gets erased wholesale. I bet those guys we took captive in the Hula Hoop aren't alive anymore, either."

"Sugitani, you said his name was?" said Tsuchimikado suddenly, leaning against the wall. "Back when Shiokishi made that video call to us, he said the name of a couple of subordinates—I think they were Sugitani and Minobe."

"Still," said Musujime tiredly, her fingertip playing with her hair. "I wonder what Dragon is, in the end."

If it was a question they could answer so simply, nobody here would be suffering, but she couldn't help asking it.

Unabara glanced at Tsuchimikado for just a moment. Tsuchimikado, a sorcerer like him, gave no reaction, so Unabara decided to put in his own two cents. "Unlike all of you on the science side, I happen to be on the magic side. If you want my opinion, the term *dragon* has religious connotations to it. For example…Angels."

Accelerator's shoulders twitched when he heard the word.

All because of one night:

September 30.

That night, Accelerator and Hound Dog's Amata Kihara had fought to the death over a girl named Last Order. And there, he had witnessed something he might call an angel. A mad dance of glowing wings, each over ten meters long. There were still parts about the incident that day he didn't fully understand, but he'd done some of his own research and figured out a few things:

The wings' appearance was connected to Amata Kihara and Last Order.

And the name of the virus Kihara used that day was ANGEL.

He lived in Academy City, so he couldn't just discard it as something magical, something occult.

It could be that Unabara's viewpoint was completely misguided, and that Dragon really was something entirely different…but if there was a possibility that angel and Dragon were connected, Accelerator wouldn't be able to stay uninvolved. It would link Last Order to Dragon, Academy City's best-kept secret.

…*What aren't we seeing?*

From the start, Last Order and the other Sisters had supposedly been created as materials for the Accelerator experiment. They should be useless now that the experiment was over. And yet, they were very deeply related to the city's depths.

At this point, he had to start wondering whether his initial assumptions were wrong.

In other words, whether there had been something else to the Level Six shift experiment.

If all these results had been in accordance with someone's plans, they could have conceived the experiment as something designed to fail from the outset.

…*What have that brat and I gotten wrapped up in?*

Accelerator didn't personally care what happened to the former Spark Signal members who had occupied the private salon. But the fact that they could have gotten clues about Dragon in that situation only to have them snatched away made him feel worse, powerless.

"For now," continued Unabara, "the string of incidents starting with the Hula Hoop has ended, so...that would mean we all go home now."

"What about Dragon?" asked Accelerator pointedly. "We gonna go hide under our beds without finding anything?"

"...What, then you'd rather raid Shiokishi's hideout?!" spat back Tsuchimikado, amazed. "Considering he wears a powered suit around the clock, he's serious about protecting himself. His home base is probably as strong as a reinforced fallout shelter. We're not going to get in so easily—after all, he would have designed it assuming people like us were the ones coming for him."

Without a word, Accelerator turned his glare on Musujime. She had a means of transportation that ignored three-dimensional limitations: Move Point.

Musujime, however, shrugged her shoulders. "I don't think how we do it is the issue."

"What does that mean?"

"Only that we can't *peacefully* invade a fortress of that scale. We're up against one of Academy City's twelve leading figures. To put it bluntly, we'd need the resolve to become terrorists on the level of those at the Hula Hoop."

"...If we could ally with someone equally prominent—in other words, one of the General Board's official members—we might get in smoothly from using politics or have the fortress itself be opened," added Unabara. "Though that's predicated on the assumption that there's someone like that we *can* ally with, of course."

Accelerator, Motoharu Tsuchimikado, Awaki Musujime, and Mitsuki Unabara each had people they needed to protect. Considering that, unraveling the Dragon mystery through terroristic brute force wasn't a very good plan.

Academy City's number one thought for a moment or two about a certain young woman, casually looking over to the camper window as he did so—and then, suddenly announced, "Doesn't look like we have much time to prepare."

"?"

Not understanding, but deciding to observe what Accelerator was staring at for now, the rest directed their gazes out the same small window.

A moment later.

Ga-boom!!

The payload of a portable antitank missile launcher collided with the camper, the explosion transforming it into scrap iron.

Naturally, it would take more than that to kill the likes of them.

The camper had several entrances and exits. Tsuchimikado and Unabara each jumped out separate doors, Musujime used Move Point to escape, and Accelerator used his ability to bust through the wall himself and flee in the direction opposite where the missile came in.

The four, however, didn't group back up and confront their new enemy—or anything of that sort.

They each fled, scattered, following different routes. That was how Group did things.

...Must be Shiokishi. We learned too much about Dragon during these incidents, and now we're targets, too, predicted Accelerator calmly, diving into a narrow alley for the moment. *Which means it's likely he put together an assault team in full knowledge of my "weakness." Instead of trying to kill me in the shortest possible time, they make it a battle of attrition to drain my electrode battery. They know I'd break them like toys if they just rushed in.*

For a moment, he wondered about the camper's driver, but he didn't spare him many thoughts. He hadn't heard any screams right after the blast hit. The driver was probably an accomplice; it was likely they fled before the attack.

...But that doesn't mean I have to stick to running away like they want me to. It's actually a plus that I know who the enemy is now.

Better than not knowing who I'm fighting anyway. If I find their group first, then exploit the right blind spots to wipe them out, I won't have any issues.

And to use a tactic like that, he'd have to shake them off for now. He took a left, then another left into an alley, trying to get a look at the enemy lines from behind.

Greee.
All of a sudden, Accelerator's electrode shut off.

…?!
Accelerator, who had been adjusting his leg force using his vector ability, promptly lost control and fell to the road. It wasn't purely a physical problem. A thin sensation akin to a numbness racked his brain, right up to the deepest parts of his mental faculties.

As though he were drunk or sleep addled, his thoughts became incoherent and lost their continuous flow.

He understood his current state of being on the ground but couldn't connect that to any thought processes that could tell him what to do next.

What had attacked Accelerator as he squirmed along like a caterpillar was a very simple phenomenon.

Someone had controlled his electrode switch remotely.

And if it had affected him despite being deep inside an urban canyon, they were probably spreading the remote-control waves over a wide area. Accelerator's ability borrowed power from an electromagnetic network composed of almost ten thousand military-grade clones, and if he was cut off from that, he wouldn't be able to use his ability at all.

Normally, Accelerator would have been able to consider all this in an instant—and even think of a countermeasure.

But in the current situation, he'd been robbed of the very ability to think.

"…"

Gritting his teeth, the fallen Accelerator looked at his right hand.

It held a homemade crutch he'd added features to for times like these.

It had all kinds of motors and sensors built in, but it hadn't retained any function to suitably carry Accelerator when his ability was removed. Right now, he faced the very real problem of not being able to get up.

In the meantime, he heard several sets of footsteps getting closer.

He could feel a sense of crisis at something, but he couldn't concretely relate that to what he should do in response.

"…"

Footsteps approached from the other direction, too, where the alley let out. He was boxed in now, but Accelerator couldn't even calmly analyze the sense of danger.

Someone grabbed his arm. Then they threw him into the passenger's seat of a sports car parked near the alley's mouth.

There was nothing he could do. The car zoomed off, driving through the nighttime streets at a high speed.

As the distance from Shiokishi's pursuit unit increased, the remote-control waves lost effectiveness, which gave Accelerator his faculties back. Number One returned his electrode switch to normal, glared at his crutch, and then looked at the driver.

"…You?"

He remembered the face.

It was the high school–age boy who'd gotten wrapped up in the explosion in District 3. He was supposed to be with the wounded pregnant woman and heading for a hospital in District 7…

"Why are you suddenly so surprised?" asked the high school kid, dropping the sports car to a legal speed. "Anyway, I guess your body really does move when it has to. Thanks to that, I didn't have to let the person I owe my life to—no, someone who protected something even more important—die."

The high schooler smiled from his eyes.

Accelerator, however, pulled his gun from his pants belt and smoothly leveled it at him.

"…You learn quite a bit, even in a bullshit world like this," he spat.

"Rescues in the nick of time don't happen very often, for example. Especially if one of the General Board members, Shiokishi, set up this raid. I'd never *coincidentally* run into a familiar face."

"..."

"You're the same as me, aren't you? Someone who lives in the world of evil. Who put you up to this? Did Shiokishi think up a two-layered trap?!"

The high schooler, gun trained on him, looked not at Accelerator but straight ahead.

"You are right...," he said, the words coming out like molasses. "I've got the same scent as you. Totally different grade, though. My job is to be a lackey and support the big shots like you. Grunt characters bought at a discount and expended wholesale. But," he added, "no matter how foul I may be, that doesn't change the fact that you saved someone more important than my own life. And I'm not rotten enough to let a guy like that die without helping."

"..."

"This isn't just some cheap I-owe-you-one situation. Totally different level. It's a *debt*, and I'm repaying this debt. If you don't like it, you can feel free to shoot me right now."

For a short while, Accelerator stared at the side of the high schooler's face.

He never looked his way.

He was probably convinced he wouldn't get shot.

Accelerator tsked, then moved his gun's aim away from him. "Keep going."

"How far?" asked the young man with a smirk.

Without thinking about it too much, Accelerator answered, "I've gotta kill that Shiokishi bastard."

Shiokishi of the General Board had bared his fangs at Accelerator and the others to make sure certain information on Dragon wouldn't get out. Once he knew his first wave hadn't been able to finish them off, he would probably go after the most effective vulnerability.

In other words, he'd take Last Order hostage.

Accelerator presumed he hadn't yet played that card. If he'd had a hostage from the start, he'd have threatened them before attacking and tried to contain them.

Accelerator had to settle things now, before Shiokishi could move on to plan B.

To defend or to attack?

He had the option of quickly grabbing Last Order and going to ground…but he didn't think that was a good idea. It wouldn't be enough. What he wanted to protect wasn't her alone, but the very world she loved. It was too difficult even for Accelerator to keep fighting while protecting everyone around Last Order at the same time, like Aiho Yomikawa and Kikyou Yoshikawa.

Then what should he do?

After thinking for a moment, a wicked grin came over Accelerator's face.

What he would do was simple.

Victory favors the bold.

Kill before being killed.

A duel of speed, of which could wipe out the enemy camp faster.

…*Well, obviously*, thought Academy City's number one deep down, letting out a low, unintentional laugh. *I'm already covered in blood—this suits me far better!!*

2

A dull, throbbing pain ran through Saiai Kinuhata's head.

Stephanie's automatic shotgun had delivered massive damage despite Kinuhata's Nitrogen Armor. Without her shielding, Kinuhata was an incredibly frail (according to her) girl. If the shotgun shells kept pelting her, one would eventually be fatal.

…Ow. Taking more than seven hits when I'm super-close, like closer than five meters, would be really bad…!!

Kinuhata did some broad analysis from the damage she'd sustained as she burst onto a slope leading out from the District 3 underground. The subterranean mall was apparently closed off because some terrorists had been running amok, but…

"Nya-ha-ha!"

Behind her, Stephanie laughed, wielding her hunk of steel over a meter long in both hands. The large firearm was extremely strange to see against the scenery of a Japanese city.

"Your escape route is quite *straightforward* considering you're running from bullets, isn't it?"

"?!"

Another volley of shots followed without hesitation.

Bshaaaaa!! A long sound from many short ones overlapping.

Stephanie would have been aiming down at Kinuhata on the slope from aboveground. In other words, the ground, that thick wall of asphalt and concrete, should have gotten in the way.

Nevertheless, a rain of bullets stormed toward Kinuhata.

It was like an avalanche. The scattershot was powerful enough to turn an armored car into a sponge within three seconds, and it took her a few seconds to realize it was even tearing away chunks of the artificial ground. And during all that, a ton of pellets struck her body.

She slammed into the floor once, then bounded back up like a basketball. As she did, she desperately balled herself up to roll over the floor and avoid the concentrated attack. Because the concrete that made up the underground mall's ceiling (and therefore, the aboveground surface) was destroyed, parked passenger vehicles and such also rolled down in the avalanche.

"!!"

Kinuhata didn't pause to think.

She grabbed a car falling at her with one hand. Her petite palm touched the door area and made an awful cracking noise. Countless wrinkles shot through the metal frame, as though she'd clutched a cushion.

She'd acquired a hulk weighing about five hundred kilograms, but it wasn't so she could use it as a defensive shield.

It was a weapon to throw at her opponent and crush her.

That was right when Stephanie Gorgeouspalace stepped on the landslide of concrete wreckage to approach the underground mall.

Her footing was unstable, creating a situation where she wouldn't be able to immediately jump left or right to avoid it.

And Kinuhata planned on using all her strength to kill her.

…Comin' at ya!!

She twisted her upper body once, fueling it, and swung around the passenger vehicle. Now she just had to let go, and an attack like a giant, building-destroying wrecking ball would fly straight at Stephanie.

She didn't know if the woman was a soldier from outside or a mercenary, but she wouldn't be able to stand up to an Academy City–made Level Four.

That was what she thought anyway.

Ga-krrsh!!

Stephanie's shotgun struck the vehicle right in the fuel tank.

It was a literal instant before Kinuhata let go.

Wha—?

The car's rear half transformed into a crushed empty can. Then, all that fluid stored in the tank ignited like a bomb.

Sound vanished.

Her vision was wiped out by a single flash of light.

Struck by the blast wind, Kinuhata's body hurtled to the side. Intense light and heat rushed into the underground mall, which had little illumination save for its fluorescent lighting, and black smoke crawled along the ceiling.

Her counterattack had been stopped by yet another.

But what surprised Kinuhata wasn't only Stephanie's quick wits.

It was the foundation underpinning them.

She's…used to this? This outsider is super-knowledgeable about how to fight espers like me…?

Logically, that was impossible. Even within Academy City, where supernatural powers were just a part of life, not many would be able to lead the Level Four Kinuhata around this easily. And there couldn't have been a whole lot of individuals who could match her technology and tactics from the outside world.

"Wait…"

After realizing that, she unsteadily looked up.

Stephanie, shotgun in hand, was descending the rubble and entering the underground mall.

"Wait, are you…?"

"Oh, you finally figured it out? Before becoming a mercenary, I was an average person who lived in a peaceful country…It was the guilt. I knew there were people suffering out of fear of bullets and artillery and land mines, yet, I could fully enjoy a relaxed peace. That was why I decided to save the people embroiled in warfare."

As the blonde pointed her hot barrel at her, she smiled and said, "Yes, I was originally from Academy City. I used Anti-Skill's arresting techniques for killing. That was why Mr. Sunazara, a sniper, looked at you so oddly, wasn't it?"

So that was why.

Why Stephanie Gorgeouspalace knew exactly how to kill espers.

"If I remember right, you can use the nitrogen in the air to block my attacks, right?"

Slip.

She pointed her light submachine gun in a completely different direction.

"I'll start by messing that up. Fortunately, there seem to be many delicious restaurants in this underground mall…How many propane gas tanks would you say there are?"

She pulled the trigger.

3

Accelerator proceeded down the midnight streets in the sports car, chauffeured by the high school student. After getting in touch with Tsuchimikado via cell phone, he learned the other members were currently fleeing using their own routes, like he thought. And then:

"Great. I think you're the first one to get out of the pursuit unit's encirclement. I want you to go to District 21 now. There's an observatory in the mountains."

"Eh? What, does Shiokishi have a shelter in the mountains, too?"

"*No. He's an official General Board member. If we want to take him down, we'll need to be prepared politically...Meaning we'll need someone with the General Board's level of authority. The twelve board members are a wily bunch. The one at that observatory is probably the only one we can hope for any cooperation from,*" explained Tsuchimikado, adding under his breath, "*Tsugutoshi Kaizumi is a good person, but the brains of his operation is Seria Kumokawa, a female high school student, who is too much of a genius for him to handle.*"

"Well, who the hell's this person who could help us out?"

"*Monaka Oyafune,*" answered Tsuchimikado immediately. "*She's having an astronomical observation event as charity with the kids who were kidnapped in the Hula Hoop incident...She's the best person out of the General Board. I don't like to do things this way, but she owes us. This might be the only chance we ever have to negotiate with her.*"

With that, the sports car Accelerator sat in headed for District 21.

This school district was the only mountainous one in Academy City. Nevertheless, its altitude was extremely low, and even the highest peak only reached about two hundred meters. The district was famous for its reservoir as well as its animal and plant research, but many also knew it as a center for astronomy.

Small parabolic antennae, each about one meter across, possibly a type of radio telescope, lined the slope at constant intervals. The mountain roads Accelerator and the student's car drove up were intentionally free of most artificial light. Skid marks were visible in several places on hilly, curved parts of the road. Maybe they held illegal street races here on weekends.

The observatory was near the center of the mountains.

It was on a large concrete land, the only flat place here, as though rebelling against the mountains' slopes. The sports car entered the parking lot. When it did, Accelerator spotted a small bus. There was nobody inside; the kids must have been having fun, safe at the event they'd planned to have from the start.

"You can drop me off here," said Accelerator, opening the passenger door and pushing the tip of his crutch onto the asphalt.

The high schooler serving as his driver frantically interrupted him. "H-hey, wait a minute! What about my debt to you? Even a grunt like me can tell you got involved in something crazy. I can't just call it quits after giving you a quick lift."

"I didn't do anything amazing. If you do any more than this, I'll be the one who owes *you*," said Accelerator, getting out of the car and standing up on his crutch. "...And if you go any deeper, you could end up a target, too. I don't care what happens to random lackeys, but if someone uses that pregnant lady I saved as a hostage, it'd leave a bad taste in my mouth."

"You're..."

"I'll contact you if I really need help. Stay hidden until then. It's important to keep the useful pieces stowed away. That's how we survive. Let me use you like that."

"All right. Hey, let's trade cell numbers. If things get bad, make sure to give me a call."

They both used their cell phones' infrared communication function to exchange phone numbers.

After that was completed, the high school student finally drove off in the sports car and left the observatory, albeit reluctantly.

*Anyway...*thought Accelerator with a short sigh.

The number he'd given him was obviously a dummy he'd set up in advance, and he'd rejected the incoming number as well. Now their connection to each other had disappeared completely. It was Accelerator's way of tying up loose ends.

He looked toward the large observatory building from the parking lot.

In there was one of the General Board members: Monaka Oyafune. The VIP that would be the key to defeating another board member, Shiokishi.

If she was the best person on the board, then she was probably Accelerator's polar opposite.

He'd never actually talked to her before, but Oyafune owed Accelerator for two things. The first was, as Tsuchimikado mentioned, the fact that they'd saved those kids at the Hula Hoop. The second was when they'd stopped a sniping attempt on Oyafune during the clash between Group, School, Item, Member, and Block.

Tsuchimikado had a forked tongue, so he probably wanted him to use those points skillfully to get her cooperation—and as was clear from Accelerator's words and actions, no job was more unsuited to him.

...This is going to be a pain in the ass.

He scratched his head, then walked with his crutch toward the observatory. Whatever the case was, he'd have to see her face-to-face and start talking before anything would happen, but...

"Please go home."

That was quick, thought Accelerator.

Incidentally, the one who had insulted him as soon as he'd opened his mouth in the parking lot a short distance from the observatory had not been Monaka Oyafune, but a short man who appeared to be her secretary. Accelerator didn't know how many secretaries the lady had or how many she'd gone through, but the man who stood before him appeared highly strung, glaring at Academy City's number one and blocking his path to Oyafune.

"And yes, even Mrs. Oyafune was very skilled in her time. She excelled in negotiation and bargaining rather than using force, but she was so feared by foreign diplomats they called her tactics *peaceful acts of invasion*."

The secretary's fists, which had never punched another person before, trembled as he spoke.

"But she's done with that now. She doesn't live a life of going back and forth between light and dark anymore. Don't you understand that? You've looked at the peaceful world from the darkness all this time. Don't you know how difficult and important it is to cast that away? Or are you so addled with your world that you don't even understand that?"

Accelerator tsked in irritation, but it wasn't particularly toward what the secretary had to say.

..."*Most likely to cooperate,*" *my ass. This just turned into the biggest pain of them all. How dare he use me like some dime-a-dozen minion. Next time I see him, I'm gonna need to put five bullets in him before I'm satisfied...*

He felt something seething in his stomach, but he didn't show it. Instead, he said, "Sorry to bother you."

"...You're...giving up?"

"Hey, you're the one who told me to. What, would you rather stand your ground and make this a bloodbath?"

"Even if I had to, it wouldn't change what I need to do."

The secretary's face paled, as though he'd only just now considered the possibility. But he still wouldn't yield the way.

Accelerator questioned, "Can I ask you one thing? What the hell happened to her?"

"...Her daughter," answered the man after a pause. "When the General Board was deciding on provisions related to the restrictions of weapon export to the outside, Mrs. Oyafune, who was anti-munitions, used her own bargaining tactics to gain advantages with it. She truly hated warfare. But then, an envelope arrived at her office. In it were an unused magnum and a picture of her daughter... Nothing came of it in the end, but I suspect Shiokishi, a supporter of the munitions business."

"..." Accelerator's eyebrow very slightly, but very certainly, moved.

As though he'd acknowledged Academy City's number one as a person now that he'd said he'd leave, the short secretary averted his eyes as he continued. "Mrs. Oyafune withdrew from the front lines after that. She'd live in a sphere that doesn't contact this city's darkness, but it also blocks what happens in the darkness without them knowing, in such a way that they won't go after her...That's how she wants to live now, foolish though it may sound. It's a very delicate balance—a golden ratio created by Monaka Oyafune, skilled negotiator...If you and yours intervene, that balance collapses. Her daughter and others close to her would end up being targeted again."

"That so?" muttered Accelerator under his breath.

Just as he was about to turn his back on the secretary, Monaka

Oyafune had finally noticed their little squabble. The old woman came running out to where he was. The secretary's expression changed, but she didn't seem to notice.

"Excuse me, but…Who might this be?" asked Oyafune, mystified, looking at Accelerator.

Accelerator had once saved her life in secret from a sniper's attempt to kill her, but because it had been secret, Oyafune probably didn't know who he was.

"…Never mind." He wasn't about to boast about it, either. Tsuchimikado had told him to use it to his advantage, but that thick-skinned, shameless bastard could go to hell for all he cared. "Just asking directions."

Finished speaking, Accelerator started to turn his back to Oyafune and her secretary.

But this time, the secretary began to question him.

"…And what about you? You must have at least known things wouldn't have gone the way you wanted them to. But you came anyway. Here's my final question: What happened?"

"Why would you need to know?" spat Accelerator in response. "You turned me down, and now you only want to know what's going on? It would just add to your burden. You're better off not knowing what sort of trouble is going on between that bastard Shiokishi and me."

"…" The secretary's expression shifted.

Details aside, he'd probably gotten a good idea of what was happening. For whatever reason, he knew that Accelerator needed to fight one of the General Board members, and to do that, he needed Oyafune's assistance as another board member. Nine times out of ten he wouldn't be able to beat Shiokishi without her help, and even if he had managed, he'd still be treated as a criminal.

Out of reflex, the secretary looked away from Accelerator. "…Sorry."

"It's my problem. Nothing you need to get involved with," Accelerator replied, sounding tired of the nonsense. "I should have just done this myself to begin with. It might cause some problems, but it wouldn't have gotten you tangled up in it."

Once the fight with Shiokishi ended, Accelerator would probably be branded a terrorist.

After losing all support, he'd be unable to live life the way he had been. He wouldn't be able to see Last Order very easily anymore, either. And if their interests clashed, he could also end up fighting Motoharu Tsuchimikado, Mitsuki Unabara, and Awaki Musujime.

But—

So what?

Hadn't he made this decision for himself? That he'd keep fighting to protect Last Order, even if he had to make an enemy out of Last Order herself? This didn't change anything. His course was set—he didn't have to drag Oyafune into it.

"Sorry for bothering you. Forget what you heard here. I'll settle the score with that shithead myself."

Without waiting for an answer, Accelerator turned his back completely this time.

But then—

"What are you doing?!"

Suddenly, he heard a new voice.

It belonged to a boy who couldn't have been older than ten. It was one of the grade school kids who had been part of the astronomical observation charity event. And it was the hostage boy Accelerator had saved at the Hula Hoop in the nick of time.

"You're the hero from earlier, right?" the kid tried again. "What are you doing here?"

"…Nothing."

"I heard you talking before."

Accelerator and the secretary looked at the boy anew. He'd come closer in the meantime. With no hesitation—right up to Academy City's number-one monster. Without an ounce of caution, probably because he'd saved his life.

"I didn't know what you were talking about, but you're going to fight again, right? To save people in a situation like I was in?"

The boy looked straight up into Accelerator's eyes as he spoke.

"Then I'm coming, too."

...Are you kidding me? wondered Accelerator, unconsciously wanting to face-palm. "Get lost, stupid brat. Who's going to fight with whom, here?"

"Well, those people said they'd abandon us!!"

The abrupt comment surprised Monaka Oyafune most of all. The secretary frowned slightly, as if he had an idea.

"I know you wouldn't fight for something stupid. And I know you're going somewhere really dangerous! So I'm going, too. I won't let you be alone. If there are people in trouble like I was, then I want to fight, too!!"

He had no idea what was happening, but he spoke sincerely.

Considering the child's practical usefulness in combat, it was an all-too-unrealistic request. Despite that, Accelerator didn't ignore him and leave. Even though he was looking directly down at the boy, he responded to his honest words with an honest reply of his own.

"...I don't need your help."

"But—"

"I was alone at the Hula Hoop, idiot. Did it look like I was ever in any danger from those terrorist insects?"

"I don't know. I was blindfolded."

"Right. Then I'll just tell you—I was in no danger then, and I'll be in none now."

That wasn't true.

Accelerator knew the truth; he reigned over the world of darkness, after all—but Monaka Oyafune and her stocky secretary knew it, too.

Accelerator *was* strong. But in order to wield his power to its fullest in the darkness, he needed the support of several departments and agencies, not the least of which was the General Board. Losing all that, making them into his enemies, turning all of Academy City's military against him—that bespoke incredible danger.

This wasn't his problem alone anymore.

It involved everyone he needed to protect.

They could freely control his electrode and block his abilities whenever they chose. Crawling through the mud and rain during the battle like he did with Amata Kihara of the Hound Dogs would be unavoidable.

But...

"I'm the strongest Level Five in the city. Some random brat doesn't have the right to worry about me."

Accelerator didn't mention any of the hardships that awaited him.

The boy didn't need to know.

What he said was simple. It was so that he wouldn't drag the boy into the darkness, so that this child wouldn't be exposed even to a fragment of the risks that would soon befall Accelerator.

"Listen up. Even if you see someone suffering, grabbing a weapon without thinking and killing the thugs makes you as much of a villain as them. Someone who can murder people just because it makes sense to them, without thinking about other people's feelings or giving them a chance to become better—you can't call that a good person. You don't need to turn into that. That's my territory. Something I need to do alone."

That was courageous, and only those who knew the details would have understood that.

Monaka Oyafune and her secretary both only understood a small piece of it.

"I can fight just fine on my own. There's no room for someone like you."

"...I still want to," said the boy abruptly, resisting the gentle words that tore him down. "I still want to fight, too."

Then the boy looked up at Academy City's strongest Level Five and shouted at the top of his lungs:

"I don't want to give Academy City to cowards like them!!"

Other people finally seemed to notice the commotion.

Several men in black, maybe other secretaries or the facility's security, came up to them, and one placed a hand on the boy's shoulder. The gesture itself was gentle, but it was clearly for the purpose of getting him away from Oyafune. Even as the man restrained him, the boy didn't turn away from Accelerator's gaze. Even when their teacher came out a few moments later, he looked into his eyes until the end.

Accelerator watched the boy for a while as they brought him back to his classmates at the astronomical observation event. And he wasn't the only one.

Monaka Oyafune, official member of the Academy City General Board, was watching the boy go as well.

"...You mentioned Shiokishi before, didn't you?"

"Mrs. Oyafune!!" the secretary said frantically, trying to stop her.

But Oyafune was looking directly at Accelerator. She knew, thanks to the incident with her daughter, how politically fearsome Shiokishi could be.

She also knew the dangers of this battleground that Accelerator was about to enter.

In contrast, Accelerator spoke his next words as though spitting them out. "Nothing you need to worry about."

"By that, I take it...you intend to fight him, like that boy said."

Oyafune gave a short sigh, considering the boy's final words.

I don't want to give Academy City to cowards like that!

The boy didn't have a particular enemy in mind. In his mind, the "cowards" were just a vague image about the darkness that lurked in the city.

But perhaps that was why Monaka Oyafune thought the way she did. As someone who knew about the city's darkness but decided to stop fighting—didn't that make her one of those cowards?

She was merely one old woman who tried to argue things out with the world, without shedding blood or relying on military force, using only her powers of negotiation. Was she not someone who could proudly object to hearing the word *coward* applied to her?

"...I wonder what I should do," she murmured suddenly.

"Hell if I know," answered Accelerator, clicking his tongue, peeved. "It's your life. You decide."

The words cut to her core, and despite herself, she smiled.

Accelerator could deliver that line so assuredly because that was how he lived his own life. Even now, he was protecting something.

Monaka Oyafune placed her hand on something nearby.

It was a black, bulletproof car.

She placed her right hand on the expensive vehicle's roof first, and then placed her left hand on it in the same way. Then, she turned to face the car fully.

Bang!!
She drove her fist as hard as she could into the car.

"Mrs. Oyafune!!" cried the secretary.

But she ignored him. For the first time in a very long time, she'd felt the pain of damaging something in her fist. She turned to face Accelerator again, her expression looking like she'd expelled all the negative emotions she had held deep down.

"...My eyes are finally open."

"Give me a break. I just decided I'd do this alone like a minute ago, you know," said Accelerator, almost like asking for confirmation.

"It's my life. I get to decide," she answered immediately. "When I received that photograph of my daughter along with a magnum, I decided that breaking my own fangs would be the most appropriate way to protect what's important to me."

"..."

"But I wonder why I didn't think like this: 'They've severely underestimated me by going after my daughter.' Why didn't I realize that if I don't root out the evil, nothing important to me will ever escape them?"

Monaka Oyafune moved to stand directly in front of Academy City's strongest Level Five.

They stood on equal terms now, not because of any trivial violent power they possessed at their fingertips, but because of something in a different dimension, something that came from a pillar deeper inside the human heart.

Accelerator knew others with eyes like that.

Aiho Yomikawa from Anti-Skill and Kikyou Yoshikawa, formerly a scientist.

"Let's pay Shiokishi a visit. That would be the best plan. His base of operations is impenetrable, whether by raw power or political sway, but if I add my own authority as another board member to the fight, I can remove the latter obstacle, at least."

Accelerator tsked in irritation.

But the secretary wouldn't let it go with just that. "But, Mrs. Oyafune, that method would be—"

"I've made up my mind. Even if this person was to leave, I would fight Shiokishi alone. In which case, working together would be ideal, wouldn't it?"

The secretary, sensing her strength of will, then gave a sharp glare at Accelerator. He'd just said he wouldn't get Oyafune involved in this so—

"This young man told me to decide. He didn't force me to do anything. And I decide how I live my life. You've no right to blame him. He afforded me the utmost consideration."

"Damn it...!!"

After cursing, something he would normally never, ever do, the secretary opened the black bulletproof car's door and groped around the dashboard. He came out with a gun.

But it wasn't to point it at Accelerator or Monaka Oyafune.

It was the opposite.

"Someone as amazing as you doesn't deserve to die over something this worthless, Mrs. Oyafune. This person has the capacity to bring happiness to many people on a much larger scale than this."

With practiced movements, he checked how many bullets remained in the magazine and then glared at Accelerator. "You! Now that you have her cooperation, I expect a modicum of responsibility!! Protect her with everything you have! If you let Mrs. Oyafune be killed, I *will* turn you into Swiss cheese!!"

"That was good. You know, you might be cut out to be a villain."

"Would you not say awful things and make them sound like

compliments?" he muttered as the three climbed into the black sedan.

Their destination, at last, was the home base of Shiokishi, the General Board's string puller.

With history's strongest villain in tow, the General Board's negotiator Monaka Oyafune rose up once again.

4

Something must have happened to Saiai Kinuhata.

Hamazura and Takitsubo finally guessed as much after sneaking out of the private salon building. The terrorists were no longer in control of it, and Anti-Skill officers were still performing a site verification.

"…I got a message from Kinuhata on my cell phone."

On the screen of her cutely designed phone was a message saying she was going to lead Takitsubo out of there and to wait for her for a little while. Time had passed since then, but Kinuhata hadn't shown herself at all. Eventually, the two of them escaped the private salon building on their own.

"Hey, did you get in touch with her? I hope we didn't pass each other by."

"I've been calling her, but I can't get through."

Takitsubo's vacant eyes stared at her cell phone. Hamazura couldn't tell whether she was like that all the time, or if she hadn't completely shaken off the ill effects from the Crystals. She'd already been using them when she and Hamazura first met.

"Hamazura, what should we do?"

"Well, Kinuhata is a lot more durable than us," said Hamazura. "I mean, she's a Level Four. And she did send a text. Maybe we shouldn't make any careless moves and wait for her to get in touch. It would take something pretty crazy to kill her—"

Boom!!

All of a sudden, a huge explosion went off in another part of District 3.

*   *   *

It didn't blow up a building; it had gone off underground. No sooner did the distant ground start to crack than crimson flames began to erupt from underneath.

Because there was more than one explosion.

Bam-ka-bam-ka-boom!! Several roiling balls of fire flared up at once. The asphalt split, swallowing passenger vehicles parked on the road into its ant-lion pit. Few people were nearby, probably because of the terrorist incident at the salon building, so thankfully it didn't seem as though any bystanders had fallen into it.

Somehow, the explosions seemed to be getting closer, little by little.

As Hamazura watched, he eventually said with trembling lips, "You've gotta be kidding me. This is ludicrous, isn't it?!"

There was no guarantee Kinuhata was directly involved with those explosions, but flashy bombings like this usually had something to do with people on the "dark" side like Hamazura and Takitsubo. The possibility was higher than zero.

"What's even exploding anyway?"

"Hamazura, it might be the underground mall."

When he looked where Takitsubo was pointing, hordes of customers were just starting to pour out of a department store entrance. The smoke had probably come up from underground, and now they were frantically evacuating.

Hamazura looked around and found an entrance to the underground mall that was also connected to a subway ticket gate. After descending the staircase, essentially a smokestack now, an orange-colored light was there to greet them.

It was a hellscape.

There were no flames near where he stood yet, per se. However, the massive, burning orange inferno farther in was flinging tiles from the floor and ceiling and glass panes all over the place, becoming almost like a thick wall made of light. The air itself was strangely warm. It made him feel like he was inside a giant oven.

Something was definitely happening, but there was still no proof Kinuhata was in there.

Hamazura wavered.

This firestorm was far too dangerous to enter to search for someone he wasn't sure was there. But it wouldn't solve anything if the flames got to him while he was trying to make up his mind.

...Keep going or turn back...?

"Hamazura, look!!" shouted Takitsubo, pointing at something.

Something was flickering beyond the orange flames. No, it was a silhouette. A small one, standing still, obscured by the wall of fire.

When Hamazura spotted it, he unintentionally cried out, "Kinuhata!!"

The young woman, surprised, turned to look. She wasn't relieved at seeing the face of someone she knew—in fact, she shouted back, her expression seeming even more tense after noticing them.

"Get down, dumbass!! Hiding behind things won't work!!"

As soon as he heard those words, he saw it.

Another figure, this one fairly tall, standing behind the flames.

It was holding something long and slender—something that looked like a machine gun.

"!!"

Hamazura pounced on Takitsubo, and they both fell to the floor. The heated tile felt like it was scalding him, but this wasn't the time to worry.

Ba-bam!!

A volley of bullets flew at them from beyond the flames.

A line of them flew horizontally at about waist height. And the bullets didn't seem like regular rifle rounds. Not only did they damage the glass-block walls, they tore big chunks out of even the concrete pillars near the stairwell.

"Nya-ha-ha!"

The firing stopped for just a few seconds.

The bullets had ripped through like a tempest, but the shooter probably hadn't intended to kill Hamazura and Takitsubo. The tall person's target was probably Kinuhata. They brought the huge gun up again and pointed it in Kinuhata's direction, and then the tall... probably woman said:

"You're using nitrogen to make walls, so I figured I could stop you by messing with the air. But it sure is hard to get all the nitrogen out when it makes up seventy percent of the air, isn't it?"

...Is she the one who did all this...? Hamazura, pressed to the floor of the fire scene, struggled to make heads or tails of the situation. Was she using the propane gas in restaurants or something to turn the mall into a sea of flames?

The way she held her gun...It seemed to vaguely resemble the bearing of the delinquent-wrangling Anti-Skill officers.

But someone who fought to protect children wouldn't be willing to set an underground mall on fire just to fight an esper.

Someone in the darker parts of Academy City like us...? That huge gun is clearly different from the terrorists'. Theirs weren't meant to be hidden...

The enemy knew how Kinuhata's ability worked and was trying to take advantage of her weakness.

After considering that, Hamazura took out his handgun.

It was good for carrying around, but with a short barrel, its accuracy at long distances was pretty poor. If he wanted to make sure he hit, he'd have to get within at least thirty meters.

...That machine gun is obviously better than my piece. If she realizes I'm trying to shoot her, she won't think twice before mowing me down. What do I do? How do I get in close without getting noticed...?

He racked his brain over the question, but his opponent didn't wait for him. The tall female figure continued, "But if I get the specific conditions right, explosions can create something like a vacuum for a moment, can't they? Like cutting winds, a strictly localized event...The hole would only be a few dozen centimeters across, but still."

"?! Hamazura, get out of here right—!!"

*   *   *

"If I shoot a bullet from that hole, you won't be able to use your precious shield, will you?!"

Ba-boom!!
Several explosions went off at the same time.

They almost appeared to be surrounding Kinuhata's small frame. Overwhelming flashes of light blinded them, and a shock wave rolled toward Hamazura and Takitsubo as if through a tube.

Hamazura immediately covered Takitsubo's mouth and nose with his hands and shut his eyes tight. If they inhaled this sirocco, it would sear their throats and organs.

Once the scorching gale had passed, Hamazura finally opened his eyes. Beyond the flames, the tall figure was pointing her gun at Kinuhata.

This was what the enemy had meant.

If she created a localized vacuum, Saiai Kinuhata wouldn't be able to cover that part with her shield. Then, if her adversary fired a bullet through that hole, the shot would hammer into her defenseless body.

"Kinuhata!!"

There was no response.

Only the awful, continuous rattling from the tall woman's smoking gun.

5

Accelerator's group reassembled.

Location: District 2. The area boasted many R & D facilities in fields that created a lot of noise pollution, like automobiles and explosives. Large soundproof walls encircled the district; the place even had noise-canceling equipment installed that worked by emitting sound waves of opposite phase.

"Given the neighborhood, it's not very populous…Lot of munitions-related facilities, too," explained Tsuchimikado, somewhat appalled.

"Considering the fact that Shiokishi is an armaments fanatic, it's basically his home turf."

They were on a street built alongside a large bypass, in an area populated by gas stations and fast-food joints. It might be easier to think of it as a highway rest stop.

Musujime, leaning against the black sedan, asked, "So do we know where this Shiokishi person's hideout is?"

"According to Oyafune, it's one of the testing shelters in the district," Accelerator spat. "They use explosives here, don't they? They set up model shelters and do endurance tests by hitting them with explosions from different angles. Shiokishi's private fortress is way tougher, and it blends right into the scenery."

"And as for Oyafune...?" Tsuchimikado craned his neck, bringing the old woman into his view. A smile crossed his lips. She had changed into a suit.

When she met his gaze, she bowed slightly and said, "Yes, I'm quite prepared."

"You were having your secretary wait 'somewhere safe,' right?" asked Tsuchimikado with a shrug.

Accelerator looked at Oyafune. "Surprised your secretary let you do this."

"Well, can't allow any dangerous acts, after all," she replied vaguely.

Tsuchimikado clapped his hands together. "We have everything we need, so let's finish this quickly. We're not exactly going for a polite visit and a pleasant tea party."

Meanwhile, Shiokishi, one of only twelve official General Board members in Academy City, frowned.

This dome-shaped building, shielded with special armor, was quite spacious but had little in the way of furnishings. The general impression it gave off was that of a battleship. Only a few lavish chairs and wardrobes dotted the area, just enough to highlight their captain's tastes.

For Shiokishi, peace and security were the greatest luxury and the result of having expended a maximum amount of work and capital. In reality, this heap of military secrets had enough money spent on it to purchase an entire European castle, complete with furniture.

And now—that peace and security, the highest and richest form of pleasure, was beginning to shake under his feet.

"An enforcement of the equal-authority inspection system by an official member of the General Board...?"

Yes, the twelve had an agreement like that, didn't they?

The General Board's main members needed to have equal power at all times. They couldn't allow one to amass significantly more influence and cause the balance to collapse. During their assemblies, all twelve members' opinions were treated equally. The objective, he figured, was that they needed to lead Academy City in an extremely democratic way.

It was, of course, all a farce.

Each of the twelve amassed power in their own fields that set them above the others and tried to control the city in any way that could possibly benefit them, all purposely at the expense of the others who nominally had "equal authority."

Normally, there was no possible way any of them would come waving the flag of such an ornamental system.

...*Can I reject it?* Shiokishi wondered immediately.

Usually, he'd be allowed to.

But it wouldn't work this time.

After checking his avenues of metaphorical escape on the General Board's network again, he saw the twelve members each had their own trivial little pacts. No one pact had very much effectiveness, but strangely, they were put together so that they would interfere with the equal-authority inspection system. If he tried to use one method to block it, that would violate a different pact, and if he tried to dissolve that pact, that in turn would trigger yet another one. It felt incredibly tenacious to him, like a spiderweb strung over many years only to finally corner its target at a dead end.

"That fox...! She kept on forming asinine peace treaties even if it meant cutting off her own authority or support divisions—but it was all for this?!"

It was terrifying that, despite its tenacity, her plan had never revealed even a hint of itself until the trap was sprung. He thought he'd been keeping tabs on Monaka Oyafune's movements this entire time.

"What shall we do, sir?" asked his hand-reared assassin Sugitani as the man stood beside him. "This shelter has equipment to physically and politically prevent third parties from entering, but almost all our political defense functions have been disabled by Monaka Oyafune enforcing the equal-authority inspection system. And…"

"If the cameras are right, we can presume that Oyafune either has Group, not the least of which is Accelerator, under her thumb, or is working jointly with them. Refusing her inspection and holing up inside the shelter won't lead to peace and security…After all, I fully prepared an assassination on her, and it ended in failure. We should assume they currently have more strategic value than a nuclear weapon."

Clad in his thick powered suit, Shiokishi kept folding his hands together nervously. In contrast, Sugitani, who served him, was more self-possessed.

"…Will they really go through with such a hardball approach, sir? Even if ignoring their official inspection gives them the casus belli they need, attacking this place would lead to a war between General Board members."

"…They'll come," answered Shiokishi, tapping the foot part of his composite armor on the floor. "This all relates to Dragon, after all. They're grasping at straws, so they'll come."

"Group aside, that wouldn't be Monaka Oyafune's intent, would it?"

"That woman's reasons for acting are even more dreadful. I'd thought her declawed until now, but she's always been the sort of woman who would fight entire countries with her life on the line just because some kid she'd never seen before was crying. There are no political methods that will work. If she's making her move, the only thing we can do is respond by force."

"Shall I capture her daughter, Suama Oyafune?"

"It might work for Oyafune, but not Group. Does it seem like we have time to do anything we don't need to?" responded Shiokishi, almost cutting him off, as though he'd run the simulation on that possibility several times. "We'd split our forces to secure a hostage. What if they occupied this shelter in the meantime? We might have a hostage, but it'd be meaningless if they pointed a blade at my own throat. Doing that wouldn't lead to a foundation for peace and security."

...If Shiokishi and his forces got their hands on something more important to the enemy than their lives, then even if they pressed a gun to his head, there would probably be room for negotiation. But this decision to pursue another path was a matter of Shiokishi's principles. He would never factor the possibility of risking his own life into his plans, not even as a joke.

Whatever the case was to be, Shiokishi made his decision for meeting it:

"We fight them here."

Sugitani didn't voice any objections. He would merely obey his master's decision.

As though he felt his attitude was peaceful and secure, Shiokishi softened his tone and continued. "All of us. Gather the Group pursuit team and the hostage retrieval team here. Hold off their invasion from within the shelter and, in the meantime, have another unit surround them from the outside as well. We'll crush them with a pincer attack."

"Oyafune has the justification for her actions. What about that, sir?"

"Yes, we can't just repel her. Have our intelligence division thoroughly scrape the inspection-request paperwork. They can claim her stamp on the paper is blurry if need be—as long as they can materialize a reason we can't accept it, we'll gain the upper hand."

Shiokishi's mind worked quickly within his powered suit. His brain was built to do calculations the fastest when pursuing peace and security.

"Ulterior motives are hidden within the reasons for action we give one another. After offering a suspicious justification, all that remains is to win or lose through violence. If we win, it will be easier to influence the other official General Board members...and I've made that happen many times before. This will be no different."

"Yes sir."

"It's time to begin. Whatever the case is, I'll have no peace of mind until Monaka Oyafune and Group are annihilated."

Having come to an area with many similar dome-shaped shelters, Accelerator and the others stopped.

The shadows grew behind parked cars, building corners, and factory roofs.

At a glance, the scenery was mundane—but professional combat specialists, geared with special bulletproof equipment and weapons like submachine guns and rifles, had blended in with it.

Shiokishi's pawns.

When Accelerator's group stopped, they took it as a signal.

Not of surrender or capitulation.

No, they took it as a gesture that they would resist until the bitter end.

Powered suits began to jump off building rooftops, each almost seven meters tall, one after another. Remote-control armored vehicles with arms equipped, often used for bomb disposal, made sudden stops, creating a barricade. Giant, tanklike turrets were attached to the armored cars' roofs.

Tsuchimikado chuckled in spite of himself. "Classic Shiokishi, so keen on his munitions. The weapons he gives his chess pieces just ooze with playfulness."

"...What do you think?" asked Musujime. "Someone on the General Board would know normal forces won't work against Accelerator."

"Haven't you noticed *that*?"

Accelerator, on his crutch, jabbed his jaw toward the sky, toward the very top point of the domed shelter Shiokishi was probably hiding in. There was some kind of basketball-shaped metal sphere on it. It looked almost like an omnidirectional transmission radar used for jamming.

"That thing interferes with AIM fields. I bet the main part of it takes up a ton of space in the dome. The juvenile reformatories in this city have AIM jammers to prevent people escaping using their abilities, right? It's a special version for the General Board. It's probably set for you, too. The scariest thing for a shelter that can stand up against nuclear detonations would be a teleport ability that ignores three-dimensional defenses."

Musujime took the military flashlight off her waist. She twirled it in her hand like a baton and frowned. "...I can use the ability itself, but it feels like my aim would be thrown off. I could warp things, but they're likely to get stuck in the ground."

"If this guy is on the General Board, and he's a weapons and munitions specialist, he'd obviously know my military value. And that these minions could never finish me off," growled Accelerator, fed up. "But if he can get an AIM-field sample from me during the fight, he might use it to calculate the data for interference waves or something. And if he keeps going, he could wipe out at least Musujime and me by forcing our abilities to go out of control."

"What will we do, then?" asked Monaka Oyafune, who had never been directly involved in combat in any way, with a somewhat tense expression.

"Same thing I always do."

Accelerator, in contrast, bent his neck as if to crack it and brought his hand to its side.

To where the button for his choker electrode was.

"Use the front door."

6

Shiokishi was famously prudent, a fact that was clear from how he kept himself in a powered suit twenty-four hours a day. His base of operations was highly sturdy, too, of course. The domed facility, about two hundred meters across, blended in with the other test shelters in District 2. People said it could withstand standard strategic weapons.

However.

"Not sturdy enough, is it?"

Accelerator's murmurs drifted on the wind.

"When something uses the catchphrase *nuke resistant* you gotta use power like this."

A massive *ga-boom* rumbled through the air.

What Accelerator fired had been simple. He'd used one hand to grab a car parked nearby and lobbed it with all his might. The physical laws he took advantage of were nothing special; the tool he used wasn't made of a unique material, either. Just by adding in his anomaly of vector control did a simple projectile throw end up smashing the shelter.

"Let's go," muttered Accelerator in annoyance before flicking his electrode back off. To save as much battery power as he could, the Level Five proceeded forward with his handmade crutch. No one present could stop him. The nearby defenders had lost consciousness from the impact caused by the shelter's destruction, the remote-controlled armored cars had been flipped over, and the powered suits' joints were destroyed.

Accelerator stepped over the remains of a blasted-away wall section and set foot inside the facility. "Should be ten or twenty minutes before Shiokishi's forces reorganize. We capture Shiokishi and have him order them to stand down before that happens."

"Such a pain," said Musujime, unamused. "If you can do something this monumental anyway, we might as well crush him to death from a distance right now."

Accelerator answered with a tsk. "We kill him after we get info on Dragon out of him."

"E-excuse me, but…," started Oyafune, who had come with them, looking behind her. "Tsuchimikado isn't following us."

"He's holding them off outside," said Accelerator. "We didn't check to make sure they're all down for the count, and reinforcements could still come later."

"It would be bad if he decoded my AIM diffusion field or Accelerator's, but Mr. Sunglasses doesn't rely on his ability anyway."

Oyafune looked like she wasn't convinced, but Accelerator and Awaki Musujime ignored her. If he died, then that was that. Group was only held together by their value as a combat team. In Group, you proved that value without saying a word.

Accelerator's strike had turned the inside of the dome to mush. The interior was now like a Swiss roll that someone had taken a fork to and mashed up as the group went through it. The normal routes didn't matter. They proceeded farther and farther inside through gaps in collapsed, crushed, and exploded walls.

Eventually, they saw several men who looked like Shiokishi's personal soldiers lying on the ground. The aftermath of Accelerator's dome-rattling attack had probably knocked them all out.

"Officially, this is an inspection," said Accelerator. "Oyafune, it's your job to have a face-to-face discussion with Shiokishi while we protect you from the flanks."

"We'll keep breaking walls until we get to his hideout, but in the end, you'll be bearing the brunt of—"

Before Musujime could finish, something changed.

All of a sudden, a partition slammed down from the ceiling like a guillotine. It blocked the passage and isolated Accelerator and Musujime from Oyafune.

"Musujime!!"

"!!"

Her ability could freely move people at a distance without regard for three-dimensional restrictions. But as Musujime stared at the partition, she shook her head. "No response. Something else must have happened on the other side. Oyafune isn't over there."

"Useless piece of shit!!" Accelerator almost reached for the electrode switch at his neck, but they heard a new set of footsteps.

"I request a match."

The one who had said that was a man in a suit. He was familiar to Accelerator. It was Shiokishi's private soldier who'd killed all the former Spark Signal members occupying the District 3 private salon using a large handgun. If he remembered right, the man's name was Sugitani.

Sugitani took a box of cigarettes from his suit's inside pocket, then pulled one of the thin tubes out of it with nothing but his lips. "I do believe I told you I'd be praying to never see each other again."

"That's rich, coming from the ones who set this all up."

"I also remember telling you it was your job to see to it that this didn't come to pass."

In order to light the cigarette, Sugitani exchanged the box for a cheap lighter. Contrary to his outfit and mood, it was a clear plastic lighter one would find for sale at a convenience store.

"Do you know about Dragon?"

"That?" said Sugitani, bringing the lighter closer to the cigarette in his mouth to light it.

At least, that was how it looked to Accelerator.

But the next thing he heard was the soft *shhhh* of gas escaping.

The sound came from Sugitani's lighter, and it knocked Awaki Musujime, who had been standing next to Accelerator, to the ground.

It was as if she'd been punched.

There was no scream.

The strange attack had completely knocked her out.

It's not lighter gas...?

The device probably encapsulated a gas of a higher pressure. By releasing it all at once, he'd fired a small paralyzing bullet. With his frontal surprise attack a success, the man spat out the cigarette and said to Accelerator, "Modern combat isn't about how many forces either side controls. It's about settling things before it gets to that point."

"..."

"Shiokishi's orders. Musujime was a higher priority to destroy than Accelerator—she can hop freely through walls, whereas you only have high destructive power."

"Who the fuck are you?"

"A Koga. Or a descendant anyway," answered Sugitani in a self-deprecating tone. "A band of cowards who have been doing this sort of thing and calling it *justice* for a very, very long time."

As he spoke, he took out his large handgun.

But that probably wasn't his main weapon. Considering his fighting style until now, he wouldn't use such obvious methods. Or maybe that was what he was going for, and he'd purposely commit to a direct attack using bullets.

With this kind of enemy, the more someone thought about it, the deeper they sank into the mire.

As Accelerator watched him closely lest he slip up, Sugitani said, "Oyafune is done for."

Accelerator's eyebrow twitched at that.

"Two old people from the General Board are now face-to-face, but Shiokishi is wearing his special-order powered suit. It's too strong for any weapon Oyafune could hide in her clothes to affect it. The woman will die, torn apart by greater force than a heavy construction machine."

"I doubt Shiokishi would give the okay if the plan involved his own life and limb."

"Think of it as a bit of selfishness on my part. I'm sure Shiokishi is surprised right now, but he should be able to carry out his duty regardless. Someone armed with a powered suit wouldn't lose to an old woman, after all."

Sugitani spoke simply, without sounding especially prideful.

"If we can eliminate Oyafune of the General Board, we will eliminate all political opposition. He will mobilize all of Academy City's forces to drive you into a corner, and if they go through the appropriate channels to secure a trump card like Last Order, everything will be over for you."

7

Two of Academy City's highest executives—two General Board members—were currently meeting face-to-face.

Between them stood a table, one with no teacups and snacks, constructed instead for honest dialogue. It was wrapped in a quiet air, characteristic of the upper class. Accelerator's attack had fractured the dome and exposed the starry sky to the two people below, but even that seemed tolerable as an element for such an interior.

Oyafune and Shiokishi.

Two elders, both deeply involved in many historical affairs, each offered the other a peaceable smile.

"Where to begin? My request of you is really quite simple. It isn't money, it isn't political sway, and it certainly isn't your life."

Oyafune was the one to touch things off.

"I'd simply like you to refrain from selfishly integrating and expending the lives of others on all projects and operations you devise and execute in the future. Simple indeed, is it not? All others, aside from yourself, uphold this rule as a matter of course, after all."

She was right in that her words, when taken in isolation, sounded simple.

But he knew Monaka Oyafune would pursue it aggressively. This wouldn't end with a verbal promise, with an "All right, I swear not to do it anymore." She wouldn't be sated unless she forced Shiokishi to dismantle his private, directly operated forces, then indirectly exerted influence on other units to steal every last drop of the power and authority he needed to hire and use mercenaries.

That would be synonymous with stealing *everything* from him.

She was essentially eliminating all that made him appear powerful and sentencing him to become a mere layman.

"Oh, yes, and I should ask you about Dragon as well."

"Is that necessary for you?"

"Not particularly for me, but my collaborators, Group, have asked me to inquire about it."

Shiokishi watched her through his powered suit helmet, focusing on her face as she sat across from him. Still, he was silent for a moment before opening his mouth to speak.

"…My dear Oyafune, how much do you know about Dragon?"

"Nothing at all. Though if my authority is what it is on paper, I'm sure I would have had several chances to find out. I expect you know best of all why that didn't come to pass."

"It is something that must remain out of sight," he said quietly, not realizing she was criticizing him. "I am doing no more than accomplishing tasks necessary to protect Academy City, one by one. That is how dangerously critical the very word is. You may refer to me as barbaric, but only because you know nothing about Dragon. And I have no intention of telling you."

"Oh, I am of the same mind," answered Oyafune immediately, without losing her gentle smile. "And I would stoop to actions considered barbaric if I needed to. If it benefited me protecting those precious to me from your evil grasp, I would have no choice but to pursue this Dragon."

"Then we are at an impasse."

"We both say we want to protect Academy City, but I believe we're referring to different things. That's why our paths have split."

"I see."

Shiokishi gave a single short sigh from beneath his helmet.

Roar!!

A moment later, he used all his powered suit's output to punch Oyafune with his special-alloy fist.

The powered suit Shiokishi wore was a custom-order piece of equipment, upgraded even beyond the ones the city used for military purposes. The remodeling was geared more toward defensive power and durability than its mobility and compatibility with other firearms, but that only meant the giant fist he flung at Oyafune was all the sturdier.

This was far beyond what a heavy construction vehicle could do.

It would smash an old woman's body to atoms.

But…

"…You never even gave it a little bit of thought?"

Monaka Oyafune's body hadn't been crushed—she didn't have a single scratch on her.

In fact…

She hadn't blocked his fist, nor had she even evaded it. His powered suit's fist had stopped mid-punch. It was like its power had shut off.

And now, it was just a heavy metal cage.

"That I might, just as you protect yourself in a powered suit, *adopt measures to protect my life as well*?"

"Wh…what…?!"

The woman gripped a knife made of obsidian in her hand.

The Soul Arm reflected Venus's light as it shone through the ceiling, cracked open by the damage from Accelerator's attack, and used that reflected radiance to dismantle any and all objects into pieces.

Naturally, however, the weapon did not belong to Monaka Oyafune.

She brought a hand to her face.

As though peeling off the cover of a carton, she stripped away the surface of her face. For just a moment, he saw darker skin underneath, but then the stranger placed a different face on their head.

And that face was…

"Mitsuki…Unabara…?!"

"Oh, you use that name? I had thought for sure you'd call me Etzali," he answered, waggling the obsidian knife.

In the meantime, the powered suit protecting Shiokishi began to fall to pieces. Every one of its screws came loose, the gaps between steel plates widened, and the motors and gears started dropping to the floor.

It didn't take very long for all the armor to completely fall apart and expose a middle-aged man in full dress to the outside air. His defenses lost, Shiokishi broke out into a nervous sweat.

Unabara gave a thin, scornful grin. "You seem quite lucky. If this spear's effective range had reached your body, your flesh and bones would be reduced to a lot of varying pieces right now," he said. Then he added, "Still, it would have been a problem if that had happened before I could ask you about Dragon."

Shiokishi, for his part, while pushing away what few mechanical holdouts still clung to him, said, "Oyafune was…I knew it—that coward is watching us from on high, from somewhere safe, isn't she…?!"

"Is she, I wonder?"

Unabara's eyes narrowed slightly.

It was the expression of someone who had just encountered harsh disrespect aimed at someone they held in high esteem.

"My talismans use human skin as ingredients, but Mrs. Oyafune didn't hesitate for a moment. It may have been from her arm, but it still must have hurt a lot to slice off over ten centimeters of skin."

Unabara's fingers crawled around the obsidian knife as he closed in, step by step.

"It's time to ask about Dragon. Or would you rather taste how much pain Mrs. Oyafune went through—the one who you called a coward?"

"Guh…!! Minobe!!"

Shiokishi, backing away, pushed a button embedded in his suit's inside pocket.

Immediately, a partition opened in the wall, and two tall men appeared. One must have been Minobe.

They moved in front of Unabara, shielding Shiokishi behind them.

"Did you think Sugitani was my sole pillar of security?"

Shiokishi, his expression still trapped and drawn, gave an unnatural smile.

"I've always had my security split into two teams in case I was betrayed from within: the Sugitani team and the Minobe team. All so that they could kill each other if things came to that." He paused. "You may be talented in combat, but you can't deal with this team by yourself."

The two tall men remained still as Shiokishi attempted to escape on his own.

Unabara's face hardened.

But when Shiokishi got near the exit, he suddenly stopped. He was looking at something past the exit, astonished.

"Why?"

He turned back to them again, forgetting his flight.

Then he shouted the question again at his subordinates.

"Why has *the rest of the security team been massacred*?!"

One of the two men opened his mouth.

But what came out was not an answer to Shiokishi's question. Instead, he looked at Unabara and said:

"You're pretty early, Etzali."

He heard a dull *thud*.

Something had sprouted out of the side of the General Board member Shiokishi. It was a knife. One thrown haphazardly. But it didn't have a normal blade made of steel. It was of a stone called obsidian, thoroughly polished, used by members of a certain people.

It wasn't Unabara's.

The man called Minobe had thrown it, despite the fact that he was supposed to be acting in Shiokishi's defense.

For a few moments, Shiokishi remained stiff, looking at the casually launched knife without turning around. But then his body swayed to the side, and he fell over.

The name Etzali.

The selection of an obsidian weapon, a material that was at a glance less practical than metal.

"No..."

"You never gave it a second thought?"

Each of the tall men brought a hand to his face.

"About the possibility that there were others who had infiltrated Academy City's dark side in the same manner as you?"

Their face skin peeled off noisily. From behind those masks appeared different features—and soon their bodies and even genders began to quickly shift. It was exactly how it had worked for Unabara: a phenomenon created by Aztecan sorcery.

It was a man in his late twenties and a girl in her mid-teens.

"Tecpatl...and Tochtli!!"

Tecpatl was from the organization Unabara—Etzali—used to belong to. He was in charge of things like planning operations. Tochtli was Xóchitl's fellow comrade.

"We had planned to place ourselves as central factors of Shioki-shi's security lineup, then eventually replace the very man himself, though. But he never takes off his powered suit. And if we physically destroyed the armor, the sensors would alert Sugitani's group. We were just wondering what to do about it when the lot of you charged in," said the brown-skinned man, Tecpatl, without sounding particularly regretful about it. "If Shiokishi's *post* was to be ruined, then it wouldn't mean anything to replace him. We'd decided to draw the curtains there, but...at the very last second, we came up with a nice souvenir."

"...I don't think the organization would gain very much from you bringing my head back to them."

"No, that's not it. You have it all wrong," answered Tecpatl with a shrug. "Finding you in the shadows and killing you was the *whole reason* we infiltrated Academy City's core and tried to replace Shiokishi. After all, belonging to a division like Group makes it impossible to locate you with conventional information networks...On the other hand, there are no problems as long as we have your head."

8

Awaki Musujime was down.

The only remaining fighters were Accelerator and Sugitani. Glaring directly at the assassin who had named himself a descendant of the Koga, Accelerator touched the switch for the electrode on his neck.

"I'm about to murder you. Hope you don't mind."

"I do not. I'm not petty enough to be enraged by a word or two of nonsense."

Boom!!

Both moved forward at once.

Accelerator controlled his legs' force vectors and shot ahead like a cannonball, but Sugitani took several lighters from his pocket in response. Casually, he threw the lighters, which were modified to constantly emit gas, then tossed his lit cigarette into them.

Ba-boom!!

The raging flames became a solid wall in the ruined passage.

But that wouldn't work against Accelerator's reflection. Without a moment's hesitation, he burst through the wall, and—

He's gone?

Accelerator jammed his soles into the floor to brake, having lost his target. But he was too late. Sugitani had distracted him and moved sharply around behind him in the meantime.

"If I recall, Amata Kihara broke your reflection by pulling his fist back right before impact."

"?!"

A voice and a fist came rushing in from his blind spot.

Accelerator hastily jumped back from his position.

"And Teitoku Kakine used objects that don't exist in this world to create vectors that are likewise unreal."

The voice and fist tracked him perfectly.

Sugitani's footwork was so smooth it was inhuman. He traced around in a curve sharper and quicker than fish in the sea, maintaining his point-blank distance.

There was a loud *grrkk!!*

Pain jolted through Accelerator's face, and then Sugitani backed off for the first time.

"I see," muttered Sugitani, shaking his wrist around. The joint had swelled as though he'd sprained it. "These are unique exceptions they found as a result of investigating their own specialties. I suppose emulation is never perfect."

"..."

And yet, he had still jarred Accelerator's brain without using an ability. That was only possible due to Sugitani's top-class skill. If he were some street punk, it wouldn't just be his wrist bones—they would have lost control of their blood flow and experienced their internal organs exploding.

"How third-rate," spat Accelerator, despite having coldly analyzed the situation. "You've got some skill, but all you can really do is follow orders from that black-hearted old man? And you're a descendant of people who called themselves defenders of justice?"

"..."

"Does Shiokishi *look* like a good guy to you? And are you right for obeying him? Don't make me laugh. The answer is so obvious a baby could see it."

"...You are right. The word *good* is always misused by those in positions of power. Even if that wasn't the case, one can't build a perfect system.

"However," added Sugitani.

Without an ounce of hesitation—

"Does that mean leaving everything to evil would solve every single one of the planet's problems?"

—Accelerator and Sugitani glared each other down.

Good had met Evil's gaze and denounced him.

"Be serious. Evil like you and Group—all you're doing is scavenging for the leftover scraps of good. We constantly stand against hundreds, if not thousands, of tragedies, and you think you've beaten us by stopping two or three? Garbage pickers like you think you can fill the world's belly with scraps?"

"You shithead."

In response, Accelerator spoke ill of Good.

"The fact that you think those scraps are garbage means *your* goodness is fake."

"Fake?" Sugitani raised an eyebrow. "You mean to say a villain like you knows what it means to be an ally to justice?"

"..."

There was a slight pause after the question this time.

Nevertheless, in the face of it, Accelerator said, "Yeah, I do—so well that it pisses me off just thinking about it."

"I see," replied Sugitani, reaching into his pants pocket. "But you won't be seeing that good guy again—because you're about to die."

A moment later.
Accelerator's electrode abruptly lost all effectiveness.

Academy City's strongest Level Five crumpled to the floor alone. He seemed to be squirming, trying to move his extremities, but he wasn't getting any real result out of it.

"You probably can't understand human speech anymore, but there's a modification in your electrode that allows us to control it remotely. Cut off from the Misaka network, you have zero combat ability."

After finishing what he had to say, Sugitani glanced at Accelerator's crutch.

It looked different than the designs from when they'd supplied it. It had undergone several modifications, probably to allow him to stand even after his electrode's power was gone. But it didn't seem to have worked out.

"This is what I mean when I say *good*," said Sugitani, taking out his large handgun.

It was the gun he'd used to slaughter all the terrorists in the District 3 private salon building. Now that Accelerator had lost his power of reflection, Sugitani could kill him with one shot.

"This is how a man does things, when he lives in a world of cowards but keeps fighting to stay good."

The only sound then was the loud *bang* of a gun.

9

Stephanie Gorgeouspalace was still pulling her shotgun's trigger.
The oafish metal heap shone eerily, reflecting light from the flames

that were inundating the underground mall. Its bullet storm contained the power to mow down a run-of-the-mill armored car within seconds from inside one meter. It was no joke, no exaggeration—it could take a car and make it into a fold-up diagram.

Saiai Kinuhata was using an ability called Nitrogen Armor to protect herself, but even that had its limits.

By repeatedly blowing up propane gas tanks, Stephanie would momentarily blow all the air away, creating infinitesimal vacuums near Kinuhata. Now that the nitrogen walls were no longer able to form up, Stephanie's pellets could pass straight through.

The woman didn't hesitate.

Her index finger moved, meaning to take advantage of this single instant and pour as many pellets as she could into her target.

Ba-boom!!
The air burst.

The tempestuous pellet spray hiding immense power within roiled the air in the vicinity, swallowed up the dark smoke, and even caused the wall of flames to flicker. Gunshots loud enough to blot out all other sounds went off in succession, the lead pellets piercing into the space Kinuhata occupied. It didn't matter what angle the situation was examined from—it would be fatal. However, Stephanie didn't stop there. She continued pulling the trigger, again and again, pumping more bullets in.

The stronger the esper, the more irregular their tactics, because they depended on their own abilities all the more—but she was the opposite. Still, that certainly didn't mean her power was ordinary or average.

The most basic form of combat was to be incredibly efficient and optimized over many long years of a person's life. By pursuing such a goal, it was self-evident how strong some people could become.

In other words—

Her bullets shot accurately toward her target without any waste.

From the same underground mall, but from past the wall of flames, she heard what sounded like a boy's voice.

"Ki…Kinu…Kinuhataaaaaaaaaaaaaaaaaaaaaaaaaa!!"

The boy seemed to be crying out in death instead of the girl.

Stephanie's face remained clouded.

It wasn't that she hadn't felt the bullets hit. She couldn't see it, since it was past the fire and smoke, but Saiai Kinuhata's body would at this very moment be transforming into a meaty pulp.

What Stephanie wasn't happy with was how easy it had been.

She was taking revenge for Chimitsu Sunazara, yet, it had ended so simply.

She needed to make her opponent suffer much, much, much more.

Why was it over so quickly?

"…Are you messing with me? Is this a joke?"

Stephanie heard the sound of her own teeth gnashing. Grating against each other so hard she thought it might deform her skull.

"There was a lot more than this that I wanted to hit you with. This was still just the opening act! Don't lower the curtains without asking for my permission!! You destroyed Mr. Sunazara! A person like that wouldn't die this easily!! Suffer more! Beg for your life!! Stand up and let me kill you!! You had damn well better come back to life so I can kill you a thousand more times!!"

The intense force of the buckshots created a gust of wind, like the air had inflated.

Smoke struck her in the face, and she snorted it up. While coughing, Stephanie finally released her finger from her shotgun's trigger.

The wall of smoke parted.

There was something on the other side.

Is that all you were? spat Stephanie.

Just as—

Bang!!

A gunshot went off.

A hole appeared in Stephanie's gut.

And then she *saw*:
Beyond the smoke, Saiai Kinuhata was aiming a gun at her.

"What...? What?!"
Her face one of shock, Stephanie stared at Kinuhata.

She wasn't unharmed. There was a large bruise on her little face, as though she'd been punched, and bright-red blood dripped from her widely exposed thigh. But that was all. She had none of the injuries that the automatic shotgun should have caused—nothing to grind her flesh and bones and organs into gruel.

Stephanie didn't understand.

For now, though, she tried to ready her automatic shotgun at Kinuhata again.

But the single bullet had dulled her movements more than she'd thought.

Before the shotgun's muzzle could take aim, Kinuhata fired again. And then again, then a third time, the bullets piercing into Stephanie's chest. Her giant gun slid to the ground.

"You told me not to die, so I decided to humor you. Should I, like, not have?"

"But how...," began Stephanie before seeing something on the floor.

It was a metal can, about the size of a hair spray canister. But the metal seemed quite a bit thicker compared to its size. And the thick can had ruptured from within, as though it couldn't withstand the internal pressure.

An English letter was written on the metal can's surface.

Stephanie recognized it as a chemical symbol.

"Liquid...nitrogen...?!"

"Does it really come as that much of a surprise? If you create, like, a vacuum between two walls and insulate it, it's not that hard to carry around with you."

Essentially, when Stephanie created a localized vacuum state, Kinuhata had tossed the liquid nitrogen into the heated air and instantly replenished a large amount of nitrogen.

As Kinuhata held the gun up at her, she smiled thinly. "I manipulate nitrogen. In other words, that's seriously the only thing I can do. Did you think someone who totally understands that she can't do a thing if the nitrogen is gone wouldn't have ever thought about what to do in a case like that? Plus, I'm one of the people who dwells in Academy City's darkness. I can get whatever I need, like, no problem."

Flames crawled over the shotgun where it lay and caused the powder inside to ignite.

But Kinuhata didn't even glance at it.

"You were in Anti-Skill, so you certainly learned a lot about how to fight espers and unlocked the ability to find their weaknesses. But it looks like you totes don't understand that I've always been the kind of person who's constantly struggled to win and survive."

Kinuhata holstered her gun as she spoke.

She wasn't letting Stephanie off the hook. She just wanted to end things for sure, with an attack she was most confident in—her ability.

"Oh, right," said Kinuhata as though in parting. "An esper like me who has a strong shield and can totally grab cars and throw them is nearly invincible in close combat. My worst enemy is someone sniping me from afar with pinpoint attacks and not giving me a chance to do anything…Chimitsu Sunazara was way more on point than a gun freak like you!"

Stephanie tried to pull her spare handgun from her waist.

Kinuhata moved faster.

The esper's arm, which could easily lift entire cars, was aimed right at her.

10

Tecpatl—the man who virtually controlled the Aztecan "organization."

He now stood before Unabara with Xóchitl's comrade Tochtli in tow. For the sole purpose of killing him, the pariah.

Unabara's gut told him it was an odd pairing.

He didn't remember Tochtli and Tecpatl being on very good terms with one another. Neither had the kind of trust required to watch the other's back in certain death situations. Was organizational hierarchy alone enough to overcome that? Whatever the case, right now, that wasn't what Unabara needed to be worrying about.

"…" Without thinking, he glanced at the obsidian knife in his hands.

The Spear of Tlahuizcalpantecuhtli.

By reflecting Venus's light onto an object, the Soul Arm could dismantle even the strongest armor back into its constituent parts. It was just as effective on human bodies. If he hit Tecpatl or Tochtli with it, their bodies would part into flesh and bone more precisely than a skilled artisan butchered cows or pigs.

Could he do it?

They had parted ways, but they were still former comrades. Would it be right?

"Hey, come on." In contrast to Unabara's waffling, Tecpatl didn't even worry about it. "That little thing is all you have? …And here I'd thought for sure that something like *this* would come up."

As he spoke, he took something from Tochtli's hand.

It was a rectangular object that looked like a flat schoolbag.

Long, thin slits were cut out of its bottom, out of which incredibly thin stone plates a few millimeters thick protruded like bread from a toaster.

Tightly carved into one surface were things one could take as characters, symbols, or even images—the Aztec people's unique information storage method.

It can't be…!

An awful chill came over Unabara, and at the same time, something in the back of his mind sparked like it'd been stabbed. It was the pain of his brain being corrupted with knowledge none should ever know.

This wasn't the first time it had happened to him.

Tecpatl smiled, as if to substantiate his suspicions, and said:

*　　*　　*

"Yes. It's an original copy."

As Unabara desperately shook his head, in a state akin to getting dizzy upon standing up, Tecpatl continued, still grinning. "You know we did some...*modifications* to Xóchitl, right? Our position is good enough that we can even distribute original texts to our advance parties. I'm the one who planned and carried this out, so it's not surprising I have one, too, is it?"

"You..."

"Bring yours out. I know Xóchitl is alive, which means you must have extracted it." He paused. "And just so we're clear, you'll need more than some obsidian knife to dismantle mine."

...Is he seriously bringing an original text into real combat...? Damn! What are those characters engraved on that stone plate?

Unabara had no intention of ever reading it again. Instead, as though tasting the poison still clinging to his brain once more, he carefully considered the text Tecpatl held.

It was probably a calendar stone, a type of complicated timekeeping from the Aztec world. They were large, disc-shaped stones with descriptions of how both the world's destruction and its rebirth functioned. The grimoire they'd embedded inside Xóchitl was derived from it, but Unabara figured Tecpatl had acquired an original of a different derivative, one which emphasized different sections.

Unabara looked up, taking care not to direct his attention at Tecpatl's original text, and said, "An account of the moon rabbit...?"

"You actually went and *read* this thing? You're a bigger daredevil than you seem."

Tecpatl must have been taking unknown measures to make sure the stone plate's knowledge didn't enter his mind; he rapped casually on the stone with his knuckles as he spoke.

"It's a story about the time when the fifth sun was created. The moon, born in the same era, shone more brightly than any of the gods had initially expected. The moon would soon grow indistinguishable from the sun. To prevent this, the gods threw a rabbit to the moon to weaken its light...And when I use the power of this legend, do you know what kinds of things I can do?"

As soon as he finished, it happened.

Ga-boom!!

Something shot out of Tecpatl's hand and smashed all the shelter walls from the inside out.

It was a single straight-line attack. Despite everything, the shelter had been created to withstand strategic weapons—and yet, it fell apart in one fell swoop, collapsing on top of Shiokishi's private soldiers, who were still fighting outside.

"Hold still," said Tecpatl with a smirk. "Twenty or thirty soldiers just died, I think. Of course, this attack was originally for destroying other celestial bodies in one hit...but it seems like its materials, the rabbit bones, aren't that good."

Unabara was surprised.

But not at the sheer force of the attack Tecpatl had unleashed.

He was looking next to Tecpatl, at Tochtli.

Her index finger wobbled...and swayed, like a squid's tentacle.

"...What did you do?" asked Unabara, his lips quivering. "What did you to do Tochtli?!"

"The rabbit bones— Oh, do I need to explain every little thing to you?"

Tecpatl had launched some kind of projectile attack. And he'd used the term rabbit *bones*. It wasn't hard to put two and two together.

Why is Tochtli obeying him...?

With a natural question in mind as his gaze remained fixed to the brown-haired girl, Tochtli opened her mouth for the first time. And from it came this.

"...*Uh...Agh...gh...*"

In that moment, all the heat drained from Mitsuki Unabara's spine. It wasn't human language. She didn't have a brain or a mind left to think with. Tecpatl, seeing Unabara dumbfounded, burst out into laughter as though he'd been holding it in this whole time.

Why was she helping him this much?

Tochtli and Tecpatl weren't on very good terms, were they?

The answer was so, so simple.

Besides…

A normal person would never give their bones away without anesthesia.

"Ha-ha-ha!! It's fun to watch her, isn't it? I'd guess less than half the bones in her body are left now. The original copy does appear to have a mechanism for swapping human bones with obsidian, but it seems using it comes with significant pain. When I first used it, it blew me away. Anyway, it doesn't really matter for me as long as I can replenish the stock."

"Tec…patl…"

Unabara's lips trembled.

In the meantime, Tochtli's tentacle-like finger inflated from within, then squeezed back down to its normal shape. Obsidian had rushed into where the bones used to be.

How much pain must that have caused?

And how much humiliation?

"Tecpaaaaaaaaaaaatllllllllllllllllllllll!!" Unabara roared, putting his hand to his face. He tore off the skin covering it, revealing his true brown-skinned visage to the world.

Then, as though in response to his rage, something moved.

The scroll-shaped original text in his suit's inside pocket unfurled on its own accord and reached out. It writhed in the air like a snake, and Unabara grabbed it again, under his own volition.

The original copy that Unabara…or rather, the original copy that Xóchitl took ownership of described its interception as a counterattack against those who took up arms. In Xóchitl's case, it created a spell that caused those who took up arms to harm themselves with those weapons, but Unabara couldn't yet draw out that much of its power.

In response, Tecpatl's original copy, the one that consumed the

bones of the girl named Tochtli, described its interception as a long-distance bombardment. Its spell was built on the folktale of the thrown rabbit giving a celestial body its current form, becoming a projectile weapon that could shoot down any enemy.

A clash of grimoires.

Unabara no longer felt aversion to using his. Tecpatl had set foot into territory he shouldn't have. His mind was seething. It could only think about killing the monster.

"I like it," responded Tecpatl, holding his stone plate aloft as the owner of an equal grimoire.

"*This* is our battle. Let us exhaust all our intellect and vie for control over the Aztecs!"

Ga-boom!!

Multiple flashes of light burst from Tecpatl's hand, and Unabara's vellum scroll unfolded itself wide to stop them. Countering, the scroll became a tempest of sandpaper-like dust particles; Tecpatl's tablet swung around and blew it away.

The shock wave alone caused the shelter dome to crack and swell.

This wasn't a normal fight. He was way beyond Unabara's specs.

But Unabara's original copy hadn't become his ally for nothing.

...Urgh...The headache...!!

Every time he fought, the knowledge would come flowing in. The pain started with his head and ended at his fingertips and toes. Unabara endured, wielding the original copy again.

Original copies of grimoires assisted those who wanted to spread the text's knowledge. Thus, they couldn't be weapons for those who simply owned them. If any were to appear who were more suitable than its current owner, it would mercilessly annihilate the "used" owner and jump ship.

It was as though it was testing him.

Kill or let live—the text was deciding for itself which would be a greater boon.

...I don't care...

Unabara gritted his teeth. Red blood leaked from between them.

...There is an enemy I need to defeat even if it destroys me!!

But willpower alone wouldn't determine victory.

Another barrage of flashing lights flew out from Tecpatl's hand. They were stronger than Unabara's defenses could take. Several of the shots wove around and through his scroll shield to stab into his upper body. Even so, possibly due to the original copy's assistance, his body was not ripped apart. Instead, it simply tumbled down to the ground.

But he didn't have the stamina left to get back up.

As Unabara held the scroll open to the air, Tecpatl walked right up to him.

"It's a matter of experience. And you possess no security against the grimoire. To use it as a weapon, you have to take measures to prevent the counterflow of knowledge."

"..."

Unabara glared at him, but Tecpatl's expression didn't change.

Yet another light appeared in his hand.

A light created from the bones of the girl named Tochtli.

"What...What happened anyway?"

"What?" Tecpatl grinned. "One major fight ended. A fight against the philistines who call themselves the world's police. We believed that once it ended, we would be able to go back to our peaceful lives. So we continued to fight."

His grinning was incessant.

"But nothing ended. Nothing about our status, nor our position, nor our ways of life changed at all. Why, then, have we fought? Such a bitter battle, and all we could protect in the end were the interests of some old men standing atop us?"

Finally, his grin faded.

"We've already purged the old men who instigated us with utter gibberish. But execute them though we did, nothing changed. That's all. We lost our direction and our objective. We no longer know where to go from here. That is all."

*　　*　　*

Ga-boom!!

This time, the strike from Tecpatl's hand was a decisive one.

However, it didn't end Mitsuki Unabara's life.

The attack Tecpatl had launched from his hand had curved back around and stabbed himself instead.

"...What...?" groaned Tecpatl as he stared at the gaping hole in his stomach.

As Unabara lay crumpled on the floor, he quietly asked, "Did you know this? An original text is not a mere tool or weapon. It allies itself with those who want to spread its knowledge the most—and if needed, it will even turn against its owner."

That was when Tecpatl saw it:

Unabara had drawn something on the floor in his own blood. It was a sentence from the stone tablet Tecpatl had.

He had just copied the original text's writing, creating a transcription of the grimoire and thus attempting to spread its knowledge when Tecpatl had made his attack. Because of that, he'd been attacked by his own original text.

"...If you had confronted your original text's knowledge, maybe this wouldn't have ended in such an extreme manner. After all, you said you took measures to prevent it from corrupting you. Not only did you not spread the knowledge to others—you didn't even want to read it yourself. You were hoarding it. Did you really think an original text would allow that...?"

There was no answer.

Tecpatl had fallen onto his knees. Then, as if prostrating himself before Unabara, he collapsed. Unnaturally long, slender shadows stretched from the schoolbag-like lump, which was packed with several stone tablets. They looked like thin, beckoning hands.

Accept me. If not, I will kill you.

That was what it felt like they were saying to Unabara.

It seems original copies quite like me.

"...Fine, then...," answered Mitsuki Unabara to the grimoire's request.

A second original copy. The speed of their corruption would reach new levels now, but Unabara didn't hesitate.

"However," he suddenly said, looking away from Tecpatl. He turned his gaze so that it reflected the girl who could no longer understand human speech, Tochtli.

He had no obligation to go this far.

But if he didn't do at least this much, he wouldn't be able to face Xóchitl.

"First, there's something I'd like your help with."

The contract was formed.

In exchange for the girl's life, Mitsuki Unabara plunged onward, down ever darker paths.

11

Sugitani stood there for a while, silent, his large handgun still pointed in front of him.

Accelerator was facedown on the floor.

He smelled the particular stench of gunpowder bursting.

The scent of blood mixed with it.

However.

It wasn't his.

A hole had opened up in his chest—the victim was Sugitani, the one who should have had an absolute advantage.

"Wh...? How...?"

The man wobbled slightly.

He leaned back against a wall and slid to the floor as the strength drained out of him.

Mirroring his actions in reverse, Accelerator slowly rose.

It certainly didn't seem like he'd lost his electrode's assistance, but the remote-control device in Sugitani's hand was definitely working. He shouldn't have been able to use the electrode...

"You noticed the modifications in my crutch, didn't you?" Accelerator growled. "All these legs for helping with independent walking, the motors, the sensors—they were all dummies. Its *actual* purpose is to jam the specific waves you were using to control my electrode."

"What...?"

"If I used only regular interference waves, it would mess up the electromagnetic waves the Misaka network uses. That wouldn't do me any good. So I waited for you bastards to use yours. Then, I did a rigorous analysis of the frequency, calculated the proper waves to jam only that frequency, and built it into my crutch."

Yes: When the camper was under attack, Shiokishi's people had been using their remote-control waves. Accelerator had taken advantage of that and acquired a sample of their specific wavelengths.

So now, their remote-control frequency would always meet with interference from the crutch and never make it to his electrode.

That meant Accelerator hadn't lost his ability, he could walk on his own, and he could hold a proper conversation.

He took the gun from his pants belt and pointed it at Sugitani.

"This is how evil does things," said the monster, sounding exasperated with the concept. "You, me—not one thing is different. And don't get me wrong—I'm not a good guy. If you used the same method, that makes you a grand villain in your own right."

Sugitani grinned a little.

A moment later, two triggers pulled back.

Two gunshots resounded.

Accelerator's bullet thrust into Sugitani's body, while Sugitani's bullet was deflected.

"...What a bore."

Accelerator flipped back his electrode switch and proceeded in farther.

"If you're going to call yourself a good guy, you could at least try to play the part."

Sugitani had lost consciousness and was just barely breathing.

This was Accelerator's own brand of evil.

12

Kinuhata sat on the underground mall's floor, breathing in the flame-heated air.

Stephanie lay nearby.

Hamazura and Takitsubo were apparently past the wall of flame, but it would be too much of a hassle to plunge through it and meet up with them. A better idea would be to get back aboveground first, then regroup.

Kinuhata rubbed her scraped-up cheek with a hand, then looked over to the assassin, who lay next to her.

"...I might be crazy strong, but you went a little too far there."

"Well, I was fighting for Mr. Sunazara. This was me holding back, I think," responded Stephanie from where she lay, coughing up blood as she spoke.

Tough woman, thought Kinuhata. "Anyway, you had that shotgun beforehand, but seriously, how the heck did you get a Hexawing attack helicopter to chase us? Do you have other allies?"

"...?"

There was an unnatural silence.

It gave Kinuhata a sinking feeling, so she insisted: "Seriously, how did you get a Hexawing helicopter to chase us?"

"What are you talking about?" answered Stephanie, somewhat taken aback. "If I could have gotten an attack helicopter in a city like this, I would have just outranged you from a distance."

Kinuhata froze.

What was that all about, then?

There had definitely been a Hexawing chasing after the stolen car Hamazura was driving. The unmanned weapon was meant for Academy City airspace defense. It wasn't easy to get your hands on.

The woman on the phone said she hadn't been involved. The girl in the dress, too, said she wouldn't be doing things the hard way if she could acquire something like that.

And if even Stephanie said she wasn't connected...

Other people besides her are coming after us? For real? And it's someone with enough authority to, like, order a Hexawing to sortie...?

It happened just as she was thinking about it.

Ba-bam!!

The concrete walls around Kinuhata suddenly exploded.

Once they fell, a black-clad special forces team immediately closed in.

They weren't for arresting Stephanie.

In fact, most of them broke off to capture Kinuhata instead.

"Hamazura!!" she yelled, now immobilized on the ground. "Get the heck out of here! They're not after me! I think it's you they want!!"

Yes.

Saiai Kinuhata was, to be sure, someone with a powerful ability and a unique position. But that meant she could guess how much value she had, and how many people would be after her.

The Hexawing from before didn't match the conditions, which meant she could assume that when it went after the stolen car, the reason must have been a more unknown factor—Shiage Hamazura.

"...!!" Hamazura shouted something from past the flames, but Takitsubo pulled on his arm, urging him to flee.

He wavered for a few moments, then appeared to go along with Takitsubo. Kinuhata knew it was the right choice. She possessed useful value as combat personnel for Academy City. The chances they'd discard her while she was still usable were slim, and she intended to maneuver things so that wouldn't happen.

After Hamazura and Takitsubo left, Kinuhata heard the clapping of feet from the mall's entrance. She looked in that direction, still pinned to the ground. A girl in a dress approached.

She used an ability called Heart Measure, and with Item and

School gone, she was supposedly one of the members of the new team assembled from the survivors.

The pair, officially allies on paper, glared at each other.

"What are you even doing?" Kinuhata grumbled.

"I didn't understand the orders one bit, either. I can't believe they'd put me on a job with leftovers of the Hound Dogs. I'd even listen to you if you could explain it." The girl in the dress waved her off. "Did you know Aleister is putting together some sort of plan and executing it?"

Kinuhata frowned.

The girl in the dress ignored it. "Irregular factors like Touma Kamijou and Accelerator are apparently controllable enough to fit inside the scope of his Plan. That's why he can keep his Plan centered, and even if they go out of control, he can take advantage of whatever happens to benefit his Plan in any number of ways," she said. "I don't know what the Plan entails, exactly. But anyway, Shiage Hamazura isn't like them."

There was a short silence.

The girl in the dress continued, "That Level Zero was a factor who was supposed to have been killed in the fight between the five units. Despite all that, he somehow managed to take down the fourth-ranked Level Five, Shizuri Mugino, by himself, and he's still alive…Even Aleister couldn't have perfectly predicted that, it seems."

As the men held her to the ground, Kinuhata desperately thought about this.

Was what this girl saying true?

"Shiage Hamazura, a Level Zero who should have had no power and no role. Now he's trying to gain something on his own. Some new, real value that even Aleister doesn't know about."

And then the girl in the dress looked down at Kinuhata as if to provoke her.

Or perhaps, to try to get answers out of her.

"Apparently, depending on how things turn out, that could damage Aleister's Plan even more than Touma Kamijou or Accelerator. That's

why he's bringing Academy City's full force to bear to erase him...
What do you think? Do you really think he's worth that much?"

He didn't know what was going on.

But he kept on running anyway.

Shiage Hamazura and Rikou Takitsubo ran hand in hand through
the city enveloped by the night. They came out of the underground
mall, burst through the crowds, and jumped onto the roof of a freight
train, which was still running despite the late hour. Hunkered down
and panting atop the freight car, they went straight through the stations and charged swiftly through tunnels. But no matter how many
deep breaths they took, the stamina they lost wouldn't come back.

But their pursuers came anyway.

They didn't seem like an average team. There were black shadows
running alongside the fast-moving train. Before they knew it, their
hunters jumped onto the train car roof, several of the figures inch-
ing closer to them. This wasn't something a person could do with a
little special training. These people were like urban legends at this
point. If these guys ever saw the bogeyman, they'd probably punch
him in the face. There was no way he could fight and win.

But Hamazura had one idea...*Hard Taping. Are they wrapping
their entire bodies in the same electrically extending cloth springs
Komaba used?!*

But the goddess of luck smiled on Hamazura and Takitsubo
then. Just before the figures could catch up to them, the freight
train decelerated, probably closing in on its destination. Support-
ing Takitsubo's small form, Hamazura jumped off the train before it
completely stopped. He nearly tumbled onto the gravel and blood-
ied himself, but he barely managed to keep his balance.

He had no idea what district this was, but he flung open a door set
into the tunnel wall and flew in desperation down the narrow corridor. How far did he have to run? How long would he have to keep
fleeing? None of the conditions were clear, which meant he couldn't
concoct any detailed plans. For now, in this moment, he ran with all

his might. Ran through a marathon that went on forever, one he'd started without even knowing the course.

But Hamazura had support.

Takitsubo was at his side.

He'd been chased once before by the fourth-ranked Level Five, Shizuri Mugino. He'd been in a life-or-death situation then, and he'd had to fight on his own. But this time, he wasn't alone. The most reliable friend he had was at his side. That meant he wasn't as nervous as before. He would shake them somehow, and he even went so far as to consider how he would rescue the captive Kinuhata.

Unfortunately—

His support was suddenly on the verge of breaking.

Hamazura felt a tug at his sleeve. That's what he'd thought anyway, but when he turned around, that wasn't what had happened. The pink-tracksuited Takitsubo had nearly collapsed on the corridor's floor, still grasping his hand.

"Hey, Takitsubo?"

He hastily tried to hold her up, but she was strangely heavy. It wasn't the weight of a person who had strength left. It was a sensation like holding a big bag of mud, and it set all his hairs on end.

"Hama...zura..."

"What's wrong? Hey, Takitsubo! What the hell's wrong?!" he shouted in a fluster, but somewhere in his mind, he'd predicted this.

To begin with, Rikou Takitsubo had just gotten out of the hospital. She didn't sound like she was feeling good when she called him from the private salon facility in District 3, either. And when they'd reunited there, Takitsubo had been unconscious.

She'd relapsed.

In her current condition, there was no way she could sprint for an extended period of time. Escape when her life was constantly in peril was an impossibility.

But the enemy wouldn't wait. All this time, their unknown pursuers were getting closer.

"Takitsubo, can you stand?" Hamazura asked as she continued to sweat profusely, trying to keep the panic out of his voice.

In response, she looked into his eyes and said, "Get out of here, Hamazura."

His heart and mind were nearly at their breaking point, and those words battered them even more.

"At this rate...we'll both be captured. So you...escape on your own, please."

Stop messing around, Hamazura thought. He grabbed the exhausted Takitsubo's arm, looped it around his shoulder, then picked her up to carry her.

"Hamazura—"

"Stay quiet," he hushed, interrupting her before she could say something more.

She might have been small, but with every ounce of strength gone, her weight might as well have been the ball on a prisoner's chain.

So what? Hamazura demanded.

His eyes remained locked ahead.

Gritting his teeth, half dragging himself along, Shiage Hamazura stepped forward. He would never abandon Takitsubo.

He couldn't leave her here. He would rescue her for sure. This senseless, crazy life of a fugitive on the run couldn't go on forever. He'd turn things around. He'd pull her right out of this danger. That was all that was on his mind as he moved his feet, one in front of the other, ever onward.

But it didn't last very long.

Though it wasn't to the degree of Crystals destroying his body like Takitsubo, he wasn't at his best, either. He'd already fought through numerous battles during the day and then ran several kilometers at full tilt. His stamina wouldn't hold out. His muscles were screaming. His legs were shaking. He knew he could collapse to the floor at any moment. And meanwhile, several sets of footfalls were closing in from behind. He also heard the clacking noise of submachine gun parts.

They'd be caught at this rate.

If they were caught, they'd be killed.

At that thought, Hamazura tried to move even farther forward, but the strength at last left his legs. They tumbled awkwardly to the floor in an embrace. Hamazura got up and tried to get under Takitsubo's body again. But he couldn't lift her. This totally normal girl's body felt as heavy as a barbell.

"Hamazura...," rasped Takitsubo from next to him. "It's okay, Hamazura. I'll buy you time."

"Shut the hell up!!" he exclaimed.

But his body wouldn't move.

Hamazura half climbed over Takitsubo, meaning to shield her from the bullets. He knew they'd have an easy time piercing through a human body, but he didn't hesitate.

*Someone...*he prayed, tears forming at the corners of his eyes... *Please, do what I can't. Swoop in heroically and save her life. I need a hero right now...*

He knew nobody so convenient would show up. If someone like that existed, Shiage Hamazura wouldn't be at rock bottom like this in the first place.

But he couldn't help praying.

Rikou Takitsubo was the one thing he didn't want to lose.

Footsteps approached. Their numbers increased. There was nothing he could do. He could tell several muzzles were now pointed at them. All he had in his hand was a single pistol. At this rate, he'd be riddled with holes as soon as he reached for it.

He was utterly cornered.

Miracles never happened.

And so it was that...

Shoo-pop!! Countless flashes of light struck out.

They knocked every one of the unknown pursuers down, instantly removing the threat.

He couldn't figure out what had happened. All he knew was that some sort of ability, or something like it, had been used. By the time he thought that, more than ten of the pursuers were torn apart right before his eyes, their entrails strewn about. This part of the corridor was stained with fresh blood. He didn't know who had done it, but someone had actually saved them. That was what Hamazura had thought in his daze, still holding on to Rikou Takitsubo.

"Heh-heh-heh…"

It began to seep slowly into Hamazura from the outside, and eventually, as though remembering something forgotten, the relief made its way to his brain.

"Hey, we made it. I don't know who just provided backup, but we survived…!!"

But then it happened.

"…Haaamazuraaaaa…"

One word.

That way of addressing him alone caused a terrible chill to wash down his back.

He knew that voice. And now that he thought about it, he knew the ability, too.

Meltdown. A form of electron-controlling ability, it could manipulate and launch electrons themselves rather than waves or particles. It was registered to the fourth-ranked Level Five, and its user, its user, its user…Shiage Hamazura had taken her down before.

But now she was coming closer.

Her.

The person who had come for Shiage Hamazura was no hero.

Clip-clap. Clip-clap. Footsteps rang out proudly, as if to boast of their own existence, and they were getting slowly closer. They stepped on the blood and organs of the torn corpses she'd personally torn to pieces, coming straight for them.

A familiar woman.

She had no right eye.

Her left arm was torn off.

A pale-blue light, like a welding arc, was pouring out of her hollow, dark-red eye socket. Her left arm was the same. An arm made of blinding light reached out of her shoulder as if to compensate for the arm that didn't exist. It must have been considerably high-energy, because he even heard the sound of its electricity, like bugs getting fried in a trap lamp.

It was from her ability.

It was from the fourth-ranked Level Five.

Meltdown.

This wasn't a cheap ability that just anyone could control. As far as Hamazura knew, only one person could use it.

A ragged voice escaped Shiage Hamazura's mouth.

He squeezed out the name, not only his vocal cords but his entire body trembling. The words didn't come out properly.

"Shizuri...Mugino...?!"

"You deserve to be hunted down by better than these lowlifes. After all, you have me—and I decided I'd have you drawn and quartered!!"

Chill!!

This time, the face of true, unbridled despair opened its jaw to swallow them.

13

Accelerator, Motoharu Tsuchimikado, Awaki Musujime, and Mitsuki Unabara were in the deepest part of the domed shelter. In front of them was the defeated Shiokishi. His powered suit had fallen to pieces, and a knife made of black stone was stuck in his gut.

"There are two things we can do that will protect our own."

Accelerator, on his crutch, put his free hand to his neck and cracked it loudly.

"The first is making you spit out everything you know about Dragon right now. The second thing is taking that knife in you, moving it up and down, and splaying your intestines all over the floor."

"Dragon, eh...," mumbled Shiokishi, not even paying much attention to his stab wound. "Have you any suspicions?"

"You'd better not be about to babble on about not actually knowing anything yourself."

"It would have been easier if that were true. Unfortunately, I did learn of it. I was in a position where I was able to. That was why I worried."

The four remained silent.

Only Shiokishi's voice continued.

"It is something no human eyes should ever see. If you demand the details, I will give them, but allow me to say this for your sakes: It's better not to know. I don't mean that in the sense of a cheap threat. It is purely the remark of one who knows. To be honest, I didn't want to know. I wish, from the bottom of my heart, that I'd never known."

"What is Dragon?" pressed Accelerator, heedless. "And where the hell *is* Dragon?"

According to Tsuchimikado and Unabara, Dragon was a code word related to angels. And Accelerator had personally witnessed something with wings of light on September 30. Wings that were apparently related to what Amata Kihara was doing, to Last Order and the virus.

"...What are you saying?"

Shiokishi chuckled in spite of himself.

It was too funny to him, seeing people talk so seriously about something they had a completely wrong idea about.

"Dragon is everywhere. Look—it's behind you now."

Accelerator thought it was a mean-spirited joke.

But a moment later, he heard dull thuds.

"Tsuchimikado?"

Without thinking, he turned around.

And then he said their names.

"Musujime? Unabara?"

They had all fallen down. Completely knocked out. No noticeable injuries, but also no signs they'd be getting up soon. The members of Group each boasted incredible combat powers. An attack by factors unknown had just taken them all down easily...without even allowing room or time for a counterattack.

And then.

Accelerator saw it.

"It's not Fuse Kazakiri."

Standing in a daze with his eyes opened wide, only Accelerator could hear Shiokishi's voice.

"That is nothing more than a simple production line used in Dragon's formation."

Saying all that he needed to, Shiokishi passed out then, possibly from blood loss. He fell to the floor with a grunt, but Accelerator didn't have the leeway to look his way.

His gaze remained fixed in front of him.

Long, golden hair.

A tall, shining body, and white garments that wrapped loosely around it. He couldn't tell the exact gender, but if he had to guess based on its appearance, it looked feminine.

An infinitely smooth face, all emotions at once—happiness, anger, sorrow, pleasure—while simultaneously having a basis in something clearly alien to human emotions.

"...Dragon, is it?"

It opened its mouth.

Accelerator had never before felt such a sense of wrongness about something with a human form speaking human words.

"That given name is not mistaken, either. I do also correspond to the symbol of *angel*...I am, at the very least, far closer to the real thing than those romanticized ideas whispered of on the streets, of extraterrestrial intelligent life-forms, holy guardian angels, or the Secret Chiefs of modern western sorcerers' societies. My existence, however, differs in concept from the angels described in extant holy books. Therefore, if one wanted to refer to me in a more accurate fashion, one should choose a term from among the following."

This thing was telling him the answer to the question Accelerator and the others had pursued.

"It is rare that one would cling to this extent. This must mean you find value and interest in what I call myself. And that is why I suppose I shall answer your question."

This thing was describing Dragon's identity.

"I am the one who once provided necessary knowledge only in necessary amounts to a strange sorcerer known as Crowley.

"...I am known as Aiwass."

CHAPTER 4

Two Monsters with an Invitation to Hell

Dragon(≠Angel).

1

Aiwass.

That was what the being, apparently classified under the code name Dragon, called itself.

Accelerator confronted the blond humanoid, very cautiously observing it.

In all honesty, his thoughts wouldn't connect with what he'd set out to do next.

The basic direction for all of Group, including him, was this: to find Dragon's identity, the highest secret in Academy City, then use it to bargain with the city's leaders. They never thought for a second that the Dragon itself would appear before their eyes.

And perhaps...

Perhaps Accelerator had considered, somewhere deep down, the possibility of Dragon's identity *never* coming to light.

But now that it was suddenly right in front of him, perhaps his thoughts hadn't caught up yet.

"That is a very mystified face," said the being named Aiwass, without changing its expression. Its very golden locks appeared to radiate a faint light.

"Is it truly so incomprehensible that I should appear in this way?"

Of course Accelerator wore an expression of shock. Academy City had been keeping this being under lock and key until now. Why, of all things, would *it* choose to appear? Accelerator considered several possibilities, then chose the most logical:

"...A servant of Shiokishi's? You're too late to serve as reinforcements."

"Are you being serious?"

Aiwass shook its head. It was clearly expressing its intent, and yet, Accelerator couldn't even guess at what it was thinking.

He stayed silent for a moment, internally coming to reject his own hypothesis. *Yes, Shiokishi must have despised...or more like, feared Dragon*, he thought. This wasn't even close to how one of his pawns would respond.

However.

If that was out, then why had Aiwass appeared before Accelerator?

"Because I have acknowledged a level of value in you, and because of that...I've taken something of an interest in you," said Aiwass—its tone casual, as if to reject everything Group and Shiokishi had done up until that very moment. "You wished to meet me—and thus, I appeared. Are you unsatisfied with that?"

That was insane.

But this being didn't appear to be hiding anything, either.

Did it mean to say it silently took out Tsuchimikado and the other two because it didn't find any value or interest in anyone but Accelerator?

Now what...?

Accelerator lowered his center slightly.

Several people had shown up before now and posed a threat to Accelerator's life, like Hound Dog's Amata Kihara and School's Teitoku Kakine, but this Aiwass was cut from a completely different cloth. He couldn't even sense malice from it.

Aiwass was supposed to be the most crucial asset for Academy City's leadership. But there was more than one way to use it; defeating Aiwass was sure to deal major damage to the top brass's scheming, but maybe there was a more effective way to use this dragon...

In the first place, he didn't know what kind of role Aiwass had.

Unless he knew that first, he wouldn't be able to devise effective ways to use the being.

He started to feel like a dog on a leash.

Aiwass realized that and showed emotion for the first time—an expression that seemed surprised. "This result differs from my predictions. I had thought you would charge at me to take revenge for your friends, then end up flat on the floor within three seconds."

"…What you just said to me is a better way to make that happen," growled Accelerator.

Yes—Aiwass had taken out Motoharu Tsuchimikado, Awaki Musujime, and Mitsuki Unabara without so much as making a sound.

If one was to ask Accelerator if that was enough to engage in hostilities, he'd have said no. As stated multiple times in the past, to Accelerator, Group was only held together by how valuable each member was to use.

First, he'd extract any information that seemed useful out of this Aiwass. He'd decide whether to be hostile after that.

Having settled on his course of action, Accelerator stared the newcomer down again. "What are you? And why do they hide it with the code name Dragon?"

"Must I start explaining from there?" said the being as if it was about to remark on how surprisingly dull he was. "My identity is nothing special. I'm naught more than a simple *hboiebeingaeb*…"

Aiwass's words blurred.

Accelerator frowned, but even the being who had spoken them brought a dubious hand to its throat, checking its voice.

"…Well. I cannot even express this level of meaning in this world. The headers are insufficient. I would struggle to explain it this way. May I take a more roundabout route? It would be simple to convey this directly, but if I did, it would cause a *wgbudcollapsewsrui*, you see."

Aiwass didn't seem like it was speaking in riddles or jokes.

To begin with, Accelerator was hearing things strangely. For some reason, at the moment Aiwass's voice blurred, the direction of the sound source itself shifted away. It sounded very unnatural to him, as though the left and right speakers in a pair of headphones were reversed.

"Do you know the words *Fuse Kazakiri*?"

"...?"

He remembered Shiokishi mentioning something about that, but Accelerator didn't know what they meant. But when Aiwass saw his face, it exhaled softly.

"It is troubling indeed to speak of things from beginning to end. Remember my words and research them on your own time later. In any case, it is a being called various things, one of which is *man-made angel*. This is accurate given its properties, but it doesn't reflect Fuse Kazakiri's true nature. She is really something of a production line for the purpose of giving form to me, Aiwass."

Accelerator didn't understand most of that, but the word *angel* did stick with him.

The wings of light that appeared when Amata Kihara injected Last Order with the virus. Even that wasn't the important part? It was just a piece of the plan prepared for this Aiwass creature?

"Allow me to use a crystal as an analogy. What substances are close at hand—water or salt? Yes, I believe I'll use salt this time. Assume that there exists highly dense saltwater called an AIM diffusion field. However, crystallization cannot occur from that alone. In order to proceed efficiently, it is better to inject impurities into the saltwater. It can be a simple twig, or a small grain of dust, or a *nsrioangegau* such as Fuse Kazakiri...Well, the crystallization itself is simple, but when aiming for the desired shape in the desired size, it then becomes necessary to consider the core's properties."

"...What you're trying to say is that you were created based on this Fuse Kazakiri thing?"

"Strictly speaking, Fuse Kazakiri was the one who was adjusted in order to create me. It would be correct to think of her as a factory assembly line. In any case, I will not deny that I was born after the stylings of Fuse Kazakiri. It would be more accurate to say *uymanifesidvif* rather than *born*, but— Blast, my words cannot catch up. I suppose I will say that I was not born, but rather *emerged*. Strictly speaking, it is different, but I cannot express it in any other way."

Aiwass brought its index finger to its chest, then moved it down toward its stomach.

"Aleister seems to love his circuitous methodology, but, well— cloning technology is not enough for me."

If Aiwass was a mass of AIM diffusion fields coming together, that would mean it wasn't human.

This was all ridiculously fantastic, but Accelerator didn't laugh it away.

In fact.

He would have felt even stranger had the being standing in front of him said it was a human just like him.

"What will you do?" asked Aiwass. "I appeared out of mere curiosity, but what will your next actions be? What would you like to do? For example, do you desire to use my information to quash Aleister's ambitions?"

"...Are you being serious?" Those words heightened Accelerator's caution. "I don't know what the chairperson's goals are, but you're at the center of all this. I mean, to crush his plans means sending you, whose existence is supported by artificial means, back to the void."

"Indeed." Aiwass nodded, long hair waving. "But what does that matter?"

"What...?"

"Let us speak of history." Suddenly, Aiwass veered the conversation in a different direction. "Those who live on the ground here do many different things, celebrating them as ecological or protecting the environment. They say things like many species of animal and plant will go extinct at this rate, earnestly picking empty cans off the road and trying to reduce the amount of smoke."

"Never seen such a master Peeping Tom before."

"You would suggest you humans do anything worthy of me watching?"

"Cut the crap. What are you getting at?"

"Only that history will not change at all," answered Aiwass with ease. "Long ago, an ice age visited this planet. The environment changed drastically, and many animals and plants went extinct...But did history itself end? The flow of time doesn't budge, regardless of whether the small creatures clinging to its surface live or die. If global thermonuclear war broke out right now, and all higher life vanished from the face of the planet, it means nothing to the thick pillars of history. Ten thousand years, one hundred thousand years—eventually, other plants and animals will appear on their own to replace them."

"..."

"It's all the same. Though I may not be one suited to speak of this dimension's history. This man, Aleister, has not learned his lesson and evidently wishes to use me, but I would not be particularly troubled were his plans to be set back. After ten or a hundred thousand years, I will *asbumanifesoagbv*...or rather, appear, at another opportunity. Even that has no real worth to me, however.

"Now, then," added Aiwass, long hair swaying, arms slowly spreading. "What will you do? It may be entertaining to kill me here and frustrate Aleister, you know. That is, if your full powers are capable of such a thing."

Aiwass was unreadable.

Accelerator felt like random gears in his mind were missing; his normal aggressive thoughts weren't coming to him. It didn't matter whether or not he had proof—he knew that even given a long period of time, he wouldn't find a way through. There was no point in merely fighting. It felt to him as stupid as running on and on, trying to reach the horizon where the sun was setting.

He stayed still, and Aiwass, its hands still spread out wide, continued. "Oh? Are you sure about that? I should say this first— Aleister, whose power you trust in a negative way, is far from a perfect human."

"What?"

"Several seams have begun to come apart in his schemes."

Aiwass spoke as though it meant nothing, despite it having to do with literally its entire existence.

"Aleister himself seems to think that each time an irregular phenomenon occurs, he can simply work it into his plan to be beneficial and recover from it. But the small cracks are beginning to grow larger. At this rate, the situation will develop into something that not even Aleister, executor of the plan, would have expected. Yes…"

He had a bad feeling about this.

He could sense he shouldn't listen.

But Aiwass continued, as though mentally cornering stunted, pitiable humans was the only thing this being could enjoy in their boring world.

"…Yes, like how the core of his plan, Last Order, is headed for certain 'collapse' down the road at this rate. Well, she is just a clone, so he might simply be able to create another with the same functions."

Those two words were enough.

His top priority eliminated all discouraging factors and determined Accelerator's next actions.

2

Where am I? thought Hamazura as he ran at full speed through the deep, dark corridor.

Where was he? He was alone. Rikou Takitsubo, whom he hadn't let out of his sight until now, was no longer there.

The reason was simple—they'd been forced apart. The figure slowly following him from behind, as if making sport of him, possessed enough strength to do that. It wasn't a matter of pure physical power or abilities. Something far more overwhelming—terror—rested in the foundation.

"…Haaamazuraaa." A voice, audible from beyond the dark.

"?!" Without turning around, Hamazura surged into a sideways leap. He hit the metal railing, his body rattling, leaning over it. By the time he realized this passage was actually a raised bridge, he was already plummeting.

But it was probably still better than the alternative.

A moment later, with a *ga-bam*, a terrible flash of light stormed past. It melted the very metal walkway he'd just been standing upon, blowing it away and leaving an orange waterfall in its wake.

The Meltdown.

The fourth-ranked Level Five.

"Gah!!"

Right after those monikers crossed his mind, he slammed into the floor on his back.

He must have fallen about three meters, down onto another suspended walkway. And below the metal grating, yet another artificial floor reached past.

This was a very large space. It was probably over a hundred meters across just in width and likely several kilometers long. And even farther below Hamazura's feet was a line of small jet fighters. A quick glance revealed over twenty of them.

...Which means I'm in the aviation capital of the city, District 23...?

It didn't seem like any old repair yard. This was probably a testing ground for conducting trials on new models. The freight train Hamazura and Takitsubo had shared had been ferrying materials here.

Then it happened:

The *clack* of her shoe.

It came from above, probably from the walkway Hamazura had fallen from.

He immediately ducked for cover, diving behind a box-shaped obstacle that looked like a crane control seat.

"Well, it looks like you're fast to escape, at least. As usual. Are you sure? You left your beloved Takitsubo behind."

"Erg...!" Hamazura's back teeth grated back and forth.

He couldn't see it from behind cover, but he could tell—Shizuri Mugino was probably dragging the limp, disabled Takitsubo along with her one arm. She had a simple reason for not killing her—it was to torment him as much as she could.

In truth, he would have liked to jump out and confront her instead. But if he attacked that monster head-on, he'd never win. He'd be reduced to cinders in a moment, and that would be that, leaving no one to rescue Takitsubo. If her goal of tormenting him was gone, Mugino would kill her without delay.

...Damn it, damn it! Damn it!! Why? Why?! Why did she have to show up now, of all times?!

His hands trembling, he took out his gun and popped out the magazine to check how many rounds he had left. In the meantime, only the demonic voice of Mugino mocking him resounded through the jet fighter testing site.

"Are you panicking because you don't know how I survived? Cyborgs, cloning, and nanodevices, oh my! If you guess right, I wouldn't mind giving you a bonus. But you probably wouldn't get it anyway. You seem pretty dull."

Ga-bam!! Boom!! Several rays of light shot down in sequence. They hadn't been aiming at Hamazura precisely, but just the vibrations from the aftermath sent fear coiling around his entire body.

"It's apparently an application of the 'negative legacy' left behind by some perverse doctor named Heaven Canceler, in any case. They said they used an oil-and-fat-based melting skeleton to stabilize my flesh's regeneration rate, then induced rapid cell division. I don't think the man himself would have used it like that...though I suppose that doesn't matter. I'm having too much fun watching you cry."

Hamazura edged his head out from behind the box to get a look at the situation.

"Haaamazuraaa. Hide-and-seek is nice, but would you mind coming out soon? If you don't, I'll start aiming at this precious Takitsubo."

Agh!! He heard a grunt. Mugino had grabbed Takitsubo's hair, then held her in front of her like a shield.

Mugino then slowly brought her other arm, the intensely flashing one made from Meltdown, a hair's breadth away from Takitsubo's skin.

"Gya-ha-ha!! Now, where should I begin roasting her? Should I melt her little face off? Or should I shove it against her little pink _____ and burn it to a black crisp?! Hey, Hamazura, what do you think? It's about to turn black like a mummy— Will you still be able to get off if you stick it in?!"

Damn it...

"I'll count to three. If you don't come out, the punishment is a brand on Takitsubo's _____. You want to abandon her? I bet you're masturbating to the smell of burning virgin."

Mugino's countdown wasn't the usual drawn-out kind.

In fact...

"Three, two, one...*Ka-boom!!*"

"Damn it!!"

When she'd rattled off her countdown, Hamazura burst out from behind the crane control box. Immediately, he leveled his gun at Mugino, but she was many times faster. Plus, she was using Takitsubo as a shield.

"There's a good boy, Hamazura."

Ga-bam!! A massive burst split through everything.

She moved her fingertips like flicking a rolled-up piece of trash. Nevertheless, what came was an attack more terrifying than even a battleship cannon. It shot straight by Hamazura, striking an oil drum sitting behind him. *Whoosh!!* The fuel ignited, a blast of hot wind whipped out, and Hamazura's body flew over five meters into the air.

If she'd wanted to, she could have killed him instantly.

But she didn't—because she wanted to torment him first.

...Damn it...

It took all his energy to flip his facedown body back up. As he did, he cursed himself. A Level Zero who beat Shizuri Mugino once before? What a joke. Now he understood very well how many coincidences and miracles had interceded on his behalf back then. This woman named Shizuri Mugino wasn't some low-level monster he could kill many times over with ease. The factor known as Shiage Hamazura did not function as a trump card against her. He couldn't win like this.

"Hamazuraaa, Hamazuraaa!!"

He heard her calling his name. When he did, he clenched his teeth and tried to get himself up.

But Mugino moved quicker than he did.

Still, it wasn't to finish off Hamazura now that he couldn't move properly. From the start, she'd been drawing out their hellish time together so she could thoroughly and completely torture him.

She then set her sights on Rikou Takitsubo.

"What, are you trying to hype yourself up to be a lone, tragic heroine? You're no normal princess, are you? Didn't you have the strength to fight at some point?"

"?!" A noise, half gasp and half choke, struggled out of Takitsubo's tight throat.

Mugino tossed her limp body aside casually, then reached into her pocket with her one natural arm. Out of it she took an object that was about the size of a mechanical pencil's graphite case.

It was a case for Crystals.

"Ability Stalker. If you put it to full use, you might have been able to reverse my AIM field and hijack my ability, hmm?"

Ping. Her fingertips flicked the small Crystal case. It clattered to the floor and rolled, coming to a stop right next to the fallen girl.

Takitsubo...and their last piece of Crystal. She was the one who could turn things around.

But if she used it, she would surely "break down." Even her current unenergetic condition was thanks to the side effects from Crystals.

She couldn't take any more. If she used them even one more time, it would be over.

But...

"You know, if you want to run, you can be my guest."

Mugino's words rattled the near-dead girl on the ground.

No, they didn't just rattle her—they were so forceful they nearly broke her.

"But then I'll burn Hamazura to a crisp, and he'll die. Because you abandoned him to his death. Gya-ha-ha-ha!! I don't really care what you do. Either way, I'm sure I'll get to see something entertaining!!"

Rikou Takitsubo moaned and reached out a hand.

This was a choice that she knew would bring her own destruction upon her.

She had one reason, but it was enough.

She had to save Shiage Hamazura, who was beaten and about to be killed.

"Oooooooooooooooaaaaaaaaaaaaaaahhhhhhhhh!!"

She groaned like a beast and, finally, her hand grabbed the Crystal case. She flipped open the lid immediately so she wouldn't hesitate, as though sticking a knife in her own chest. Mugino cackled when she saw it. She seemed amused beyond all else that her feelings of wanting to save someone precious to her would lead to a nightmarish outcome.

*...Hamazura...*Takitsubo firmly shut her eyes and opened her mouth.

Her shaking hand moved, trying to fling the contents of the Crystal case inside it.

Then it happened.

"Muginoooooooooooooooooooooooooooooooooooooooooooooooooooooo!!"

Shiage Hamazura unleashed a scream.

A moment later came the sound of a giant motor. The arm for the crane they used to do maintenance on the jets had shuddered, and when Mugino realized it, she took a few quick steps backward. The hook on the end of the arm, still holding a load, swung around in a wide arc like a giant morning star on a chain. And instead of hitting the one who had dodged it, it struck Takitsubo in the side, just as she was about to take the Crystals.

Grkkk!!

It was an awful noise.

The Crystal case burst open, and Takitsubo went over the railing and disappeared into the level below.

"Ha-ha-ha..."

Despite herself, a grin had formed on Mugino's lips.

The result wasn't in her script, but coincidences sometimes brought even greater amusement with them.

"Gya-ha-ha-ha-ha-ha-ha!! What the hell was that, Hamazura?! Who were you trying to protect?! Some friend you are, finishing her off personally!!"

But then, as Mugino laughed uproariously, a damp chill suddenly came over her.

She'd been jeering at and mocking Hamazura endlessly, but he'd never reacted. He'd shown no humiliation or regret.

Mugino realized it too late.

Hamazura had been going after Takitsubo from the beginning. He'd both stopped her from using the Crystals and removed her from Mugino's clutches. Even if it meant harming the person he wanted to protect, it would at least let her avoid a decisive, fatal blow.

She thought back.

The stuff hanging off the crane hook—hadn't it been a worker-use powered suit, the kind for working with hazardous aviation explosives? Yes, one to give to the frail Takitsubo to raise her chances of survival even a few percentage points.

"...Shizuri Mugino..."

And why would he go that far?

That was obvious.

"It looks like one death just wasn't enough for you."

Then, the Level Zero who had once brought down the fourth-ranked Level Five stood up once more.

And ironically, for the same purpose—to save a girl named Rikou Takitsubo.

3

Accelerator switched on his choker electrode.

Now he could use the number-one Level Five ability whenever he wanted: the ability to alter vectors. The power to reflect every possible attack, a power that could bring forth from that trivial capacity catastrophic destruction. As long as he had it, there would be no enemy he couldn't defeat.

Aiwass had said this to him, a hint of scorn passing across its face.

That if Aleister's plans continued, Last Order would "collapse" not long into the future.

And implicitly, it had told him this as well:

If you believe you can kill me, then do it. But I'm sure power on your level couldn't eliminate my existence even temporarily.

…Well, you asked for it. Manipulating his leg force vectors, Accelerator exploded forward. *I don't know if you're a clump of AIM fields or an angel or what, but nobody who intentionally tries to harm that brat deserves any mercy. I'm wiping you out of existence and making things easier for myself, just like I said!!*

Aiwass didn't even try to dodge. It gazed upon Accelerator, its hands still loosely spread.

Accelerator dove straight into range. He thrust an open hand as hard as he could—and with it, all he had to do was manipulate its vectors, and he'd be able to destroy Aiwass from the inside out.

However.

Ga-bam!!

An instant later, a shock wave of causes unknown pierced through Accelerator's upper body in a diagonal line.

He'd been cut right through, as though with a heavy katana. Immediately after he felt it, his body slammed into the floor, and he tumbled backward a few times.

An unbelievable amount of fresh blood spewed. It wasn't only from the gaping wound in his upper body, but from his mouth and his nose as well. All joking and metaphors aside, the wound was so huge it was strange none of his organs were leaking out of him.

"Gh…bh, *gaaaaaaaahhhhhhhhhhhhhhhhhhhhhhh*?!"

He didn't know what had just happened. Several had gotten through his reflection technique before, like Amata Kihara and

Teitoku Kakine. But Aiwass was different. It wasn't using some strange logic exception to slip through. Even after he'd taken a decisive blow, he couldn't analyze what had just happened to his own body.

"Oh. That was my mistake," said Aiwass, its voice relaxed in contrast.

Something sprouted from its back, parting through its long, blond hair. Wings. Wings that shone, radiated far too much for human eyes, brighter than a nuclear explosion. Had those wings been what sliced through Accelerator?

They were abnormal.

They weren't simply golden. They glittered in a pale platinum, with white mixed at its core…Words may not have been enough to describe it, but that was the only way Accelerator's brain could express it.

Not being able to comprehend something he was physically seeing gave him a strong sense of unease.

"I see you've planted some sort of *snconstructionbozl*-use virus, Aleister. You went through Last Order to embed self-defense *bseouabilitygbu* in my *beuomanifesdnn*? Well, I do indeed apologize. It seems he *nbspgaddnpsir* something like a suicide preventer. If you want to *sbgpkillnapedv* me, please do something about the *nspidhwinggorws*. They move of their own accord."

Aiwass's words were growing stranger and stranger.

But Accelerator wasn't exactly listening. His eye color shifted into a red more baleful than the red of the blood spurting from his body. Still fallen, his hand reached out and found the ground, smashing the floor tiles.

"Abeoughabaeougbaokillwobnoweuferya…!!"

Ga-bam!! Accelerator's back burst. Jet-black wings carved out from it. Dark wings, in contrast to the pale platinum ones Aiwass had. His upper body bleached in crimson, even his lips and teeth turned bright red, the demon swayed and rose with a gravity-defying smoothness.

"——'Do what thou wilt.' That shall be thy law?"

Accelerator had no way of knowing, but that sentence was written in the *Book of the Law* and described the pillar central to a certain sorcerer long ago.

"Unfortunately, you have the wrong *rggtimerigeneration*. Yours are, in the end, the *rsgpowernophe* from the eon of Osiris. You cannot *hosefenemygierd* me, one who lives in Horus."

There was a massive, thundering roar.

It was the shock wave created by the two types of wings, jet-black and pale platinum, clashing.

The collision created a storm.

Ga-baaaahhhh!! Blazing-hot winds whipped up around Accelerator and Aiwass.

But the battle was far from equal. With the first attack, Accelerator's black wings shredded apart from their base, and with the second, they came completely off. Something more howl than scream rang out. Meanwhile, Aiwass's pale-platinum wings swung. Fresh crimson blood scattered, dancing into the air, erased by the whipping winds.

They were in two completely different dimensions.

Despite the power of Accelerator's black wings, it was like swinging around a heavy wooden club. Aiwass's, on the other hand, were like swords of legend, thoroughly sharpened by advanced technology.

There was the sound of something falling.

No—a *person* falling.

"Is that all?" said Aiwass simply, watching Accelerator sink into his pool of blood.

A normal human would have died for sure, but Accelerator was still breathing. He had unconsciously used his vector-altering ability to force his blood to circulate from torn vessel to vessel. Hence, a lot of red liquid now flew around him like juice spilled in space.

But that was it.

All he could do was cling to life. No resuscitation, no miracle, would come from it.

"I had mentioned Last Order as an easy way to tempt you, but this went faster than expected. Your level of maturity wouldn't even be able to cope with Fuse Kazakiri. You're getting impatient again, aren't you, Aleister? ...Teitoku Kakine is worth thinking about as well."

Once it was finished speaking, Aiwass turned on its heel. Using its legs, it left that place. It was actually stranger than seeing it suddenly disappear or take flight would have been.

Until—

Grick!! Aiwass felt something small breaking at its core.

An error had occurred in the AIM diffusion field aggregate's bonding that governed its existence. Aiwass considered the cause and then turned around. It began to break into pieces, starting with the tips of its golden locks, and even then, Aiwass's face remained stoic.

"If I'm right..."

A ragged voice.

It belonged to Accelerator, but they weren't indecipherable words like Aiwass's speech. He spoke in a human language, saying, "...You're using...Academy City's...AIM fields...to emerge...And to control it, you made...this Fuse Kazakiri thing...and put a virus in that brat... Which means—"

"Yes, you've thought this through."

Aiwass smiled, its fingertips crumbling and losing shape all the while.

Its eyes gazed at Accelerator's crutch.

"Your jammer for blocking waves that remote control your choker—you reconfigured it for the entire Misaka network. The network is essentially a signpost for guiding all of Academy City's AIM fields. So yes...Blocking the Misaka network's interference from this space, in this location alone, is indeed like removing the crystal's core and reverting it to saltwater. However..."

As it spoke, Accelerator's legs were trembling madly.

Even though Aiwass hadn't done anything.

"Do you understand? It is also cutting off the only lifeline you have right now."

"..."

There was only the continuous *plips* of dripping blood.

Accelerator had been just barely stopping the blood loss by using his ability and forcing his blood to flow through broken vessels. If he blocked off his own vector-altering ability, only one thing could happen.

"...Shut...up...," he said, lips trembling. He'd set the jamming to grow stronger as time passed. Eventually, he wouldn't be able to talk or walk. Mustering what strength he had left so he could finish things before that happened, he drew his gun.

——Not a strange, unknown power belonging to an angel or a demon or what have you, but a weapon he would wield as a human.

He'd walked this bloody path in order to save one girl named Last Order. To that end, he was determined to make even Last Order his enemy and reign as a soot-black king of evil.

He was a villain—and not the kind who would prostrate himself to save his own life in a place like this.

It was petty and not the type of villain Accelerator presented to the world.

Therefore, he didn't hesitate to make the decision.

No matter how much of his blood spewed, even if he collapsed, even if all his innards were exposed by his enormous wound—in order to save Last Order, he would pull the trigger his finger was already touching. That was his evil.

"Do what thou wilt. That shall be thy law."

Aiwass spoke in a singsong voice. Its hands had already broken apart up to the elbows, and its palely shining wings of white-cored platinum were as still as a device with the cogs removed. Its body was partly transparent, and an object that looked like a triangular prism appeared briefly in the center of its head, only to disappear again. Its surface moved around without end, like a keyboard, clacking and clacking and clacking.

When it realized the muzzle was suddenly pointed at it, Aiwass spread its arms—which only went down to the elbows—and spoke with a smile as though welcoming him.

"I see. Then show me thy law."

A gunshot rang out.

It left behind only two sounds: one like a crystal shattering—and another, the dull thud of a person falling.

4

Shizuri Mugino jumped down to the next level of walkways. The metal grating clanged, echoing through the jet testing center. Hamazura was there, leaning, wounded, against the outside of the crane operator's box, glaring at Mugino's one real eye.

"One death just wasn't enough, hmm?" she mocked. The arm of light she'd created in place of her lost limb crackled. "You're right. It's nowhere near enough—if you wanted to face me with words, your complaints could use the help of a few more brain cells!!"

Za-spark!! Her flashing arm swelled explosively.

But Hamazura moved first.

His limp hand held the gun, so he could've raised it up, taken aim, and fired. If he'd taken that much time, Mugino would have used it to blow off Hamazura's limbs quite cleanly.

Instead, he immediately pulled the trigger while his arm still hung low. The bullet naturally flew off in an unexpected direction...and struck a fire extinguisher nearby.

Ba-bom!! Pressed by the gas, a cloud of white powder closed around his profile.

...Hiding in the fog, are we?

"Are you still screwing with me, Hamazuraaa?!"

Giving the impression of someone in the audience throwing a tomato onto the stage during a poorly written play, Mugino's Meltdown launched a bright beam. A second pure-white ray, then a third, fired off in sequence, carving fatally into the silhouette beyond the fire extinguisher powder and blasting it away.

"Damn, I wanted to take my time crushing him. Did I accidentally kill him instantly?" muttered Mugino in spite of herself.

But the results begged to differ.

The thing she thought she'd blasted away had been one of the cardboard boxes stacked haphazardly next to him. While Mugino was preoccupied with the dummy, Hamazura had immediately jumped off the grated walkway and onto the lowest floor.

"Ha-ha-ha-ha-ha-ha-ha. Escaping with a smokescreen and a dummy? ...I had no idea you were a goddamn ninja!!"

She fired light downward, mostly out of irritation, then jumped down to the lower level herself.

Several jets were lined up in the vast space. Even for testing purposes, they were already completely finished, paint and all. Missiles and bombs of various sizes were even attached to the underside of their wings—maybe they planned to do tests fully equipped to see if they could bear the loads.

Now, then.

Mugino looked around with her one remaining eye.

Shiage Hamazura was probably hiding somewhere, watching, waiting for his chance. He'd at least realized that she'd shoot him in the back if he kept running at this point.

"..."

She glanced at a jet and briefly wondered if he would use one to counterattack. If he used its 20mm or 30mm Gatling gun and a variety of missiles, she'd probably have a little trouble.

...But no, that would be a bit much, she thought, rejecting the idea. She was sure a street thug like Shiage Hamazura wouldn't know how to control a specialized vehicle like that. And even if he could, that didn't change the fact that they were in a warehouse. As for any jets that could fight while standing still—with Mugino's ability, she could vaporize it in one attack.

She walked slowly down the kilometers-long passage, her soles clicking, and she smirked. This was it, this was *it*. If he walked up right in front of her, she'd send him to his death in one hit.

But he had to do his fair share to get there.

"Wheeere in the wooorld could you beee, Haaamazuraaa?" she sang with a random rhythm, her flashing arm swaying to and fro.

And then...

"I'm right here."

Suddenly, she got a stupidly honest response.

"?!"

It came from right next to her. She'd been on the wrong end of a crazy handgun counterattack last time. She twisted around quickly and fired Meltdown before getting a read on her target. *Bra-zakk!!* A brilliant flashing light surged out, and the jet in the direction she'd released it melted in an orange color.

But just before that, she saw it.

She saw, in the place she'd attacked, a maintenance tractor alongside long and slender bombs loaded like drainpipes at the park...and on top of them, a wireless headset on maximum volume so the sound would leak to its surroundings—plus a wireless LAN-attached fiber scope, probably used for maintaining the planes.

There was no time to consider her options.

Before she could think, the single two-hundred-kilo bomb her heated attack had blasted went up in a brilliant explosion—and caused the bombs, missiles, and airplane fuel nearby to ignite instantly.

Hamazura, who was hiding somewhere far away, didn't get off scot-free, either.

He'd been working quietly but swiftly after spotting what looked like an electric-powered tractor for pulling around the fighters, and now he was behind cover about five hundred meters away from the explosion. He'd used a small truck loaded with a complete set of painting supplies for changing a jet's color and used one of the maintenance crew's wireless transceivers to project his voice. The huge blast had knocked him to the floor.

"Guwaaaaahhhhhhhhhhhhhhhhhhh!!"

His eardrums felt like they were going to explode. He felt a strange pressure from within, as though his eyeballs were going to pop out. But what worried him more was Takitsubo. He couldn't find her. He'd left a radio for guidance somewhere far from where he'd knocked her down and given her a work-use powered suit with the crane, too. It was too heavy to move in normal mode, and its high-mobility mode seemed to require a special electronic key, so she couldn't use it for battle. It should have given her a little protection against the blast... though he hoped she wasn't still in the explosion's radius.

Whatever the case, Shizuri Mugino must have been caught up in the blast.

Fortunately for Hamazura, she still tended to look down on all her enemies. It certainly wasn't a mistake, necessarily speaking, but it gave way to openings and missteps she didn't need to have.

...That was a two-hundred-kilo bomb meant for busting pillboxes made of thick concrete. You're not supposed to use them on unarmed humans. Mugino should be out of the way with that...Now to find Takitsubo and get out of here...

Hamazura tossed the transceiver and the small fiberscope monitor away, then ran back along the path he'd come.

Hot gusts blew madly.

The floor near the site of the explosion was completely collapsed, having caused a cave-in to a basement space under it. Walkways above them had twisted and fallen. Hamazura walked through their midst. He searched high and low, shouting Takitsubo's name, mindful that a secondary or tertiary explosion could happen at any moment.

And then he heard a rustling.

"Takitsubo?!"

Hamazura looked in that direction.

However...

*   *   *

"Haaamazuraaa…"

A chill.

For an instant, all his body warmth left him.

But by then it was too late.

From inside the dark smoke reached an arm of glinting lights. Hamazura did his best to twist aside, but an awful noise and smell dispersed from near his ear. A sizzle. Like oil dripped into a well-heated frying pan.

"*Ugahhhhhhhhhhhhhhhhhhhhhhhhhhhhhhhhhhh?!*"

Mugino stepped through the smoke to look down at the writhing boy. "Did you think this…this mass-produced weapon could defeat the city's number four, Hamazuraaa?"

"Shit, shit shit fuck shit!!"

Hamazura desperately clamped down on the pain devouring his ear, grabbed his gun in both hands, and fired.

But suddenly, Mugino disappeared.

She'd unleashed Meltdown like a rocket engine. She'd probably made the same quick maneuver to avoid the two-hundred-kilo bomb. With a muffled *whoosh*, she escaped outside his field of view and said, "Your counters are all obvious— Do you really think they'll work?!"

A massive roar rose up.

It was the sound of the tip of her boot digging into Hamazura's back and kicking him several meters into the air.

He couldn't even grunt at this point. He'd stopped breathing, and his body fell—but not onto the floor, oh no; it fell through one of the cracks the bomb had made.

Bam-slam. Ka-bam.

Several shocks hit him, one after another.

Intense pain washed over him, so terrible he honestly thought part of his spine had fallen out of place, but he didn't have the time to cry about anything. He sensed a chilling intent to kill from above him and used all his energy to roll to the side. A moment later, Mugino's light stabbed toward him, time and time again.

"Run! Run!! Run away, little piggy!! Let me enjoy this hunt a little longer!!"

Pieces of the floor were stuck all over him. He started to lose track of whether he was the one rolling, or if the tempest of fragments was rolling *him*. Nevertheless, he twisted and dove behind cover. Perhaps aggravated she'd lost sight of her target, Mugino immediately jumped into the basement space as well.

…Where is this? Is there an exit…?

Hamazura, hiding behind an obstacle, eventually glanced around.

It was an odd sort of room. It was around a hundred square meters, but there were protrusions in the wall at even intervals. And past those protrusions, he could see what looked like an air conditioner vent covering the entire wall. One of the sides was reinforced glass, and he could spot what looked like a control room for something on the other side.

This was an airplane-testing facility.

Which meant…

…a room where they test durability against air friction…?

Hamazura was up against a capsule-shaped model of about three meters. It was made to be the same size as a fighter cockpit. Though it was a model, the reinforced-glass canopy moved up and down properly, and it was made out of the same combination of materials as the real planes.

The stepladder-looking thing had probably kept it in the air, but it had been knocked on its side by the blast. The reinforced-glass canopy covering the cockpit was half-open, too.

"Haaamazuraaa…"

He gave a start. Just hearing his name called made his shoulders jerk. He frantically searched for an exit door, then found one. But it was far away. If he jumped out from behind the cockpit model, she'd shoot him five hundred times before he opened that door.

He couldn't use that exit.

He'd have to end things here.

But the gun in his hand alone didn't seem able to kill Mugino. She could use her ability like a rocket engine to flee outside the range of a two-hundred-kilo bomb going off. A normal person wouldn't even be able to aim a 9mm bullet at her.

He had to use something stronger, something more overwhelming; something that wouldn't even let her escape. But he wasn't a powerful esper, and a mere Level Zero like Hamazura couldn't bring anything like that to the table.

"I swear, this is all so idiotic. It might have bothered you a lot, but it's bothering me a hell of a lot, too, I'm telling you."

Click-click. Her footsteps drew closer. If she went around his cover, it was over.

"Anyway, maybe I'm better off than Teitoku Kakine. They picked the number two up in a way worse state than me, apparently. They had to put him in a container with this sticky liquid in it, get all three pieces of his brain back together, hook his side up to this machine bigger than a fridge to make up for his crushed heart—that kind of thing. I hear he's basically just a big clump of meat they keep around so he can spit out his Level Five ability now."

Hamazura desperately looked around.

"The General Board chairperson must really want to reuse us. I wonder why? Anyway, the only thing I can say for sure is that you're dying here."

He searched for a clue to turn the tables. And…he found a last ray of hope.

"Hey, Hamazura."

And then it happened.

"Why…?"

Suddenly, he noticed a change in Mugino's voice. He thought for a moment, then shook his head. He didn't want to think about it. If he did, he wouldn't be able to take action. He would hesitate in a situation where a moment's delay would be fatal.

But Shizuri Mugino still said:

*　　*　　*

"…I wonder why I had to turn into such a horrid monster."

Damn it!!! Hamazura was just about to raise his voice.

The one thing he wanted to think about the least right now: the fact that Shizuri Mugino was both a monster *and* another human woman. He didn't know what she meant by "why." Was it that she'd escaped death with technology unknown to him? Was it starting to work for the shady Item organization? Or was it becoming a Level Five? Whatever the case was, Shiage Hamazura didn't have an answer for any of those questions. All it presented him with was agony.

Hamazura, toying with the small clue he now had, thought once more.

Was it okay to kill her?

Could he bury her as a simple monster and still deserve a happy, smile-filled ending?

"Was that what you wanted me to say, Hamazuraaa?"

An incredible *whump* rang out.

Mugino, having come around the cockpit in an instant, whipped a kick into Hamazura's gut. But her assault didn't end there—seven or eight fast, sharp strikes later, and Hamazura was in deep pain not only on the surface but down to his internal organs.

"Gya-ha-ha!! You're all twitchy now! Hmm? I don't know, is blood supposed to be coming from your mouth? Do mouths *do* that? Maybe I'll get a fun, super-rare scream out of it!!"

"Guh…gah! Gvbhr…?!"

…Damn…it…What the hell just happened to my organs…?

The inside of his body shook unnaturally. His organs weren't working right. They were moving like individual creatures packed into a leather bag. It was the first time in his life he realized a human body could work in this way.

Are they still where they're supposed to be…? …They're not all shuffled around in there, are they…?

"Oh, come on, don't be so down. If I give you a nice, gentle rub, maybe your senses will come back, hmm?"

Crrrick!! The tip of her toes dug even more deeply into him.

She tossed him into the half-open cockpit with the force of someone tossing something into a garbage can.

A crackling came immediately after. Mugino's flashing arm had swelled larger than he'd ever seen it.

"I'll mix you up with the melted metal, cool you, and make you into a neat house decoration."

He didn't have time to think.

Hamazura fired his gun. But it wouldn't hit Mugino; instead, the bullet veered away...and shattered the reinforced glass on the one wall. Mugino's smile became even more vicious, but Hamazura's expression didn't change. That had been his goal.

It would never have hit her anyway. The weighty glass, shattered by the bullet, collapsed inward...Right on top of the control panel. The pieces pressed down on all kinds of buttons, sending unplanned orders to the giant "device."

Vwooom. It was a low, dull sound that echoed.

Mugino looked around in confusion, then located the thing that looked like an air conditioner vent set up on the wall, now squirming. Meanwhile, Hamazura edged deeper into the cockpit. Inside the model, all the instruments but one had been removed. He pressed it, and the half-opened glass canopy shut fully, closing him tightly into the cockpit.

Shizuri Mugino, realizing something, finally turned back to Hamazura.

Her lips moved, but he couldn't hear her through the reinforced glass.

But.

It looked to him, at least partly, that her eyes were like that of a girl about to burst into tears.

A moment later.

Everything outside the cockpit turned into an orange explosion.

* * *

The room they were in was a room for testing air friction durability. When fighter jets exceeded the speed of sound, they experienced massive air friction. Their surface temperature would rise to hundreds of degrees. This durability testing room was for making sure the jets could withstand such friction. They obviously couldn't create air moving at supersonic speeds, so instead, they used a large amount of iron filings to create a wind that would artificially increase how much friction there was.

Hamazura was protected by the model cockpit.

But Mugino had no such luck.

Ga-boom!!

An incredible explosion went off. The entire hundred-meter-square space was filled with hellish winds hundreds of degrees Celsius. Mugino had a way to move at high speeds like rocket engines, but with the entire space filled at once, she had no chance to escape. It really was like a giant fly being swatted aside. Her body was flung straight through the air into the back wall.

After that, he couldn't see what happened.

Everything outside the clear reinforced glass was orange, leaving him no clear views. It was like he was looking out the window of a space shuttle reentering the atmosphere.

Hamazura covered his face with his hands.

This was not the joy of victory.

He had his eyes shut, praying only that this hell would disappear as soon as humanly possible. Was this really the only thing he could have done? He questioned himself over and over, and it was the only thing on his mind.

Eventually, the hellscape calmed.

For a short while, Hamazura didn't move a muscle, but eventually, he sat up in the cockpit seat, albeit slowly. He pressed the button, opening the reinforced glass canopy, and fell out of it. A hot, humid air struck his skin. It was like being in an oven.

What had become of Shizuri Mugino?

He didn't have time to check.

"Hamazura. Hamazura!!"

From somewhere else, he heard a familiar girl's voice. He looked up and saw Takitsubo looking at him from a crack in the ceiling created by the two hundred-kilo bomb. Hamazura waved. "I'm okay," he said.

He had chosen Rikou Takitsubo, and for that, he had discarded Shizuri Mugino.

He gave the thought one more moment in his mind, then decided to move forward on his own two feet again.

That, however, was when his cell phone rang.

He picked it up. On the other end was Saiai Kinuhata.

"Hamazura!! Listen to me— Get out of there, like, as fast as you possibly can!!"

"Kinuhata…?!"

"I totally know you're in the District 23 fighter testing site! That totally doesn't matter! Another Academy City unit is heading that way to arrest you. And not the good kind of arrest! I can't, like, totes guarantee you'll survive!! Take Takitsubo and get away from there now!!"

"What?" Hamazura frowned. He would understand them sending a team after Takitsubo or Kinuhata. But he was just a street thug. Why had things gotten so dramatic? Mugino's appearance had surprised him, but now that he thought about it, what on earth was that team chasing them before that?

Either way, he didn't have time to mull it over.

He ran to the durability testing room's exit, ran up the stairs, and hurried back to Takitsubo's side.

"Hey! How far away are we supposed to run?! Academy City may be big, but it's still walled off. If they keep sending people after us forever, they'll catch us eventually!!"

"Jeez, don't you have some kind of Skill-Out safehouse or something?!"

"Yeah, but those are just to hide from rival gangs. There's no way we'd ever be able to get a secret spot that would stay permanently hidden from special forces!!" he shouted into the cell phone, running through the hangar-like area and pulling Takitsubo by the hand. Their pursuers were surely closing in. They'd be killed at this rate.

And then Hamazura stopped running.

There was one—and only one—route that was sure to escape Academy City's pursuit.

"Hey, Kinuhata. Academy City's supersonic passenger planes have autopilot features, am I right?"

"Hamazura, you're not—"

"I know I don't know how to take off or land, but once we're in the air, it'd be fine! Isn't there some kind of manual or something?! For now, we just have to get up there, and we'll be good. I won't think about landing. We can jump out in parachutes if we need to, so that's not an issue!!"

As he spoke, he looked in front of him again. Along with all the fighter jets, there was a huge plane almost eighty meters in length. It was a supersonic passenger jet that could soar at over seven thousand kilometers per hour. If they wanted to get away from Academy City's special forces, they would just have to flee outside the city.

With its gigantic fuselage, they wouldn't be able to climb aboard without a specific boarding ramp vehicle.

But possibly due to the two-hundred-kilo bomb's effects, a walkway was jutting out diagonally. Hamazura and Takitsubo moved up it and into the air, clinging to the side of the passenger jet. Fortunately, it wasn't locked. They opened the hatch, then climbed aboard.

"Hamazura, can you hear me? The underground hangar you're in has this scramble liftoff feature thing. Speaking super-broadly, it can set up an electromagnetic catapult hill."

"What should we do? How do we escape to the skies?!"

"The catapult's firing function is, like, linked to the cockpit. If you boot up the control computer, you should totes be able to touch the screen with an index finger and lift off."

He ran to the cockpit in the nose and opened the door to find over a hundred buttons and a flight yoke waiting for him. It almost made him feel dizzy, but he followed Kinuhata's instructions—she must have been looking at a manual—and began pressing buttons.

Several screens flickered to life, and the four huge engines began a low groan. One of the monitors showed a diagram of the catapult.

Following directions, his fingers flew across the monitor, and several of the items on it changed from red to green.

And then:

The underground hangar door flew open wide, and men in black uniforms who must have been the pursuit team flooded in. They looked at the supersonic passenger jet just as it was about to take off and took immediate action.

Without wasting any bullets, they brought around a construction tractor and parked it in such a way that it blocked the catapult.

"Shit!" cursed Hamazura in spite of himself, but he couldn't stop the commands he'd given at this point.

With a massive *gshhhh* noise, the supersonic passenger jet made its way quickly down the catapult rail. He saw one of the black-suited men, the one moving the tractor, hastily climb out of the vehicle, and knew that the supersonic passenger jet was headed straight for it.

They'd crash.

So Hamazura thought, until—

Zzzap!! A tremendous flash of light burst out and knocked the tractor to the side. Before Hamazura could consider where it came from, the electromagnetic catapult launched the supersonic passenger jet from the climbing tunnel up above the surface.

Hamazura didn't touch the flight yoke; it would have been foolish to do so. Instead, the autopilot program steadily brought the plane horizontal. As long as they didn't hit any turbulence, he'd be better off leaving it alone.

Mugino...

The flash he'd seen at the end had probably been hers. He didn't know what reason she had for firing it, but he got the keen feeling they'd meet again somewhere.

"Hamazura...," came Takitsubo's voice suddenly from next to him.

Hamazura found he was naturally able to wrap her in a hug. That seemed to finally release the tension, and the two plopped down onto the cockpit floor.

One battle had ended.

And in his arms was but a single girl.

5

Accelerator was slumped on the bloody floor. The amount of blood loss was insane, but strangely, he didn't feel pain. His limbs wouldn't move properly, but he felt no fear. Or maybe he'd lost the ability to feel it.

...Is it...over...? he thought, dazed.

One last attack with his life on the line. The bullet he'd fired at the end had pierced right into the triangular prism thing he saw in the Aiwass's semi-transparent head region. Then there had been the sound of a crystal shattering. He didn't quite understand what that had been, but he figured it was Aiwass's weak spot.

However...

"I suppose I should rate that at so-so."

This time.

This time, true despair washed over Accelerator. Before he realized it, Aiwass was standing in front of him. He didn't know when, exactly, it had happened. Or how the being before him had recovered, or if the damage really affected it at all, or what that triangular prism was. They'd been engaged in a death match until now, and yet he still hadn't gotten a single scrap of real information.

"In actuality, I might have gone down there just like Fuse Kazakiri. Even if it hadn't been as bad as as a clean kill, I wouldn't have been able to come out for, say, several years. Aleister's plans would have needed drastic revisions, and you might have been able to rescue Last Order in the meantime.

"However," continued Aiwass casually—as though saying it didn't matter if it survived or died—"the security Aleister built seems to be more careful than I'd anticipated. Perhaps he's a worrywart. In any case, it seems my defenses were made to be less penetrable than I expected."

"...You piece of shit..."

Accelerator desperately tried to get up.

But he'd lost too much blood. He couldn't even move his limbs properly. While he struggled, Aiwass continued.

"I feel bad, since you fought with everything you had."

Aiwass smiled thinly.

Above its head appeared a shining angel halo.

One with a pale platinum glow, a hint of white at its core.

The blond monster that held interest based on objective value and had appeared before someone out of that interest said one final thing.

"...It seems I have a transformation feature."

Ga-baaaaaaaaaam!!!!!!

Accelerator's consciousness was cut off without mercy.

And thus, his last hope to save that one single girl disintegrated.

EPILOGUE

I Won't Let This End in Tragedy

Brave_in_Hand.

The blond monster, Aiwass, walked on two legs, a run-of-the-mill cell phone at its ear.

It was near the edge of an exposed steel beam in a building still under construction. It walked while looking at the moon, not paying the slightest attention to its oh-so-narrow footing. The precarious metal perch held no value, so it had no interest in the thing. That was the only reason.

"Is it truly so mystifying, Aleister?" said Aiwass slowly into the cell phone it had acquired from parts unknown.

The other person was silent for just a moment, then answered, *"If you wanted to, you wouldn't need to move on foot. And the same applies when it comes to conveying your intent. Your actions are indeed perplexing and seem quite inefficient."*

"To stand on two legs and converse through a convenience of civilization...Is that not an act from which one can draw significant value? Perhaps, though, it is perplexing to a man who floats upside down in a glass container in the pursuit of efficiency first and foremost."

Efficiency and value.

That seemed to be what distinguished the two monsters.

"Oh, yes. About the 'number one' you finally succeeded in creating by building this whimsical city for over fifty years."

"Are you about to tell me things haven't proceeded as expected?"

"Well, you can allow it, can't you? You have margins of error. Still, I must say, his mind was more puerile than I thought. He bemocks himself as evil, but I wonder if he realizes it is only because of a fervent thirst for goodness…Even though the one who he pursues, the Imagine Breaker, doesn't act according to good or evil in the first place. That boy simply acts in line with the mental activity that bubbles up to the surface, only to be arbitrarily deemed 'good' by others."

As Aiwass looked at the moon, it smiled very, very thinly. Its expression seemed to say that a short moment's idle conversation held more value and interest than even destroying the world.

"And perhaps," it said, "you admire them, hmm?"

"…"

"Heroes come in many shapes and sizes: those who try to stay on the straight and narrow, obeying the emotions that well up within them, even if nobody teaches them; those who have committed a grave mistake in the past and try to walk a proper path even as their sin causes them agony; those who can become a hero for one person alone, even if they don't have the talent and weren't chosen by anyone. Each sort of hero is someone who will rise again and again, no matter how many times they are beaten."

"…Aiwass."

"These three types of heroes seem to be equipped with what you lack. I cannot blame you for admiring them…After all, there was a time when you could do nothing except fall to pieces and wail."

"Aiwass."

Aleister said its name one more time.

He who appeared both male and female, both adult and child, both saint and sinner, let a sharp twist creep into his voice for a mere moment. Normally, his voice was clothed in all emotions: joy, anger, sorrow, and pleasure. But now something was different.

Aiwass's expression never changed.

Perhaps Aiwass didn't even find that reaction worthy of its interest.

"I will be using whatever I can. Even if that means you. You may

laugh and speak of errors in my plan, but allow me to say something as well—that absolute superiority of yours is by no means an eternal guarantee."

"I didn't particularly gain this power out of desire, nor do I maintain it through effort," said Aiwass into the cell phone. "Well, that's fine. I'll emerge here again if I find value and interest."

Moments before daybreak, Aiho Yomikawa awoke for some reason. Even she didn't know why. She was a talented Anti-Skill officer, and as a result of her training, she could accurately sense the presence of others. Without turning on the lights, she left her bedroom and found her apartment's living room window had been opened.

On alert, she searched the room and discovered two things. The first was that a roommate, a girl named Last Order, was nowhere to be found. And the second was the sticky trail of blood leading from her room to the living room window.

Yomikawa's expression changed, but then she found a third clue.

It was a small note.

A short sentence had been written on it using bright-red blood, the characters shaky. There was nothing indicating who had written it, but Yomikawa recognized the words right away. She couldn't glean deeper meaning from the words, but this one, abrupt sentence was written there:

I'll save this brat's life. I promise.

Only the periodic sounds of shaking disturbed Accelerator. He was in a dark space—a freight train container. And this freight train, which ran before the first commuter trains started, was set to keep chugging along and head outside Academy City. There would have been freight checks near the outer wall on their way, but Accelerator, active in the dark underbelly of the city, knew that certain processes could get a stowaway through them.

There were no voices.

It was so silent it seemed strange that this served as the hiding spot for two people. In Accelerator's hands, as he lay curled up and unmoving, was another person, a girl, who was also still. It was Last Order, fully unconscious, the brunt of her weight on Accelerator. Aiwass's appearance must have placed considerable stress on the girl; she was exhausted beyond what he'd ever seen.

"The girl presents a problem."

Accelerator recalled the words, delivered from on high after he'd been completely trounced.

"It depends on Aleister's plan, but whether it's right now or far in the future, there is no doubt she will eventually be destroyed. She will die during the process of him integrating me into his plan. I wouldn't rely on that doctor. Bluntly speaking, he's just another human. His skills aren't perfect, and if the technology in this city could do something for her in the first place—well, Aleister would never leave any causes for concern sit and not do anything about it. Still, though, losing this body if and when his plan crumbles is just one of myriad possibilities. If you want to save yourself tears later, walk a path besides the one that already exists."

What was the intent behind those words?

As though he'd seen value and interest in something, Aiwass's words alone continued to flow.

"Go to Russia."

Accelerator had stayed silent and listened.

Aiwass wasn't someone he could deal with in anger, a problem that he could tear limb from limb, and that fact alone disturbed Accelerator enough to fry his nerve cells.

"More specifically, head for the Elizina Alliance of Independent Nations, which broke off from the motherland. That place is beginning to transform into the center of a planet-scale war. Every civilization's knowledge and technology will be honed into militaries and weapons and converge there...and something you've never seen before will appear as well—a completely different 'law.'"

Aiwass, mindless of others' thoughts and feelings, continued uttering words alone.

"The index of prohibited books—remember that term. The index itself is not there, but there is something crucial related to it."

" "
...

Accelerator's puny evil didn't stand a chance against power that overwhelming.

What should he do now? It felt like he'd been using a GPS map to cross some flatlands, but suddenly his screen had gone dead. He couldn't figure out what it was he needed to aim for.

Academy City's strongest monster. Nobody could see him hiding in that freight train, but if they had been able to, everyone might have felt the same.

They would have seen an abandoned child, one who had been wandering around the vast city's streets and had finally curled up in abject exhaustion.

There was a crunch.

It was the sound of him crushing his cell phone in his hand—his only connection to Group, Aiho Yomikawa, and Kikyou Yoshikawa.

Accelerator brought the young girl in his arms close again, and his lips moved very slightly. In words that were almost unspoken, he said:

To Russia.

The supersonic passenger jet Shiage Hamazura and Rikou Takitsubo rode pierced through the heavens, maintaining its balance and a fixed course on autopilot. But that wouldn't last forever. Hamazura had no way of safely landing the jumbo jet.

...We'll have to use parachutes to get off.

Hamazura was busy placing bombs from the testing facility all over the plane as he thought out their next move. This passenger plane, though, was another part of Academy City's top-of-the-line technology. They couldn't let another country recover it, and he didn't want such a huge mass falling intact anyway. It would be best if they detonated the jet above a sea or a flatland.

After he finished setting a bunch of explosives, Hamazura headed for the passenger seats rather than the cockpit. Takitsubo was there, tiredly leaning against the wall.

"Everything's set. Will this really be okay?!"

"...Yeah. This plane has a built-in security package that melts all the important circuits with strong acid when it crashes to prevent technology from being salvaged. There should be almost no risk of secret information winding up in another country's hands where it can be used as a weapon..."

There was no firmness in her voice.

Hamazura was no scholar, so he couldn't even guess as to how much the Crystals had damaged her. But she probably wouldn't heal if they did nothing. And he got the feeling that no outside medicine could do anything about it.

In the end, they would have to rely on Academy City technology if Takitsubo was to have any chance at survival.

...Our victory condition isn't to escape from Academy City. And it's not to destroy the entire science side.

Shiage Hamazura made the decision on his own.

...It's about surrendering to Academy City in the most optimal way. I mean, we'd obviously never be able to beat them. I should narrow my focus to how well I can lose.

At the very least, he'd negotiate and get a guarantee for Takitsubo's safety.

In the same way this supersonic jet was built using technology secret enough to warrant installing acid to erase its traces, Takitsubo's Level Four body and DNA map were also secrets they couldn't let fall into another nation's hands. He would use this as leverage to cut a deal with the immense City. That was the only way to survive.

No matter...

No matter what dangers he had to face after getting Takitsubo back safely and losing his only bargaining chip.

"??? Hamazura, what's wrong?"

"It's nothing."

Hamazura forced himself to smile, then placed a bomb on the door leading outside the passenger seating. He took Takitsubo by the shoulders and veered her away from it so she wouldn't be caught in the blast.

And then Takitsubo put her arms around his neck.

Their faces drew closer, then their lips touched.

It lasted only a few seconds, but it was enough to completely shatter all of Hamazura's pessimistic plans.

"Don't leave me."

That was all she said.

Hamazura understood how much meaning was packed into those few words, though.

"All right..."

He embraced Takitsubo again. *Whatever happens, we'll both survive.* "I'll never leave you," he said with trembling lips. "Damn it, I promise. I swear I'll never leave you!!"

The frantic words brought a faint smile to the girl's face.

The supersonic passenger jet slowed down. Hamazura didn't understand it, but while he was setting the bombs all over the inside, Takitsubo had messed a little with the autopilot settings. She didn't seem to have any more luck in taking control of the flight yoke to fly the plane but, after reading the manual a bit, she had apparently learned how to make a few small setting adjustments.

"I wonder where we are," Hamazura said.

"If the GPS is right, probably Russia. I think we're near a country called the Elizina Alliance of Independent Nations. There won't be any civilian facilities here, so there shouldn't be any damage if we blow up the plane here."

"I see," said Hamazura. No matter where they were, he'd keep running. He'd make use of anything and everything to keep Takitsubo safe, and in the end, they'd both find happiness. After steeling his resolve again, he remotely detonated the bomb attached to the passenger seating exit.

The door blew off instantly.

Because of the air pressure, a gust of wind launched Hamazura and Takitsubo out into the wild blue yonder like air escaping a balloon. With parachutes on their backs, they held hands as they fell, as though it were a skydiving competition.

They flew to their new battlefield, intending to grab hold of hope with their own hands.

Meanwhile, a certain spiky-haired boy was also headed for Russia.

The battle with the Roman Orthodox Church and the Russian Catholic Church had entered its climax. As a result, a girl who had memorized 103,000 grimoires had been put in mortal danger. In order to rescue her, he would have to defeat Fiamma of the Right, the apparent mastermind based in Russia, as soon as possible.

"Wait for me."

That was all the boy said.

To rescue a certain girl, his legs carried him unhesitatingly onward, into the heart of the worldwide war.

I won't let it end in tragedy.

Several protagonists, each with their own feelings in their hearts, unerringly assembled in one place.

Their paths, which had been separate once, would intersect.

And that would be when the true story began, with the stage standing atop the most terrible battlefield in the world.

AFTERWORD

To those of you who have been reading since Volume 1, it's good to see you again.

For those of you who purchased all twenty-one volumes at once, thank you with all of my heart.

I'm Kazuma Kamachi.

As explained in the beginning, this book's story is closely linked to Volume 15 of the novels. It's chock-full of science terms, centered on the key word *Dragon*, which appeared to hint at deeper goings-on at the end of Volume 15.

Aiwass says this as well at the end of this story, but heroes come in many different varieties. Accelerator, a villain who desires good above all others, and Shiage Hamazura, who became a hero by crawling up from his position as a bargain-sale grunt character whose death would have made perfect sense. They're different kinds of heroes from Touma Kamijou, and I have to say it's a lot of fun having them show up out of the blue…Of course, that said, it's only because Touma Kamijou's story is central to the whole thing that we can get excited more effectively in contrast by this one, a story about villains and street thugs.

Maybe I just can't help liking characters who fight with their lives on the line for someone or something precious to them, whether it's

Kuroko Shirai or Acqua of the Back. I was thinking at first that I'd make the subtitle for the epilogue Hope_in_Hand, but I changed it to Brave_in_Hand to denote their bravery, and it struck me as much more suitable for these protagonists!

I'd like to thank Haimura, my illustrator; my editors, Miki and Fujiwara; and Iwakura, who kindly assisted with the powered suit designs for this novel. To be honest, with the unique atmosphere of the villains' side that clings to Accelerator and Shiage Hamazura, I think the illustration really has its work cut out for it more than the prose. Thank you very much for your support once again.

And a thank-you to all my readers. The only reason I can continue this irregular series whose mood completely changes depending on the volume is because you all decided that way of doing things can be okay. I'd like to try various things in the future as well, so I look forward to your continued support.

Now then, as I humbly close the pages here.

And as I pray that the heroes' battles will grace the pages of the next book.

Here, now, I lay down my pen.

What form will the battle of these protagonists, each with bravery in hand, take?

Kazuma Kamachi

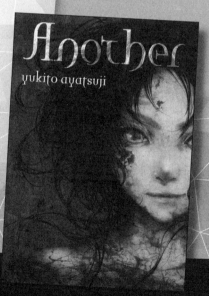